CONFRONTATION

Jim Goldmann

1

This book is a work of fiction. Names, characters, places, and incidents are products of the author's imagination or are used fictitiously. Any resemblance to actual events or locales or persons, living or dead, is entirely coincidental

Prologue

"Ladies and gentlemen, that concludes today's briefing. As always please leave your handwritten notes at your stations. We will convene again tomorrow, same time."

With those remarks the Deputy Director for Homeland Security, Winifred Flint, terminated the meeting. The Operations Directors for each service under Homeland Security oversight met daily at 6:30 am for half an hour; an attempt to assure interagency cooperation and coordination.

As the members stood and strolled toward the exit, talking in small groups, the Deputy Director continued, "Ms. Sterchy, Mr. Martin, and Mr. Gage, stick around." The announcement had the effect of hastening the departure of everyone else.

The named individuals returned to their seats and waited for the room to clear. Once the door closed, Flint looked up from her computer and said, "Jeanette, would you please share with these gentlemen what you told me last night?"

"Winifred, I hardly think this requires any further attention at this time."

"If you deemed it important enough to call me at one in the morning and wake my husband, it's important enough to brief your colleagues from the CIA and the FBI."

Jeanette Sterchy, Operations Director for the National Security Agency began, "Over the past several weeks we've intercepted seemingly random chatter which may point to a potential domestic terrorist attack. The references are obscure and impossible to source as of yet. However, when processed through the latest eleventh order encryption algorithms," Sterchy nodded at Harrison Gage, "we are detecting a pattern of highly-coordinated activities. However we can provide neither conclusive nor directive counsel at this point."

Fred Martin, Operations Director for the CIA, jumped in, "With all due respect to Mr. Gage and his colleagues, these algorithms have not been sufficiently vetted. I hardly think we should issue an alert based on a few random interceptions."

"And last month's foiled Jakarta attack?" replied Gage. "Those same algorithms proved sufficient for you to inform the Indonesian government in time to prevent a major catastrophe and round up the perpetrators. The sooner you accept our help the better it will be for everyone."

"Gentlemen, there's no need to play 'my dick's bigger than yours'. On the basis of the Jakarta success, I am issuing a level two advisory alert. Keep your ears to the ground. That will be all. Harrison, one more minute, please."

After the other two exited Flint asked, "Was that necessary?"

"Yes. He knows the algorithms work and the sooner he gets over his paranoia the better."

"He's not alone. I'm worried for you. The upcoming Senate hearings will not treat you or your colleagues kindly."

"And where do you stand, Winnie?"

"It doesn't matter where I stand."

"But it does. The public needs to hear what you really think; understand the progress we've made. Don't let our detractors confuse and misinform. Just be clear on the facts."

"Harrison, I am not unsympathetic to your Movement but this is a political town. Has the Ulysses Treatment rendered you naive?"

Harrison Gage sat forward in his chair, "Our adversaries may be able to turn the flow of the Mississippi at bit here or there but it will come at great expense and in the end, the current will still reach the Gulf. A time will come when you will join us."

"Perhaps."

As Gage rose to leave, Flint offered, "I heard what happened in Italy."

Gage's face lost its resolve.

"What are you going to do?" asked Flint.

"It's a matter for the Italian authorities. The Bureau will not get involved."

Flint nodded, leaned back in her chair and watched her friend's back as he left the briefing room, wondering how she would remain neutral.

Chapter 1

Water ran dark and clear along the curb cascading over refuse gathered by the torrent and spilling into the cavernous storm sewer. It had been raining heavily for hours. A bright fluorescent glow passing through neglected windows cast a dim yellowed hue on the wet, uninhabited sidewalk.

Inside, the diner smelled of an admixture of coffee and grease with just a hint of cigarette smoke, a legacy of a different time and different sensibilities. Two twenty-something's sat in a booth across from each on faded plastic cushions of an indeterminate color gobbling up what passed for a very early breakfast. They guzzled coffee chasing the beer they'd imbibed earlier at McGee's down the street; hoping to detoxify and make it home safely without a ticket. It was past closing time and a few regulars remained nursing their late night coffee unwilling to leave the warm, dry establishment for the cold, wet streets and whatever grief awaited them at home.

There were two waitresses at this hour, standing together and waiting for everyone to leave so they could finish cleaning up. One might describe them as a female version of Mutt and Jeff. Teresa stood tall, a big-boned woman with a natural laugh. Her counterpart, Dawn, the quiet, unassuming one, was perhaps three-quarters Teresa's height with fine features, like a china doll.

"Is he still out there?"

"Don't look!" Dawn cautioned her friend and co-worker, hiding behind her ample frame.

"I'm telling ya, you oughta call the police. It's not safe." Teresa warned.

"I'm fine. And what would they do anyway? He hasn't done anything."

"He's followed you home. You said you saw him from your apartment. You're not bein' careful. You gotta do something."

"I'll walk ya home," Cory, the short order cook, offered as he cleaned the grill. Dawn found herself reluctant to ask any favor of Cory. He was nice enough but she didn't want to lead him on suspecting his intentions were more than protective.

"That's okay, Cory. You don't need to. I'll be fine."

Teresa pulled Dawn out of Cory's earshot. "I'm serious. How many times have you seen him out there? He's been comin' around for what, three weeks? Do you recognize him?" Teresa asked as she looked beyond Dawn to the lone figure standing in the rain across the street seemingly oblivious to the weather, his face obscured in shadow by a wide-brimmed hat; his form practically blending in with his surroundings.

"We aren't safe."

"See I told ya," Teresa said as she looked at the wall-mounted TV.

"He's some guy on TV. He's not talking about my mystery man," Dawn countered as she turned to look at the television set.

Sitting behind a desk to lend himself gravitas the well-dressed commentator continued his attack in his subterranean baritone. "They threaten our very way of life. These Samsamites could be anyone, anywhere. They could be your neighbor, your boss, even your wife. They bring their

9

brand of socialist atheism. It's the same old story. But with a new twist: they aren't human.

"Oh, they look like the rest of us. Pretend to be normal, to be our friends. But they have more sinister aims. In despair they have taken an extreme step and left their humanity behind hoping for an escape no different from the drug addict searching for his next high. But these villains want nothing less than to hijack *your* life, too, with promises of a better world. They sow dissension, fear, and mistrust offering hollow promises in place of the values this country was founded upon: hard work, individual freedom, and faith in God.

"They have placed their faith in science. But even mainstream science disavows them. And they offer what they call the BRIDG, nothing less than enslavement to the very technology we created to make our lives easier. The BRIDG, they can't even spell, ha ha.

"And what is their goal? World domination.

"And what kind of world do they want? One without free will. One without God. One without commitment to country and family. A shallow world where everyone thinks alike. One they can control.

"Well, I am pleased to report that our President has today directed the Senate to convene special hearings under the direction of the Committee for State Security. And their task? To root out these mutants and shut down their enterprise. I have it on good authority that Senator Paul Gregory will be chairing the Committee. And their first order of business? They will call Michael Neumann: the so-called leader of the so-called NextAge Movement.

"You remember him. He's the guy who started all this. He's the guy who pretended to be crippled just so he could be 'healed' and testify to the miracle he created in concert with his wife. But make no mistake. There is untold power and money behind this movement. Neumann may be their front man but in name only. This is the brainchild of Arthur Paulson and his BioDigiTech Corporation, the largest privately held company in the world. And why is it privately held? You know why. They don't want anyone looking at the man behind the curtain. They don't want the scrutiny that Wall Street would bring. Well, now they'll have their day in court. They'll be shown for the charlatans we all know them to be.

"People, be careful." Jeremiah Barnum held up his hands to ward against the perceived threat. "They aren't human. Oh, their story is alluring enough. They weave their spells with promises of peace and 'connection'. But trust me, they offer nothing but dust and ashes. Stay tuned. As always my eyes and ears are open keeping my commitment to you, my listeners."

"Teresa, turn that guy off. I'm sick of listening to him." Teresa reached for the remote, pointed it at the set and pushed the power button. The diner was now empty. Cory had left Dawn and Teresa sitting across from each other in a booth.

"Would you take the Treatment?" Teresa asked.

"Yeah, right, like I could afford it."

"I hear they don't charge you for it if you can't pay."

"Well they'd want something. I learned a long time ago you don't get something for nothing. Why would I do it anyway? What would I get out of it?"

"I s'pose you're right." Teresa admitted. "Anyway, what are we going to do about your problem?"

"Which one?"

11

"You know, Mystery Man." Theresa reached across the table covering Dawn's hands in her own. "I have an idea. You know that nice young policeman? I think his name is Jeff. He keeps coming in here and the way he looks at you, well, you know."

"Are you trying to fix me up or solve my Mystery Man problem?"

"Could kill two birds with one stone."

"I'm really not interested."

"In him or anyone?"

Dawn shot her friend a look both withering and tired. "Drop it."

"No I won't. It's like you're dead. You don't do anything but come to work, go home, and come back. You have no life. You're nice enough but you don't connect with anything or anyone around you. It's like you're going through the motions. I know there's someone in there but you're buried so deep."

Dawn looked down in her lap, tears welling in her eyes. "What does it matter if I live or die? I'm no one to anyone. Just leave me alone." Dawn tried to get up but Teresa held her hands fast.

"No, I won't. I won't hear talk like that. You're young, you're pretty, and you're smarter than you think you are. You could do much better than to hang around here."

"You don't really know me. I've made some big mistakes, mistakes I can't live with. Maybe the Dark Man is here to take me out of my misery."

"What Dark Man? You mean the Mystery Man? What are you talking about?"

Dawn sighed. "I've been having a dream. It started a couple of months ago. It's storming outside and I feel scared.

There's a kid in it. He's looking at me and reaches out with his arms. I sense that he's a sweet kid but he looks like he's in pain. And his eyes. They're creepy like in a horror movie, you know, with dark circles around them. He's empty. Like me.

"Anyway, all of a sudden there is this dark man in the dream. He appears out of nowhere. He just stands there shrouded in a black cloak and then slowly moves toward me. But he isn't walking. He kinda floats or glides. And as he gets closer, the kid moves away and everything gets darker around me and I feel a crushing pressure making me sick."

Teresa looked at her friend with undisguised compassion. "You poor thing."

Dawn started to get up from her seat but doubled over in pain clutched her belly and sat back down. "I'll be okay in a minute."

"Honey, you gotta get help. You need to see a doctor. These pains have been going on for over a week now." Teresa reached into her purse, pulled out a roll of bills and pressed them into her friend's hand.

"What're you doing? There must be a coupla hundred bucks here. I can't take this."

"You can and you will. You need to see a doctor."

"Simon will kill you."

"He's worried about you, too."

"Terry, I don't know what to say."

"Don't say anything. Just go home and rest. Promise me you'll get help."

"I promise."

After locking up, Teresa watched as Dawn walked down the deserted wet street toward her apartment. The mystery man was nowhere to be seen.

"Poor thing," Teresa thought as Simon pulled to the curb in an old, beaten up Plymouth.

Chapter 2

Lead Petty Officer Tom Talbot sat straight-backed in the firmly cushioned gray steel chair; his feet planted on the floor, knees together, hands in his lap. Just back from a six month deployment, he had been summoned to the base commander's office. Tom's re-enlistment date was coming up and he figured it was time for a pep talk; though he was surprised the base commander was getting involved. He thought the whole thing unnecessary but went along anyway. What else was he going to do? Tom took pride in his role as lead petty officer in his Seal platoon hoping for a promotion to Chief Petty Officer. At the same time, the events of the last few weeks forced Tom to question whether he belonged with the Seals or whether there was some other purpose out there waiting for him. Perhaps that was the why behind Foley's summons.

Well, if they want to sell me I'm willing to listen. Maybe I could get something out of this: a better billet, a promotion. Maybe they decided to send me to school so I can get my college degree. Tom eagerly sought new challenges and would welcome an escape from his current frustrations.

The commander's adjutant sat at a desk not far from the door to the Captain's office. Sgt. D'Giacomo was concentrating on his computer screen when the phone rang.

Tom thought to himself *"I'd go crazy if I spent my days sitting in front of a computer like that."*

"Tom, you can go in now. The Captain's ready."

Tom stood, walked to the door, turned the knob and entered Captain Jason Foley's office. Foley sat behind his meticulously ordered desk. The only light in the room came from the windows behind the Captain. The pale tan and brown walls in the sparsely furnished office were covered with photographs documenting exploits from more active times. There was also a photo of Foley with the then sitting Commander-in-Chief. Tom had been in this office only once before with three others from his platoon to accept recognition from the base Commander's predecessor. They laughed about the event afterwards in the cynical fashion of the jaded enlisted man, but Tom secretly took pride in the recognition for a job well done.

As he entered, Tom was taken up short by the man he saw standing to the Commander's left. Dressed in a blue sport coat, gray polo shirt, and khaki slacks the man stood a full foot shorter than Foley. But even without the uniform Tom recognized Brigadier General James Scott. Scott had been responsible for coordinating Special Forces in the Pentagon several years before. Tom had been attached to one of Scott's units at that time.

Tom stepped into the room, saluted sharply to his superior and nodded his head toward Scott who returned the gesture. "Tom, please sit down," commanded the Captain and motioned for him to take a chair facing the desk. Tom sat and General Scott took the chair next to his. Surprised to see Scott, Tom couldn't help but wonder what was up. He decided to take the initiative. Perhaps there was some new assignment that they wanted him to volunteer for.

"Sir, permission to speak?"

The Captain nodded. Tom turned to General Scott, "General, it's good to see you. What has it been, four years?

"You have a good memory, Petty Officer. I believe it has."

Turning back to face Foley Tom began, "Sir, I appreciate that you called me in to talk about my reenlistment but it isn't really necessary. I have every intention of re-upping."

"I expected nothing less. Tom, we are considering you for a new assignment, one that is truly the opportunity of a lifetime."

The Seal's heart swelled with pride wondering what was coming next but hardly caring. He knew his record spoke for itself. General Scott turned to speak to him.

"Son, I'm putting together an elite fighting force and I want you to be a part of it."

"Sir, I don't understand, I'm already a part of the world's most elite group."

"I might disagree with you. You know I'm a Ranger?" the General offered amiably.

"Yes, sir."

"Tom, even though it's been four years, I've kept my eye on you. You consistently demonstrate the finest qualities even when compared with your peers. Have you given much thought to where you might go from here?"

§

Tom enlisted in the Navy right out of high school. He qualified easily for Dive School and then entered Basic Underwater Demolition School or BUDS, the first step to qualify as a Navy Seal. The six month program typically washed out over half the candidates but Tom scored near the top of his class. Upon completion of the course he trained as a corpsman catching some good natured ribbing from his more testosterone-addled fellow Seals. He rose swiftly earning the rank of Lead Petty Officer after only six years.

Just one week prior to the meeting in San Diego Tom found himself sitting in a bar in an unnamed Central American country following the completion of a joint operation with Army Special Forces. It was late. Most of the patrons had left and so Tom nursed one more beer with a Staff Sergeant from the Green Beret Company with which they had conducted a joint operation.

Tom had watched as the other Green Berets left the bar, the members of his squad having left earlier in search of other forms of stimulation. Rather than leave, the sergeant walked over to where Tom sat, pulled out a chair and asked as he sat, "Mind if I join you?"

"Suit yourself", Tom responded without emotion.

The thickset solider held out his hand, "Brent Daly."

Tom took his hand, "Tom Talbot."

The Sergeant nodded, took a swig from his bottle, and offered, "Sorry about the ribbing back there. Didn't mean anything by it. Just venting."

"Yeah, I get it. Doesn't matter. Sometimes I think we deserve it."

"Not you."

Tom took another swig from his nearly empty bottle.

"*Bartender,* dos cervesas, por favor" said Daly. The bartender came over with two bottles for the two combatants.

Daly continued, "I heard a story once: a group of Seals on a training exercise somewhere on an island in the Pacific. They were supposed to hijack a truck and use it kidnap their target. They hadn't prepared adequately for the mission; the heat really got to them while they lay in wait for several days and so ended up drinking all their water, even the fluid in their IV bags. Finally, the truck drove by and saved their lives with the water they had aboard."

Tom took a long drink and stared straight ahead. "It was Guam, and I was there."

"Sorry man. Didn't mean anything by it."

"No big deal. Someone once described the difference between Seals and Green Berets to me this way: let's say we're both charged with a mission to capture a cache of weapons held in a room. You Green Berets would prepare in great detail going so far as to understand which way the door swung and the placement of materials and personnel behind the door. Given enough time, you might even build a mockup to thoroughly plan for any contingency."

Tom smiled, "We Seals, on the other hand, would just shoot through the door, gun at waist level, raising holy hell. You know, we're too young and fit to be shot, or so we'd like to believe."

"Maybe, but I saw what you did back there."

The previous day found Tom and his squad lingering in an open area in the jungle alongside a fast-moving river waiting for a group of Green Berets who were to arrive prior to the squad's extraction. They had just returned from disabling a well-armed riverfront facility supporting a faction of drug-running insurgents currently out of favor with their government. Tom's squad staked out their target without discovery for two days waiting for the right time to strike. The Seals strategically placed the explosives without detection waiting for a supply boat to arrive. As the boat rounded the bend in the river Tom was gratified to see the supply boat carried a large gray metal tank mounted amidships and loaded with gasoline. As the boat pulled up to the dock the demolition expert detonated the charges resulting in an immense fireball and causing a chain reaction taking out three buildings including one housing a large weapons cache. Satisfied with the success of their mission; the Seal team quietly made their way through the jungle to the rendezvous point; their targets never suspecting their presence. Exhausted from days fighting the heat, bugs, and boredom, Tom's squad lounged along the bank of the river waiting for the Green Berets.

Never letting their guard down, the troop nevertheless waited with a sense of relaxed ease expecting to get back to their base before sundown. Tom had just finished losing to his friend David at cards, the two of them laughing at the bonehead play that cost Tom the game. The Green Berets, who had been on a reconnaissance mission targeting a different rebel group, neared. Tom heard two of them arguing as they approached along the river bank.

"Corporal, when we get back I'm putting you on report." Tom saw a sullen soldier walking in front of the incensed lieutenant. Behind them he saw the rest of the squad, one burly warrior carrying a fallen comrade.

"Soldier, I'm talking to you," said the second lieutenant in a slight Southern drawl.

"Lou, leave Jerry alone. He feels bad enough as it is. Don't pile on," said a sergeant, Daly, walking just behind the two. But the newly minted officer kept it up. Sensing something wasn't right Tom stood, the others in his squad following his lead.

"Soldier you will turn around and look at me when I am addressing you."

The corporal stopped in his tracks. Tom saw the vacant look in his eyes. The soldier turned around raising his rifle in a slow arc and shot the officer in the stomach. The lieutenant looked down at the red stain slowly spreading from the wound, dropped to his knees and looked up into the eyes of death.

The corporal raised his rifle just high enough for a kill shot to the head when all pandemonium broke out. Tom reacted faster than the rest of his squad and was on the corporal before anyone else. Tom's friend David was close behind and took a rifle butt to the side of his head. The shooter fought like a man possessed but was soon subdued as the others joined Tom and held him fast.

Rising slowly over the restrained soldier Tom turned back toward the bank of the river where David fell. He was nowhere to be seen. Looking downstream Tom saw the unconscious Seal trapped under a tangle of fallen branches against the steep bank on the opposite side of the river, his head underwater. Tom hesitated for just a moment. Another Seal, Billy, grabbed his arm. "Tom, don't, it's too dangerous."

Tom shook off caution diving headfirst into the raging torrent. A wicked undertow found him but ultimately couldn't hold the impressively strong swimmer in its grip.

Tom fought his way to the surface, took a ragged breath and dove deep again. Battling like a man possessed he reached his fallen friend. Diving beneath the branches he wrestled with the tangled tentacles trying to free David.

He rose to the surface several times, to get his breath, the moments ticking away, diving again and again attempting to extricate his comrade. Finally releasing him, Tom pulled David deeper underwater to break free of the branches and, continuing to fight the current, swam to the other bank and pulled the unconscious Seal to safety on firm ground.

Years of training and experience kicked in as he began reflexively resuscitating his friend in a vain attempt to restore life. Finally, his fellow Seals pulled him off, his efforts coming too late to do any good. Tom looked around taking in the mayhem, one shot dead, one drowned, another having lost his life in the earlier enemy action.

Tom sat cross-legged on the ground unable to move, staring at nothing and muttering to himself. One of his fellow Seals, Billy again, squatted, put his hand on Tom's shoulder and asked, "You okay?"

"Yeah," was all he said. He knew he should have been able to save David. It wasn't enough to have pulled him free, it was never enough. Tom stood and helped the others clean up the site while the radioman called for extraction.

Returning with his platoon to the States and decorated for heroism, Tom took pride in the recognition, but still felt a nagging feeling in the back of his mind that he should have done more; somehow he had failed again. Everywhere he went, try as he might; no matter what he did triumph eluded him escaping through his fingers like sand. Something didn't seem right. He felt incomplete. He wasn't where he belonged. His sense of purpose still eluded him.

Chapter 3

"Let me get this straight. You're telling me you want me to resign, leave the Seals, the Navy?"

This is coming out of left field, thought Tom.

"It's necessary, son. The Pentagon doesn't get it."

"Begging your pardon, General, but I'm not sure *I* get it."

"I understand your reluctance. Let me back up a bit. When I retired from the Army I joined the Peacemakers." Scott laid his business card on the desk in front of Tom. The Peacemaker logo, a clenched fist holding an M-4 inside a blue circular field featured prominently on the card.

"You're a mercenary," Tom's voice barely concealing his contempt.

"This isn't the 19th century, son. I represent a private military company. We hire people like you to defend this county. We supplement the regular military. We're employed by the State Department to provide protection in danger zones where it might prove difficult to utilize conventional forces. We support and train local militaries from Central America to Africa so that the US military can stay in the background avoiding difficult political decisions. The military is constrained by the Congress and needs us to supplement the regular army. The Captain here knew your enlistment was coming up and recommended you for a strike force I'm putting together. It will be a corps functioning at a level that will literally transform the face of combat.

"Okay, I'm listening."

"The character of war continues to evolve driven by competitive tension, just as in business or biology. It is survival of the fittest at its most basic. And victory is determined by whichever side has best mastered the three sided triangle."

"The three sided triangle?" Tom asked. *And aren't all triangles three sided?* he thought, but decided not to correct the general.

"Technology, strategy, and organization; the competence of any war machine can be characterized by these three capabilities. And we're falling behind. We may be unmatched in technology but our nation's enemies are better organized and they have a strategy that our current technology can't match. If we're going to win this war against the terrorists, we've got to change our strategy and that starts with a whole new technology.

"Sir, I'm sorry, but I'm a bit lost," said Tom. "How does this matter to me?"

"It matters to you a great deal, son. But I'm getting ahead of myself. Let's talk about technology."

"The club and the spear go back over 35,000 years. Slings, maces, and arrows have been around for about half that long. Then about four thousand years ago along comes the chariot, first pulled by oxen and later horses: the first true war machine. But chariots also changed the organization of war and brought about specialization. You have a charioteer maneuvering the vehicle with a bowman or spear thrower standing next to them to deliver the attack. Different duties based on different skill sets.

"Imagine riding in an open chariot on the plains of Central Asia traveling at breakneck speed toward your opponent's

24

forces, the wind blowing through your hair, dust and dirt churned up by your wheels and those of the other chariots around you. The smell of the horses mixes with the dirt while adrenaline courses through your veins. You're standing next to the charioteer, holding a bow with an arrow cocked in the string, ready to fire, reload, and fire again."

Seeing Scott staring off into space Tom thought the General looked almost wistful.

Turning back to Tom, he continued, "Can you see how technology and organization have become companions in the evolution of warfare?

"I guess."

"And how different is it today? We have highly sophisticated armored tanks. The horse is gone but we still have drivers and we still have the archer, so to speak. The more things change the more they stay the same, right?"

Tom knew Scott wasn't looking for a response so instead asked "What about the third side of the triangle: strategy?"

Scott nodded. "Sun Tzu offers us the first documented treatise on strategy in war in his Thirteen Principles describing strategies from planning and tactics to the use of spies.

"Throughout the middle ages and into modern times the art of war continued to evolve building on refinements in each leg of the triangle. In fact, the developments in technology, strategy, and organization act synergistically with each other to accelerate progress. Nowhere is this more evident than in the present day.

"Our current technology has delivered terrific strategic advantage for us here in this country. Computers, lasers, drones, among other innovations have dramatically altered the role of the soldier. Imagine the D-Day invasion if we had the technical superiority we now possess. Rather than suffer the massive casualties we did when those brave men stormed the beaches at Normandy; what if we could have taken out the German defensive positions with smart bombs instead of all those exposed men? Sounds wonderful, but there's one problem. As technology evolves so does strategy just as in business or sports."

Tom found himself both entranced and confused by Scott's exposition. Scott's take on the evolution of human conflict fascinated Tom offering him a whole new perspective. At the same time he felt Scott separated himself from the immediacy of war. While Tom found himself inspired by the grand sweep of Scott's vivid and provocative description; the sterile picture he painted ignored the brutality of war. Soldiers died. Non-combatants died. And so many came home maimed physically, mentally, or both.

"General, I beg your pardon but I don't see how any of this applies to me."

Scott ignored the statement.

"We have a sledgehammer which can crush anything in its path but when you use it on a hill of fire ants, you may kill a few but all you really do is scatter them enabling them to regroup and attack again.

"We are failing in the war against terror. The enemy has adapted its strategy so that brute force won't work. We've stopped more terrorist acts than the public will ever know but we haven't come close to cutting off the enemy at its source. Conventional warfare doesn't work against the current threat. We're playing defense when we should be dictating terms.

"What do we do when we're threatened? We bring out our vastly superior technology, no more than modern saber rattling. Sure that worked to subdue Iraq's conventional forces but we're still mired in a Middle East stalemate.

"Now ask yourself this question: with the character of global conflict evolving and terrorist cells subversively sowing disruption and distrust, how are we going to change our strategy to effectively defeat this new foe? The enemies' strategy has evolved as ours must now evolve to defeat it.

"We will use organization and technology to move to the next level. In business the fundamental strategic question is: How can I differentiate my business sufficiently to create a sustainable advantage against my competitors? International conflict is no different. And I believe I've discovered a method using newfound technology to deliver the advantage we need to root out evil and restore stability. But before I go into that I need to add one more dimension to our discussion."

Tom wasn't sure this was a discussion but in an effort to impress the general asked, "Sir, begging your pardon but haven't you forgotten something?"

"What do you mean?"

"Didn't Clausewitz say chance played a major role in war? I mean, look at Pearl Harbor. In the lead up to the war our leadership was committed to our battleship fleet and all but ignored the coming importance of air power at sea. At the same time, Japan knew that aircraft carriers were the future and so built a fleet very different from ours. They destroyed our battleship capabilities at Pearl but, as chance would have it, our four carriers were at sea during the attack. As a result we got a jump start on this new technology and had a core to build upon to win the war."

"Son, I'm impressed. You've been paying attention. Chance plays a major role in any conflict, and as a result, we have to mount strategies which minimize the impact of chance. Are you familiar with the role Special Forces have played throughout history?"

"I'm not sure what you mean, sir," Tom admitted, lost in the General's words and impatient for him to get to the point.

"From time immemorial Special Forces have played a key role in warfare. Unlike conventional units, Special Forces focus on disruption, sabotage, and reconnaissance. I bet you didn't know that during the Crusades, small units of the Knights Templar were organized to attack Muslim units for intelligence or to seize supplies. At the same time Muslim units used soldiers who could pass for Crusaders and board European ships to either capture or destroy them. In fact, the Nazi's borrowed from the strategies of the Muslims when they infiltrated behind Allied lines during the Battle of the Bulge posing as MP's in captured jeeps sewing disorder through misdirection. You've hear of Ninja's."

"Certainly. They were Special Forces, too?"

"And mercenaries. Here were soldiers highly trained in the martial arts using the latest technology in firearms and explosives augmented by advanced tactics in camouflage and psychological warfare. They engaged in the full range of black ops from assassination to political and economic destabilization.

"At the start of World War Two Winston Churchill created a group of specially trained troops from the 'hunter class', as he called it, to harass and subvert enemy positions from Europe and North Africa to Southeast Asia. Heck, the US and Canada formed a ski unit for sabotage in Norway called the Devil's Brigade. The first Ranger unit was formed in 1942.

"More recently Special Forces have received greater prominence given political sensitivities around conventional warfare. We have been able to intervene where no war exists. Name the hot spot and our Rangers, our Seals, and others have been there supporting our aims when those in Congress have been unable or unwilling to act. The list is long: Vietnam, remember we were advisors there before we went in full bore. Add to that list Northern Ireland, the Gulf Wars, Afghanistan, Chechnya, Bosnia, the Lebanese war, the Japanese hostage crisis in Peru, in Sri Lanka, and, of course, the assault by you Seals on the Bin Laden compound.

"No matter how the conduct of war changes, in the end, success or failure rests with the soldier. And in the end it's the soldier who makes the difference in war. But, also in the end, Seal, these bodies and minds are limited."

The General tapped his forehead. "You've seen the toll war can take on both. We will change that equation. What if I told you we're now able to augment your physical skills to make you almost indestructible? Imagine the advantage. Imagine being a part of such a fighting force." Scott paused to let that last comment sink in.

Tom couldn't help but be entranced. *"What's he getting at?"* he wondered.

Scott leaned close. "Son, we need you. You recall that operation I recruited you for four years ago? It's on again."

Tom had been recruited for an initiative called "Operation Achilles". He never learned the particulars of the mission other than to know it would require some type of 'augmentation' as they put it. He also recalled being disappointed it had been dissolved at the last minute. He now remembered some scuttlebutt going around at the time that General Scott retired from the Army as a result of something going wrong with Operation Achilles.

Something didn't seem right and yet Tom was intrigued. Maybe this 'elite force' he was talking about didn't fit with the Pentagon politics and bureaucracy. That must be it. Tom felt flattered that they had come back to him after all this time.

"No one ever told me what Achilles was about. What would I have to do?"

It was like peeling an onion for General Scott. Tantalize the recruit with a scrap of information, just enough to get him asking for more.

"Tom, you're strong, but strength isn't enough. What if I told you I could create in you the agility, the reflexes, and coordination to match your strength? You know, don't you?

"You could have stopped that soldier from shooting up his lieutenant. You might have been able to save your friend from drowning. It's what you need and it's what we, as a nation, need to give us the advantage in this new war."

"But why do I have to leave the Navy?"

"The Pentagon can't get involved at this time. Think of this as pilot project. When we've demonstrated success you'll be in a pivotal position to help lead this new force. Imagine yourself at the center of this latest evolutionary step. You will be the kind of warrior all soldiers hope to be.'

Scott didn't share with Talbot that the Brass had no idea what he was up to.

"So how do you do this; some kind of suit or machinery? It isn't a chemical enhancement or drug is it?" Tom recognized that route wasn't for him. He knew people who took performance enhancing drugs and wasn't tempted.

Scott shook his head from side to side emphatically. "There are no steroids or other drugs like that involved. I'm not at liberty to tell you more until you commit. I can't have this bandied about by every soldier on the base."

§

Four years prior General James Scott found himself on the verge of greatness only to have his ambitions dashed by a group of amateurs. For several years he worked in concert with Arthur Paulson at BioDigiTech, or BDT as it was more commonly known. The plan had been to develop a means to alter human brain anatomy, particularly in the cerebellum, a collection of nerve cells located at the back of the skull and the top of the neck right above the spinal cord. That collection of neurons integrates sensory perception, coordination, and motor control.

As leader of Special Forces coordination for the Defense Department, Scott recruited a group of operatives to be his guinea pigs. He intended to inoculate the recruits with a retrovirus armed with the means to rewire the cerebellum as a means to create an elite fighting force. Scott anticipated that the altered brains of the soldiers would permit them to fight with a whole new level of skill. Coupled with their technical superiority America would possess an unassailable advantage in war. When the bureaucrats at the Pentagon saw the success of his efforts Scott believed he would have a clear path to appointment as Army Chief of Staff, maybe even Chairman of the Joint Chiefs.

But he found his hopes dashed by Paulson and a small band of co-conspirators. The primary researcher on the project, Dr. Gabriella Neumann, had conspired with Paulson against Scott, developing her own brain altering virus to cure her dying husband. When Scott arrived at BDT to claim his virus, Paulson prevented Scott from taking the specimens with the help of the FBI and Scott's superiors. Worried the whole affair would bring unneeded notoriety; the Army did Scott a "favor" and allowed him to retire.

But, like any good strategist, Scott had plans within plans within plans. He joined the Peacemakers, a military contracting company, in a bid to reinstitute Operation Achilles. He brought in Bob Arnold, Chief of Biological Research at BDT, and Neumann's boss, to help him restart the Achilles project. It had taken several years, but he was ready to start up again. And this time there was no one in his way.

The Peacemakers proved to be a good short term solution and a way to make more money than he'd ever seen before. He now stood in a position to leverage his eventual success to become Secretary of Defense. Anything was possible. No one outside a very select group knew what he was up to and how it fit into a larger, grander strategy. By the time Operation Achilles launched, it would be too late to stop him. He had finally allied himself with real power.

§

Tom sat back considering the offer. The Navy had been good to him, very good. But there was something in the way General Scott approached him that caused Tom to feel there was more here; a real opportunity for him to excel, to make up for past shortcomings. Though only in his early 30's, Tom wasn't easily conned. He knew Scott was appealing to his sense of duty as well as his ego. And yet, here was a highly decorated general officer telling Tom he had been selected among how many others for this honor, this opportunity. The General must have checked into Tom's background and known of his past; and not just the recent past. Scott must have gone way back, to another incident which set in motion a chain of events beginning even before Tom hit puberty.

Arising as a bubble of air from deep inside a dark well, a memory intruded on Tom's consciousness; but, try as he might Tom found the details just out of reach, something about destiny and purpose fulfilled. Maybe his mind was telling him this was the right thing to do.

He didn't realize it, but Tom was nodding to himself.

"I wish I could tell you more about your assignment but I am sure you understand the necessity for secrecy."

"General, your word is good enough for me. I think I'll take you up on your offer."

"I'm pleased to hear it. The job pays well. As an E6 you make what, $40,000 a year? What if I offered to double that, throw in a signing bonus?" Scott paused. "But, as I think about it, you might appreciate the income but I think you're doing this out of a sense of duty."

Tom looked stricken.

General Scott laughed as he stood.

"Tom, I was only kidding. The pay comes with the job. We'll be contacting you shortly with all the particulars. I don't want you saying anything specific to anyone in your squad. Just tell them you've received a great offer from the private sector and leave it at that. Welcome aboard, son." Scott held out his hand and Tom stood as he took it enthusiastically.

Tom turned to the Captain as Foley spoke. "Tom, we'll start processing your discharge. You'll be out in about three weeks. I think you've made a good choice. Good luck, sailor." The Captain saluted dismissing Tom who returned the salute, turned crisply and left closing the door behind him.

Tom walked with a spring in his step as left Captain Foley's office. He found himself engaged with the thought of joining Scott's team, his heart racing with the prospect of embarking on a whole new career. Here he was, so young and already being singled out for something significant. There were still numerous unknowns but that didn't matter. In fact, the prospect of finding himself on the cutting edge, jumping off into a whole new world, learning new skills, energized him. He started to realize how the events of the past few weeks weighed on him making him feel as though he was swimming upstream. Maybe this was the purpose he'd been looking for. This could be his chance for redemption.

Scott stood looking at the closed door through which Tom Talbot departed.

"Thank you, Jason. He's just what I'm looking for. His psychological profile predicted his reaction to a tee."

"That boy's in for quite a ride. I hope you know what you're doing."

Scott turned slowly to face Foley, the dark menace in his voice palpable. "That 'boy', as you put it, will serve me well. I have every expectation of success but if not," Scott shrugged, "there have always been casualties in war. Sun Tzu said 'All warfare is based on deception'."

"And I'm certain you've heard the same quote translated another way: 'Never will those who wage war tire of deception'. That's a big difference. And what's in it for you? I'm not certain whether you're motivated by your own ambition or settling a score with Arthur Paulson. His Ulysses Project seems to be gaining momentum."

Scott's eyes turned cold. "Don't get any ideas. If your conscience tries to get the better of you I will remind you of a debt. You sit in that chair because of me. And if not for me you would be in a much more confining position, if you get my drift. I can still put you there. Never forget it."

Jason Foley said nothing knowing full well he had made a pact with the devil years ago and now must fulfill his part of the bargain.

Chapter 4

The Nameless Man remained at ease. From his vantage point he gazed through the crystalline panes of the picture window taking in the truly breathtaking sight; gazed through pupils encircled with irises black as the blackest night. Behind him stood his closest lieutenant; a man he had served with on other missions, most more successful than the last.

Beyond the stone patio the well-manicured lawn seemed to go on forever until ending abruptly in a stand of trees. Though the calendar announced the advent of spring some time ago; at this elevation the aspen branches remained bare. Scattered patches of snow dotted the more shaded corners of the property. Beyond the trees the Rocky Mountain peaks rose in majesty blessing the estate which had been in the owner's family since time immemorial; each successive generation adding a room here, a wing there, until the building rivaled the Biltmore estate in grandeur. But this armed fortress could not be mistaken for a tourist trap.

Crossing the lawn toward the house the Man made out the form of the home's owner striding purposefully in his direction; a shotgun resting its butt in the crook of his right arm, the barrel resting comfortably against his other elbow. A game bag with the fallen prey slung down from the barrel.

Stanford Gates wore what one would consider typical hunting attire, lace up boots, dark brown pants, a plaid long sleeved shirt, a light suede vest and a hunting cap. Gates' guise appeared conventional in every respect but for his left hand. The story goes that he lost it battling a black bear. The animal held the man's hand in his jaws while Gates had the presence of mind to grab his hunting knife with his right hand jamming it upward with inhuman force into the base of the beast's skull severing its spinal cord. The feat seemed even more amazing when one considered he had been left-handed prior to the attack and subsequently taught himself to use his right hand.

He could have easily afforded the latest bionic technology to replace the severed appendage but instead chose a dark gray (the color commonly referred to as arsenic) iron fist, his personal badge of courage. The Man had no clue whether the story was true but it made for good press. For all he knew Gates cut off his own hand (a feat of which he was certainly capable) with the sole intent of distinguishing himself, making an unambiguous statement. Now, the primitive appendage sent a clear message to anyone who might attempt to gainsay him.

The room in which No Name waited held multiple hunting trophies with the head of the bear who had dined on Gates' hand occupying the place of honor over a walk-in fireplace. The opposite wall held a 72 inch flat screen television with a state-of-the-art computer and sound system below.

The hunter leaned his shotgun against the outside wall and opened the game bag releasing two red foxes. Dropping the bag on the patio, he walked to the door, opened it and called, "Come here, Lady. Come see what I have brought for you."

Lady, a sleek melanistic jaguar padded out the door without so much as an acknowledgement of No Name's presence. That was fine with him. He would have hated to kill the animal if attacked, not because he cared whether it lived or died, but the repercussions would be quite unpleasant.

"Hello my friend," said Gates. "It gladdens my heart to see you here. Please allow me a few more minutes to feed my darling and I shall join you." No Name watched as the cat devoured the still warm meat.

No Name remained standing. It might have been acceptable to sit in the Great Man's presence but he didn't want to chance it, not without permission.

When the animal finished Gates released the cat to run the property. The collar around her neck held a device which would prevent her from roaming far. Gates picked up his shotgun, unloaded the breach placing the shells in a pocket on his vest and entered the study.

As he crossed the threshold, and as if in response to his presence, the sound system blared the opening bars of Tchaikovsky's *Swan Lake*. "Softer", he spoke and the volume decreased sufficiently for the men to converse.

Gates walked deliberately to his desk raising the champagne flute placed there earlier. It didn't hold the pale yellow carbonated liquid. Instead, the Man observed a ruby red concoction, probably cranberry juice. Gates drank only fruit juice, and only in its natural state, room temperature.

"Well my friend, will you join me in a toast or will I be disappointed?" Gates looked both benign and quizzical worrying No Name to the core. He placed the glass back on the desk.

Despite his uneasiness the Man stood parade straight and said, "No sir, we were not successful."

38

Gates raised his hand and brought it firmly down smashing the flute into a thousand pieces and splintering a corner of the desk in the process.

Gates looked up from the damage. "Your colleague appears nervous." He was now stepping around the two men.

Despite the Nameless Man's prior counsel to the contrary the lieutenant spoke.

"Sir, we did everything we could. I don't see a way we can enlist these Samsamites. Death is the only solution."

"I believe you are right," said Gates as he brought the iron appendage down on the skull of the unsuspecting subordinate with mortal force sending a spray of blood, bone, and brain across the room as the man collapsed in a heap. Gates walked to the door, opened it and called out, "Lady, come here, I have a special treat for you." The panther gently padded into the study and went straight for the carcass.

Gates returned to his desk, picked up a cloth and wiped the organic matter from his fist. As if nothing out of the ordinary had occurred he continued, "Do you know the word sinister derives from the Latin root for left? In the Middle Ages people thought left-handed people were possessed by the devil. Quite poetic, in this case don't you think? You don't find me sinister, do you, my friend?"

"Sir, good, sinister, these are the value judgments of the weak."

"So true. Now, back to your recent adventure; I would like to hear the details."

The Nameless Man began, "We followed your instructions to the letter. We selected three males and three females whose personal backgrounds indicated they would not be missed for a few days. We began with a simple interrogation which, of course, proved fruitless and then moved on to chemical agents. Interestingly they proved ineffective as well. Usually we would see some intoxication but they seemed impervious to the effect. From there we moved to electrical stimulation and when that didn't produce results we resorted to more traditional methods. Though I could sense fear, the subjects exhibited remarkable calm. If I may say so, I was impressed. There is something in this Ulysses Treatment which bears further examination."

"If you are suggesting that you take the Treatment, you would be wasting your time", countered Gates. "I am certain that it would render you useless to me. What did you do with the remains?"

"I considered burying them in a mass grave, covering the bodies with lye to destroy the evidence but found a discreet crematorium just outside a small town in the Italian countryside. There will be no DNA to trace the bodies. And I made sure the owners would never talk. Where should I go from here?"

"I must consider other alternatives. It is essential we obtain access to the BRIDG. It is integral to the plan. The other elements are falling into place nicely. Time is short. I will find you when I need you, my friend.

The Man glanced at the cat hunched over his former comrade, the iron laced smell of blood filling his nostrils.

"Don't bother yourself. One of my servants will be happy to clean up this mess."

The Nameless One bowed to the Great Man and exited heading for his SUV and a trip to the desert to clear his head.

Chapter 5

Dawn gazed through the window to the street passing in front of her second story apartment. The growing buds on the shade trees in front of the building did little to conceal her apartment or the street below. From time to time she would find herself studying the goings-on: a car passing by, young teens hanging out on the corner. The structures across the street offered little interest for her, looking pretty much the same as her two story building with two units down and two up, constructed almost a century earlier, not that she knew or cared. She suspected it had been a nice neighborhood sometime in the distant past. Now plywood covered the windows on every third building. Of the residents in the remaining apartments she knew little; not because she was a recluse, she just told herself she wasn't interested.

Her living room, if one could call it that, faced the street with plenty of natural light streaming through its two windows. Dawn stood to the side of one of the windows, confident she couldn't be seen from the sidewalk. He stood, across the street, his face obscured by his wide brimmed hat. She was convinced he was looking at her apartment; and her curiosity was starting to get the better of her. She found herself tempted, despite Terry's warnings, to go down and confront him. As she imagined what she might say she heard three quick knocks on her front door startling her out of her speculations.

Dawn's home consisted of four rooms. While faded linoleum covered the floors in the bathroom and kitchen, the bedroom and contiguous living area were covered in natural wood. Insulated wires painted white ran along the off-white baseboards and terminated in electrical outlets nailed to the surface of the wall. She had covered the floor with a green threadbare throw rug which helped immensely to shield her feet from the winter cold. The fireplace, which might have kept her warm, had been sealed off decades before. Instead heat was provided by steam radiators in each room which would have been fine if the boiler in the basement worked properly.

It wasn't unusual, in winter, for Dawn to wake up in the wee hours of the morning shivering under the covers, her breath visible in the dim light. Her only solution was to climb out of her formerly warm bed and walk to the rear of the apartment. She would open the back door, cursing the whole time, walk down the back stairs in bare feet to the first floor and reach behind her to raise those same stairs, with the help of a counterweight, to reveal the spider-infested basement below.

Once in the cellar, she would pull the string to turn on the bare bulb hanging in the middle of the room and walk quickly across the dusty concrete floor to the boiler which served the radiators in her apartment. She would reach up and turn a spigot filling the tank with water cursing herself for forgetting to fill the tank before bed as she made her way back up the stairs to crawl under the covers and wait for sleep.

And the summers were worse. She couldn't afford an air conditioner and even if she had one she figured it would blow out all the fuses in the apartment.

Dawn walked over to the door to see who knocked. Her front door opened into her bedroom through which one could see through to the kitchen beyond. Three more quick knocks. There was no peephole so instead she asked "Who is it?"

"It's Mrs. Flynn."

"It's not a good time."

"It never is. Open up."

Irene Flynn stood in the doorway. Dawn looked down to make eye contact with the 4'10" landlord dressed in nothing but a housecoat and slippers and smelling of corned beef and cabbage. Dawn smiled inwardly bemused that she called herself Mrs. Flynn. Dawn had heard Irene and her husband arguing violently one evening months before and hadn't seen anything of him since.

"What can I do for you?" Dawn tried to sound accommodating.

"You know very well. You're behind in the rent. I need you to settle up."

"I'll have the money next week. I can pay you then."

"That's too late. I've warned you. No more promises. I'm going to have to evict you. You'd better find somewhere else to live, and quickly."

Dawn stood there in shock not knowing what to say or do. She had nowhere else to go. As Mrs. Flynn turned to walk back down the stairs, Dawn remembered the $200 Terry had given her the previous evening. *She'll kill me.*

"Wait, Mrs. Flynn?"

Dawn turned and walked to her dresser. She opened the top drawer, blindly reached in, found the roll of bills, returned to the door and handed the money to the landlord who wrenched it out of Dawn's hand.

As she counted the bills she said, "This will hold you for another week but you have a long way to go to catch up. I'll be back again next week."

And with that she walked back down the stairs. Dawn slowly closed the door trudged over to her bed and laid down covering her face in her hands.

"I can't keep going like this," she said softly to herself overwhelmed in her desperation. "This can't go on much longer. I can't live like this. What am I going to do?" Dawn couldn't imagine where to turn, petrified by hopelessness, unable to see a way out.

"They'll probably find me some day frozen to death lying here weeks or months after I've died. And no one will care."

As Dawn lay on her bed, numb, with not enough energy to muster a thought, a way out, any way out, she considered walking into the kitchen to retrieve a half empty bottle of vodka from the freezer. She was interrupted again.

There came three quick knocks on the door.

"Go away."

She'd had enough of Irene for the week.

Three quick knocks . . . again.

Dawn sat up on the edge of the bed.

"What do you want?" she asked, exasperated.

Three quick knocks.

Now she was angry. Dawn rose from her bed, stomped across the room and flung the door open. It wasn't her landlord. Dawn gasped. The man who had been looking up at her apartment from across the street now stood in front of her.

She took one step back. She tried to remember where she left her cell phone and realized it didn't matter. He was too close. Even if it was in her hand there was no way to call 911 in time. Looking for something close at hand to defend herself, she felt uncontrolled fear rise within her.

"There's no need to panic. I'm not going to hurt you."

The man removed his hat. He stood a few inches taller than her; he seemed of average build and shouldered a backpack. He wasn't young, he wasn't old. Dawn pegged him at about 40.

"My name is Michael, Michael Neumann. May I come in?"

Chapter 6

He seemed familiar but she couldn't quite place him. As her mind searched instinctively, trying figure out where she had seen his face before, recognition struck her, connecting his countenance with his name. Her eyes widened while her right hand involuntarily rose to cover her gaping mouth. She remembered where she'd seen his picture; those eyes staring out at her from the TV, in newspapers, on the internet.

"You're . . . "

"Apparently. May I come in?"

"Look, I don't know you. I don't think . . ."

"I'd just like a few minutes of your time. I'm trying to figure something out and I'm hoping you can help me. You can ask me to leave anytime and I'll go, okay?"

Her eyes narrowed, confusion written across her features. *What's he doing* here? *What does he want from me?*

Dawn stepped aside at a loss for words. She recovered her composure and showed him into her living room feeling flustered, embarrassed, and baffled.

He looked around as he entered the room. "May I sit down?"

"Sure." Dawn shrugged not sure how she should react.

He chose a worn high back chair near one of the windows.

"You're wondering why I'm here." A statement of fact.

Dawn nodded as she sat in a rickety wicker chair across from him.

"Well, I am, too," her guest admitted.

"I don't understand."

"Nice place"

"Gimme a break."

"Fair enough. Would you have any clue why I'm here? Are you interested in the Treatment, want to help out somehow?"

"Me? How would I know why you're here? Are you recruiting or something; goin' door to door like the Mormons or Jehovah's Witnesses? I'm not interested."

"This isn't a sales pitch. Look, I know I'm fishing here. Perhaps if I knew more about you I might know where this is going."

Put off by this unwanted intrusion Dawn countered, "I'm sorry. I heard you could read minds."

Michael smiled, "No, not really. That's a common misconception. It's more like we can sense mental states; happy, sad, confusion, anger. But you're a tough read. Your emotions are jumbled and you don't seem to connect with them."

Dawn found herself at a loss for words. Her conflicting emotions coalesced in anger torn between a feeling of violation and the recognition that this stranger could know her so easily.

"That's better, you're upset", Michael observed. "I apologize for being so blunt. You don't know me and I barge into your home, invading your privacy. Perhaps it would help if I told you a little bit more about myself. Then you can decide what you're willing to share. Maybe we can make sense of this together. What do you know already?"

"Not much really. I don't pay attention to the news. I don't spend much time on the internet. I know that you and your friends seem to frighten a lot of people. Should I be afraid?"

"Of what?"

"I don't know. Are you really trying to take over the world?" Dawn smiled as she uttered the accusation hearing how silly it sounded as the words exited her mouth. She considered herself a fair judge of people and this guy didn't seem like some nut job; but who knew these days.

"Yes, we're taking over the world. And, it's not a silly question." Michael paused. "Why don't I start from the beginning?"

Dawn nodded; increasingly disoriented by his perceptiveness and easy manner. "Are you sure you're not reading my mind?"

"It was almost eight years ago; I suffered a serious brain injury in a car accident and developed a slowly spreading paralysis. I was dying a little each day. My wife, Gabby, a neurologist, worked for BioDigiTech in their medical research division. She'd been working on another project for them and used the same methods to find a way to regrow the damaged nerve cells in my brain. But she didn't anticipate the Ulysses Treatment would significantly increase the connections among my nerve cells." He paused. "Would you like to understand how the technique works or should I continue?"

"It probably wouldn't make sense to me."

"I understand. Doesn't really matter, not at this point. When I woke up from the Treatment I found I'd changed. Not only was I able to walk again but I had this whole new set of abilities."

"What are you, some kinda super hero?" Dawn asked with more than a hint of contempt in her voice.

48

"I don't blame you for being skeptical. I was too, in the beginning, but I couldn't run away from what I found to be true. Think of it this way. You live in a community where everyone is blind; has been so since birth. It's the assumed way everyone lives. Somehow you gain sight. You can now perceive things you never had before. You can see a painting, a rainbow, the people around you. How would you communicate what you're experiencing?"

"Are you saying everyone else is blind and only you can see? That's pretty arrogant, don't you think?"

"Have you seen the Wizard of OZ? The movie starts out in Kansas in black and white and only becomes color when Dorothy arrives in OZ. Now we all know that Kansas is not black and white but the director intended to show that the land of OZ was so much more vibrant than our own world; something beyond what we usually experience as color. It's like that."

Michael continued, "The simplest animals consist of only one cell and are capable of only the most primitive actions. As animals evolved and became more sophisticated they developed reflexes, instinct, emotions, and intentions. We see human beings as the pinnacle of evolution with our capacity for organized thought and self-awareness. We have been taught to believe we are the culmination, the end point of development.

"But evolution doesn't suddenly stop. Humans have continued to evolve and adapt. The Tibetan Highlanders live at an altitude of 14,000 feet. Their close cousins, the Han Chinese live at sea level. Over a period of only 40 generations starting about 3,000 years ago the Tibetans evolved to produce lower blood hemoglobin levels to better adapt to the lower oxygen of the Himalayas. In fact, closer to home, my wife tells me that in the past several decades we've seen an increase in the number of years that women are fertile."

Dawn noticed Michael pause as if lost in thought but he quickly recovered.

"Some have argued that the development of agriculture caused human evolution to accelerate. Others have argued geographic and geologic changes such as the Ice Age forced adaptation making possible the superficial physical differences we erroneously call races."

"What do you mean?"

"The genetic evidence is inarguable. In fact, there's more genetic variation within 'races' than between them. We all began in Africa and migrated across the world from there. For example, those who migrated to Europe from Africa developed lighter skin to absorb more sunlight to make vitamin D. Those who remained in Africa needed darker skin to protect them from the sun. As you can imagine, these changes took place over thousands of years. But, occasionally there are leaps in the evolutionary tree. Biologists are debating how these leaps occur; possibly through random mutation and the resulting genetic drift as one possible explanation."

"I'm sorry, you've lost me, but, anyway what does this mean to me?"

"I know this is a little technical. In my case Gabby's cure, the so called Ulysses Treatment, created one such leap through forced mutation. I woke up from her induced coma able to do things I could never have done before. The mind is a powerful thing. More than you know. The treatment heightened my intuition and insight. Imagine your mind being able to process many more facts at a time, to see patterns that seemed obscure before and being able to draw

50

meaning where before there appeared to be none; to see into the future by understanding the effects each action you take might have. Are you with me?"

"I think so. You're saying you're smarter, right?"

"Close, but there's another facet, far more important than any of that. Remember I spoke a moment ago about being blind?"

Dawn nodded.

"We're taught there are five senses and only five. But the Treatment seems to have enabled another sense. There are realities around us that are more subtle than what we perceive with our five senses and yet they exist none the less. Let me give you an example. Our eyes pick up radiation in the narrow band of the electromagnetic spectrum we call visible light. But there are other wavelengths around us all the time we can't see. We feel long wavelength radiation with our skin and call it heat, also known as infrared.

"In my case, and for others who have gone through the Transformation, we can perceive or sense the connections among people. We don't thoroughly understand the scientific basis for this but we are all part of each other in some fashion, connected somehow. And that perception is independent of space and time. I can perceive not only the connection you and I share but I am aware of my wife at the same time."

"What do you mean? Do you know what she's thinking?"

"No, but I can sense our mutual connection like a presence. I know it's difficult to understand unless you've experienced it."

"So you can't really communicate," Dawn observed.

"No, we can. Let me show you."

Michael reached down, lifted his backpack, unzipped a compartment and withdrew a device which looked something like a computer. The largely featureless brushed stainless steel device was about eight inches tall and held a small light tan screen embedded in its surface. Dawn saw no buttons or switches other than what appeared to be a power switch.

"What's that?"

"It's called a BRIDG Communicator. It utilizes BRIDG technology, a new type of circuit developed by a colleague of mine, Peter Keyes. BRIDG stands for Brainwave Receiving Integrated Digital Gateway. The BRIDG circuit simulates the number of connections in the brain of someone who's undergone the Treatment but configured in a whole new way. Let me show you."

Michael held the device so Dawn could see the screen. Suddenly, as if unbidden, the words "Wait 'til you see the latest version. Much better than that clunker you're using." appeared on the screen.

"I just told Peter that I'm demonstrating the BRIDG Communicator and this is his response. Unlike trying to connect with another person, I can connect mentally with the BRIDG circuit and use it to communicate."

"So it's like a radio or a cell phone?"

"After a fashion, but there's no transmitter."

"How do I know it isn't high tech magic 8 ball with the answers already built in?"

"Ask me a question." Michael handed the apparatus to Dawn.

The device felt cool to the touch and lighter in her hand than she expected. Without taking her eyes from the screen she asked, "Would you leave if I asked you to?"

Immediately words formed on the viewer. Dawn read, 'Of course. But I'm convinced this meeting will lead to our mutual benefit. Give me a few more minutes, OK?'

Dawn looked up from the screen. "OK, I'm impressed. I've heard all this talk about the BRIDG and it's just a glorified cell phone? Why don't you just call each other?"

"Like you I value my privacy. I don't want to that worry someone will be listening in on my calls. As I said there's no transmitter and we don't use the internet. But more importantly, this is just one small application. Imagine coupling the speed of a computer with the consciousness of the human mind. You would be amazed with what we're just starting to do. Predicting weather with any precision daunts even the best meteorologists; there are just too many variables. We utilize sensors all across the globe measuring temperature, humidity, wind, and air pressure. Now couple that data to satellite tracking and then to what we can measure in the temperature gradients and currents in the oceans. We have developed software algorithms to process all the information using the BRIDG technology. We have demonstrated we can predict the path of violent storms, both hurricanes and tornadoes with stunning accuracy. We might not be able to stop them but we can get people out of the path of destruction saving countless lives."

"Mr. Neumann . . ."

"Please call me Michael."

"Michael. As cool as that is, I don't get why you say this connection perception is the most important part of this. It seems to me being smarter would be a real plus not to mention being able to connect to this thing." Dawn handed the device back to Michael.

Michael shook his head as he returned the BRIDG Communicator to his backpack.

"Someone else thought the same thing. But he discovered the real gift in all this. Years ago I wrote a blog under the name Samsa. You might have heard of it: 'Unbiased Opinions of the Clearly Confused'."

Dawn shook her head.

"Look at the world around you. We human beings are hardly humane. Our actions are motivated by insatiable desire coupled with profound insecurity. Life is so uncertain. We don't know if we will be able to put food on the table or have a roof over our heads tomorrow. I see your situation. *You* know I'm right, but even those with wealth worry constantly that someone will take their things from them whether it's the government or the free market. And so we find ourselves at war.

"We're torn between our animal nature and something much harder to define and we don't even know why. There are wonderful acts of kindness and charity all around us but they often take a back seat to our more primitive needs. We're stuck in the middle. In order to serve ourselves we have to work with others to foster our own wellbeing whether it be in a marriage, a job, a community, or a country.

"As we identify with whatever group we feel a part of, it must follow any group we're not a part of is, to us, inferior or suspect; gets back to that whole security thing. But those differences are just social constructs. Biologically, there is little difference among us so it must be where we grew up, what we were taught, which causes us to identify with any particular group. Our differences aren't real, or they are, by their very nature, superficial. And so we struggle with those affiliations recognizing we never really belong anywhere.

"Now take your situation."

"What do you know about my situation?"

"I don't see you as a part of any group. You don't feel like you belong anywhere." Again, a statement, not a question. "I know this because what few connections you have are weak and it's tearing you up inside."

"I don't know who you think you are . . ."

"Am I wrong?"

Now a real question. This guy set her on edge. But she had to acknowledge he was right. And she found she couldn't help liking him. She appreciated how he met her head on speaking with real passion. Despite his directness she saw gentleness in him and something else . . .

"Let's say you're right. So what?"

"Before taking the Treatment I became convinced our biology limited us, that we were wired for our own self-destruction forever descending into defensive posturing despite our higher nature. But with the Treatment I learned we really have a higher nature and how to tap into it. We wander blindly through life searching for meaning when in fact we crave connection, we just don't know how to achieve it. With the Ulysses Treatment and the BRIDG we have the capability to move to the next stage in human development. How can anyone turn their back on the chance we now have to make our civilization truly civilized? You asked earlier if we want to take over the world. With what you know now, what alternative do I have?

"There is so much suffering everywhere: war, famine, disease, poverty. And even here in this country we struggle daily with alienation and fear. You sit here in this land of plenty cut off from those around you; no life to speak of; barely able to make ends meet. Some battle day-in, day out hoping to see daylight. But you, I sense you're giving up, losing hope. Or have you already lost it entirely?"

Dawn found herself unable to argue. How could this stranger know so much? At the same time she dimly sensed that he wasn't accusing her but reaching out, trying to connect, to understand.

As if in response to her thought he asked, "Please, tell me about yourself."

Surprised by her own willingness to confide in a total stranger, Dawn began, "there really isn't much to tell. I grew up in a small town about two hours away. I moved here a few years ago with a guy I knew from back home. I thought he was the one, you know, the one I'd spend the rest of my life with. We were making a go of it, had a decent place. But then it all started to fall apart. He was coming home later and later from work, lying about what he was doing. I knew he'd been out drinking. He'd come home, drunk, yell at me, made me feel like crap. I followed him one night, saw him leave the bar with some skank. When he got home that night I let him have it. At first he denied everything. Called me every name in the book, said I was paranoid. Finally came clean; promised to turn it around. I came home from work a couple of weeks later to find him gone, with the car. He'd cleaned out the bank account and I had no clue where he went. That was about a year and a half ago. He left me with a bunch of bills and now I can't seem to get my head above water."

"Have you thought about taking the Treatment?"

"I don't see why. Won't change my situation."

Michael nodded.

Dawn felt torn; stuck between the possibilities there might be something in this for her and the reality of her desperation. *Who am I to hope? Get real.* She knew from sad experience that hope was nothing but the harbinger of shattered dreams; and as of late, even her dreams had been dark, foreboding reflections.

56

Yet, despite her feelings Dawn trusted this stranger, this crusader. There was something about him; a sense of confidence and a kind of magnetism which made her feel safe. In a corner of her mind she found herself wishing he would find a solution, however hidden, and show her a way.

Dawn asked, "So did you figure out why you're here?"

"Nope. I almost thought I had something earlier but it escaped me. In any event, I won't be stalking you anymore."

"Must be hard doing what you do, trying to solve all the world's problems." Dawn looked down at her feet, "I can't even get a grip on my own."

Michael stood, replaced his hat on his head and grabbed his backpack. "It's a struggle. We have a solution and yet we're fought at every turn. I expected as much but it gets so tiring after a while, dealing with the ignorance and fear."

They walked to the door.

"Don't you have anyone to help?" Dawn asked.

"Hundreds of thousands all over the world have gone through the Transformation and more every day. But everything has to be organized and it seems I've become something of a lightning rod."

Standing in front of her opened door Michael continued, "Thanks for your hospitality. Sorry for the rant. Old habits die hard."

Michael held out his hand and Dawn took it. She found herself at a loss, disappointed he was leaving so soon.

"Don't get discouraged," she said. "It sounds like you're doing a lot of good. In the end, that's what really matters. And if no one else appreciates it, it's their problem."

Michael smiled shyly, "Thanks. How far behind is your rent?"

"How do you know?"

Michael looked into her eyes. "Do you really need to ask? I'm a pretty observant guy. How much?"

"Twelve hundred bucks."

Michael reached into his pocket, removed a roll of bills and peeled off twelve Benjamin's.

"I can't take this."

"You need it more than me."

Taking the bills gratefully a thought struck Dawn as Michael turned to leave. She had no clue why she asked him, "Do you have any kids?"

Michael stopped at the top of the landing motionless; his back to her.

"Yes. Twins. They're about three and a half."

He turned slowly and she noticed his eyes had narrowed as if assessing her in a new light.

"What is it?" she asked.

Michael smiled, put down his backpack, reached back into his pocket and took out another thousand dollars. "Settle your affairs. I have to leave the country for a little while. I'll be back here in a week. All you need to bring are your clothes."

"You figured out why you're here."

"I want you to work for me."

"And do what?"

"Does it matter? You'll have a nice place to live and you'll make a living wage."

"I don't want charity."

Dawn wondered why Michael smiled cryptically as he replied, "This is a real job. Believe me; you'll have to work for it."

"I want to know what I'm getting into. You think I can just pick up and leave?"

"What's keeping you here?"

Dawn stared back at him, challenging.

"Gabby and I are pretty busy, as you can imagine. We need someone to watch the kids when we're working."

"You're hiring me as a babysitter? You've been stalking me all this time for that?

"Do you have any experience?"

"Yes, but that's not what I'm asking you."

"Look, I'm not sure what's going on but you're tied to the kids somehow. Why did you ask me about them?"

"I'm not sure. Just making conversation."

Michael shook his head. "There's more to it. You asked that question for a reason, even if you don't know why. I'll be back in a week."

"I don't know . . . ."

Michael's demeanor shifted in a flash almost throwing Dawn off balance. His features took on a dark, determined cast. He appeared to grow in her sight.

"The river's flowing swiftly, now. It's carrying all of us along. Like it or not you're swept up in its current. I'm sorry but it can't be helped. You're destined to play a role in all this. I just don't know what it is."

Michael turned abruptly and began walking down the stairway.

"Who in the hell do you think you are?"

Continuing to walk down the stairs and without turning Michael said, "You have a week to decide."

"How will you know?"

"I'll know", Michael said without turning around as he continued walking toward the door.

I bet you will, Dawn thought ruefully as she stared after him. *What do I have to lose, anyway? Might be an easier gig. At least I can get out of this rat hole*, she reasoned.

Michael stopped at the bottom of the stairs, his hand on the door knob. Without looking back he said, too softly for Dawn to hear, "Good for you."

Michael walked down the street to his car. He got in, placed his backpack on the passenger seat next to him and removed the BRIDG Communicator from the bag.

He was staring at the screen waiting for Gabby's response to his latest contact.

"I'm glad you finally figured it out," she began. "I told you all you needed to do was talk to her. Now, will you come home and rescue me?"

Michael messaged her back and she responded:

"Yes, I know they're cute but they're driving me crazy. It's your turn for a while."

A pause while he messaged her.

"What do you mean you have to go to Europe? I've got work to do, too."

Michael explained his response.

"Makes sense given the circumstances. Should have seen it coming. See you when you get home. Wish us luck."

Michael turned off the power and returned the BRIDG Communicator to the bag. As he pulled away from the curb headed for the airport he considered what he had to do next. Events were moving quickly now. He sat at the center of the storm. While he drove, his mind wandered playing out several scenarios hoping against hope Gabby and Jules could forestall the inevitable.

Chapter 7

"You're gonna get in trouble", cautioned Bobby

"Don't tew Mom. She doesn't understand."

"Anyway we're not hurting anything."

"Now Kerry, what word were you wooking for?"

"I need a synonym for ignorant"

"What's a synonym?" asked Bobby.

"How about 'uninformed'"?

"It's a word that means the same thing as another word."

"Then why do you need a different word?" asked Bobby.

"That works."

"If you use the same word too often readers get bored."

A light spring rain slapped at the window pane. Inside the study three children faced a computer screen. The oldest of the three, Bobby, sat in a high-backed chair swiveling back and forth in an unconscious effort to work off excess energy. Two younger children stood on either side of him gazing at the monitor. They were just tall enough to see over the top of the light beige wooden desk.

"You know, Thomas Jefferson invented the swivoh chair."

"Awex, you can be so random."

"What's random?" asked Bobby.

"Awex is random. He spouts these usewess facts whether we're interested or not."

"Oh, you wike it. It's just one of the many ways I add to your knowedge."

"OK then brainiac, when wiww my pawatt harden enough so I don't sound wike Emmah Fudd?

"What're you talking about?" asked a frustrated Bobby.

Kerry rolled her eyes in exasperation as words appeared on the computer screen.

Bobby read, "'When will my palate harden enough so I won't sound like Elmer Fudd?' Oh." Pause. "What's a palate?"

"By the time we're four. Not too much wonger," said Alex as he stuck an index finger in Bobby's mouth grazing his hard palate.

Bobby spit as he said, "Thanks a lot. Remind me not to ask you any more questions. What're you writing about now?"

"I buweeve that's a question," said Kerry.

An application appeared on the computer screen activated by the twins utilizing the BRIDG processor.

"I wish I could do that", said Bobby.

"Mom and Dad don't think anyone should have the Treatment before they're eighteen," said Kerry. "Issues with maturity and free wiww.

"It's not fair. You guys were born with it."

Alex looked at his sister. "You know, we could induce him oursewves."

"Mom would have a cow," said Kerry.

The three turned their attention again to the screen which displayed a window with a blinking cursor. In the title bar stood one word: Dialogos.

In the Fall, Peter Keyes had introduced the twins to the principles of software development. Over the ensuing months they created and published an application which permitted up to five persons to have a conversation and, at the same time, allow others to view the dialogue.

Unbeknownst to their parents they developed Dialogos for the express purpose of influencing public debate around the NextAge movement.

As Bobby looked from Alex to Kerry, the twin's amiable banter evaporated as the two stared at the computer screen. They scared him a bit when they got like this.

The first dialogue box appeared displaying the name: Jennings "Recap: we were considering Barnum's contention that our society has decayed, perhaps beyond recovery. He's right. There's no respect for real authority anymore. Everything's relative from morality to marriage. We have to get back to the fundamental beliefs and values that created our country and society. I remember when I was growing up we lived in fear of our elders, parents, teachers. That fear engendered respect. And that respect produced order. We knew where we stood but now we suffer the shifting sands of moral relativism fostered by the godless and uninformed. We've lost our foundation."

The next Dialogos box appeared with the name: Claire. "Give me a break. Do you think time moves backwards? Can you put the Genie back in the bottle? Why go back 50-100 years? Why not a thousand years to medieval Europe? Everyone certainly knew their place then. No. The men who founded this country rejected wholesale the European caste system. Those great men shook off the chains of a repressive history when they created this country. America isn't just another nation-state. It is an idea: an idea that man can govern himself and thereby take control of his own destiny. That's real progress. You would have us stagnate wallowing in our imperfect recollections."
Jennings:

"Progress? Look at the world around you. Does this look like progress? Decay ridden cities, celebrities as heroes, graft and corruption rampant, prisons overcrowded with felons and population out of control. We need a strong hand to rule over us. Unfettered freedom breeds chaos."

"Kids, where are you?" Bobby heard Gabby call as she came down the hall.

Kerry turned her head while Alex focused on the screen. Claire:

"Whoa, I need to think about that. We'll talk again later. Readers, let us know what you think."

Alex blinked and the computer screen reverted to the game the kids had been playing.

Gabby rounded the corner and poked her head in the room.

"Are you two giving Bobby a turn?"

"Yes, Mom," came the innocent-eyed response in perfect unison.

Gabby lowered her chin looking over the tops of her glasses.

"Do you think I don't know what you two are up to? You've been posting again haven't you?"

Bobby slunk down in the chair.

"OK, show me."

The twins looked at each other and shrugged.

The computer display came alive with the latest dialogue.

After reading the conversation Gabby nodded.

"You'd better be sure you know where you're going with this. There's a lot at stake here. You know what your father and I are fighting for and what we're up against."

"Its onwy what Dad used to do," explained Alex.

"And have you the experience to know what consequences you might create?"

Kerry looked her mother in the eye. "We may wook and sound wike we're three years ohd, but you know better."

Gabby crouched in front of the kids at eye level. "My dears, I'm only trying to protect you. Despite our abilities I can't help myself. You may not be children mentally but you're still my babies; you always will be and I will worry about you for the rest of my life. You'll understand when you have children of your own."

Alex looked at Kerry and smiled. "Some things never change."

He turned to Gabby and said, "We understand but we have a row to pway as weww."

"I know that."

"Mom, we're taking every precaution," said Kerry. "No one knows who we are. We're being carefuw.

"I'm sure you are. Now, I have to go out of town with your Uncle Jules. I'll only be gone for the day. I've asked Mrs. Prosser to come stay with you."

The children groaned. "Mom," said Kerry, "she doesn't understand us."

"An' she makes my peanut butter and jewwy sandwiches with butter," complained Alex.

"Bobby?" asked Gabby.

"She's OK, I guess. But she's kinda strict and the twins freak her out sometimes."

Attempting to put on a strict face, Gabby said "You two behave. I won't be gone long."

She stretched out her arms, "come here."

The twins rushed to her embrace while Bobby held back.

"You, too."

Bobby scurried to join them, all four holding tightly to each other.

Gabby felt a low, bass rumble shaking her very soul. She pulled back and it stopped.

"What was *that*?"

The twins, tight lipped, just looked at her. "We don't know," said Kerry. "It started a few days ago."

"We're still trying to figure out what causes it," said Alex.

The doorbell rang.

"That will be Mrs. Prosser. I spoke with your father earlier and he seems to have found someone more permanent. You two, be careful. Bobby, try to keep them in line."

"I will," responded Bobby with an expression serious beyond his eight years.

Gabby rose and went to answer the door wondering what this latest development might mean.

Chapter 8

The Senator's aide stepped cautiously into the packed restaurant, the murmur of the lunchtime crowd instantly masking the noise from the street. She was certain, well, hopeful, this place was sufficiently distant from the Capitol that she wouldn't be recognized; not that she was all that recognizable, yet. She stepped up to the maitre'd station.

"Good afternoon, do you have a reservation?"

"I'm meeting two people here. I'll look for them."

"As you wish," uttered the maitre'd as he stepped out of her way with an exaggerated gesture.

Cheryl scanned the crowd and didn't immediately see her lunch companions; but the Italian restaurant was dark, as she had hoped. Wandering among the tables she could smell beer and wine mixing with the aromas from the plates, indicators that the patrons were sufficiently well-heeled that they could return to work unguarded. Jules had chosen well.

She found them in the very back of the restaurant. Jules Allen stood as Cheryl approached, a broad smile creasing his face. Without hesitation he reached out and embraced her in a massive bear hug, and, given his large frame, she found herself totally engulfed. She surprised herself by joyfully returned his affection.

"It's so good to see you. I've missed you, Cheryl."

"I've missed you, too. How's Peter?"

"Never been better. Truly." As he released her Jules motioned to the other person sitting on his side of the booth. "Cheryl, this is Dr. Gabriella Neumann."

Gabby reached out her hand in greeting and said, "Please call me Gabby. We're practically family."

Cheryl took Gabby's hand and then sat across from the co-conspirators.

"I don't understand," said Cheryl, "how are we 'practically family'?"

"Cheryl, there's no need for you to be antagonistic," Jules countered.

"Jules, you read me so easily. The Ulysses Treatment seems to have worked for you," Cheryl replied, no attempt to hide her sarcasm.

"Jules, this was a bad idea. Perhaps we should go," Gabby suggested though made no move to rise.

Turning to Gabby Cheryl said, "I apologize. It's just that I haven't seen Jules in so long. He has always been one of my favorite people and still a part of my family even though Peter and I may be divorced. And you introduce yourself saying you're close enough to be in my family. It put me off but I was being unfair. Again, I apologize."

Cheryl then turned to Jules. "It really is good to see you. I wish it was under different circumstances. Of course, I've been following your exploits, all of you. What's Peter up to? You said he's doing well."

"He was directing BRIDG development for a while but became bored quickly with management so Arthur has him back in the lab where he belongs."

The waiter walked over with a plate of bruschetta, took their orders and as he left Cheryl said, "Jules, you remembered. You know I love this stuff."

She reached for the appetizer and before putting it in her mouth said, "So Peter's still relating better to things than people."

"He's not the same Cheryl. Not by a long shot."

"Yeah, yeah, I know, the Ulysses Treatment."

Attempting to change the subject Jules said, "It seems you've done well for yourself. I understand you're one of Senator Gregory's senior aides. I knew you would rise fast, but this is remarkable. Peter's very proud of you."

"But he didn't come with you."

"We discussed it but he didn't want to taint our get-together with your history. Perhaps you'll come to BDT for a visit?"

Despite feeling less comfortable by the minute Cheryl shocked herself when she asked, "Is he seeing anyone?"

"No."

"No time I suppose".

Jules said nothing in response. They continued with small talk until the waiter brought lunch.

After he left, Cheryl asked, "So, why am I here?"

Jules began. "We understand the Committee for State Security will be holding hearings soon. We also understand some of us will be called to testify and we want to know what the Senator and his committee are looking for. Are you involved?"

"I shouldn't be telling you but my appointment as chief of staff for the hearings will be announced later this afternoon."

Jules smiled proudly. "Congratulations."

"Thank you. We will be investigating whether, in fact, laws are being broken by BDT and its leadership. That includes you, Dr. Neumann. I expect we will call you, Arthur, and your husband. Jules, you probably won't have to testify, for now."

"Michael isn't an employee of BDT, never has been. Why would you call him?" Gabby asked.

"You're kidding. Look, he's at the center of this whole thing. He's the person people identify most with the NextAge Movement."

"Now the truth comes out," stated Gabby. "This isn't about the law. This is a show trial. You intend to shut us down and demonstrate the power of the Congress. You aren't interested in what we've been able to achieve."

"And what have you been able to achieve? Hmmm? An army of brain addled mutants to do your bidding? Computer technology designed so that only a designated few control the flow of information? You are a threat, you are both a threat."

Gently Jules asked, "And you believe that bullshit? Cheryl, you know that isn't true."

"I know no such thing. And even if I did it wouldn't matter. There are powers at work here beyond any of us. This thing has too much momentum. Jules, you have always been so rational, so grounded. Can't you see where this is leading?"

Before Jules could respond Gabby asked, "Have you considered that your strategy might backfire? What do you hope to gain?"

"First of all we need to take control of the BRIDG technology. It's just too dangerous. No one private company should have a monopoly on something that powerful."

"We don't have a monopoly," Jules replied. "We're sharing the technology with other companies around the world."

"And how many have taken you up on the offer; one company in Japan, a few smaller firms in developing

70

countries? Everyone's afraid. It's like you're selling technology with a built-in back door that can't be closed. We will find a way to control it and prevent you from using it for your own ends."

"For our own ends?" Gabby interrupted. "Using the circuit's incredible processing power we've developed new, genetically- tailored cancer treatments at a fraction of the cost of older chemotherapy drugs; and with fewer side effects. How is that for 'our own ends'"?

"You know what I'm talking about. And this Ulysses Treatment you've developed. Where are the level 3 human trials? You should know better."

"You're right", admitted Gabby. "But there have been no reports of negative side effects other than a few odd headaches. I'm not arguing the ethics or legality of what we've done but if you would just have an open mind, talk with Peter, you might learn something."

Cheryl responded, measuring her words, "What I believe doesn't matter. You're breaking the law. I can't help you."

For the next few moments no one said anything. Finally, Gabby broke the silence.

"Cheryl, we've started off on the wrong foot. I know there's no way you can put the brakes on this. I'm confident Arthur and I can handle ourselves just fine."

"But . . ?"

"We would prefer that you not call Michael to testify", said Jules. "There's nothing he can tell you that Gabby and Arthur can't. If necessary, I can testify in his place".

"What's he afraid of? We're only looking for the truth. We'll subpoena him if we have to."

"That's not the issue. *You* don't *want* him to testify," said Gabby.

"Me? Why should I be worried?" asked Cheryl, incredulous.

"The collective you. Senator Gregory, the panel, and you." Gabby continued. "We came hoping you would listen to reason. You don't know Michael, what he's capable of. You don't want your first high profile assignment to go down in flames, do you?"

"Are you threatening me?"

Gabby leaned forward in her seat. Her eyes seemed to sparkle when she spoke. Cheryl found herself unable to take her attention away.

"If I were to threaten you, you would know it. Don't think I'm just some mousy research physician tucked away in a lab somewhere."

Cheryl's heart raced trapped between exhilaration and sheer terror. Her breaths came in short gasps. In Gabby she sensed surpassing strength and power, a force of nature. The world around her receded, only the doctor's words seemed real.

"The work we do transcends the petty concerns of your committee. We are working for nothing less than the salvation of mankind. We have the potential to eradicate disease, eliminate famine, oppression, and war; usher in a golden age of humanity. Do you really believe that tool you work for has the best interests of this country and its people in mind?

"A moment ago you said 'there are powers at work here beyond any of us'. Not beyond us."

Cheryl looked from Gabby to Jules. He seemed to glow. She looked back at Gabby and saw the same shimmer.

"*What's happening?*" she wondered through her alarm. "*Is this real?*" Memories tried to intrude, memories from childhood. But they were just out of reach. And as quickly as the feeling came, it subsided; the glow, gone.

Gabby sat with her back against her seat cushion.

"Cheryl, we are offering you an opportunity to save face. That's all."

Emotionally exhausted and somewhat disoriented Cheryl said, "I'll consider it. I really need to get going. Maybe I should come by and see how Peter's doing. Perhaps I can work it into my travel schedule."

Cheryl stepped out of the booth practically tripping over herself, her lunch half finished.

"Jules, it was so good to see you again."

With a curt nod and barely audible, "Doctor" Cheryl left the restaurant into the beautiful afternoon.

As she walked the short distance to her car, Cheryl didn't notice the warmth in the air, the chirping birds, or the blossoming cherry trees; the promise of spring eluding her. Instead, she found herself confused and drained. She had expected a nice visit with Uncle Jules even though she would have to deliver what she expected to be taken as bad news.

Cheryl unlocked the door to her car, sat down, started the engine and pulled out of her space. She felt a headache coming on. At the stop light she breathed deeply while massaging her temples.

She didn't expect the exchange to end as it did. As she considered what had just happened, she determined that seeing Jules must have triggered memories and feelings from her time with Peter, a simpler, more carefree time. She didn't realize how much she missed the comfort of those days. But look where she was now. She had really made something of herself. She was on the fast track. Someday she would be elected to the Senate. Neumann displayed her ignorance thinking Senator Gregory a tool. She might be a brilliant researcher but the celebrated doctor knew nothing of politics.

Cheryl was now more determined than ever to call Michael Neumann to testify. *Who do they think they are? They have no idea what they're up against.*

As she drove back to her office, Cheryl planned her next moves; the memory of her experience and its aftermath lost in the labyrinth of her mind.

Chapter 9

Gabby and Jules watched as Cheryl exited the restaurant.

"Did you know?" Gabby asked.

"That she was a Natural? No clue. I started to feel it shortly after she sat down. She was sensing us but I don't think she was aware of it. I believe that's why she reacted the way she did. She seemed to be off her game."

"She was uncomfortable and didn't know why", observed Gabby. "She tried to be cordial but was too stressed to maintain the façade. You've been studying the phenomena. What do we know about Naturals?"

"Not much. Apparently some people are born with rudimentary Ulysses capabilities; in all likelihood it's something in their neuroanatomy but it's too inconspicuous to detect with our current technology. We don't know if it's hereditary, random mutation or both. In any event the capabilities are not nearly as developed as in someone who has gone through the Transformation."

"How long have they been around?"

"At the IFS we study the future. But in understanding the future we gain insight into the past. As best we can tell, Naturals have been around as long as there's been recorded history, probably longer. We've classified three types: the shaman, the rejector, and the impair.

"In some societies the Natural has been accepted, even valued. These are mystics: respected, even treasured, for their wisdom and seemingly otherworldly vision. Other societies, especially modern ones take a different tack, especially when the shaman departs from orthodoxy. Under those conditions they're marginalized, seen as eccentrics or crackpots. That's in the best case. In the extreme the shaman will be persecuted as a heretic or nonbeliever and shunned or murdered. This was the case with the witch trials, for example. Now, I'm not saying all people branded as witches were Naturals, but I'm certain some were."

"Now Jules, are you calling me a witch?" Gabby asked with a smile.

In response Jules raised his eyebrows and shrugged his shoulders. "On the other hand Cheryl displays the traits of a classic rejector, the result of societal ignorance, personal misunderstanding, and defensiveness. Our society doesn't value the shaman. Rejectors have been taught to distrust their abilities. Cheryl's emotional intelligence being what it is knew she wouldn't fit in proper society if she were open with others about her abilities. If she was going to get ahead she'd have to 'reject' her natural gifts. She probably doesn't even remember. She appears to be deep in denial and I suspect it began even before she met Peter. We'll have to ask him."

"And the impair?" asked Gabby.

"Some Naturals don't have the strength of personality to contend with their nascent abilities and the effort pushes them into mental illness. These people aren't grounded in the day-to-day and are so torn the inner conflict becomes unendurable. After observing Cheryl I worry that if we confront her too directly again we may push her over the edge. We'll need to be more careful when we're around her."

"What do you think will happen if she talks to Peter?" Gabby wondered.

76

"I don't know. They were close once."

Changing the subject Gabby said, "Michael tells me the two of you are going to Italy. What do you hope to find?"

"I'm not sure. The loss of six of the Voyagers under suspicious circumstances is cause enough for concern. We strongly suspect they were tortured but to what end?"

"Michael thinks it's connected to his latest dream. Has he told you about it?"

Jules became more attentive. "No he hasn't." He knew from experience that Michael's dreams, though often cryptic, were truly prophetic.

Gabby sat for a moment, thinking. "I won't bore you with the details. You can ask him on the flight to Rome. He sees a series of catastrophic events coming. Apart from the reason we gave Cheryl for not wanting Michael to testify he believes if he goes before the Committee he will set events in motion from which there can be no return. Jules, he's deeply worried and I'm worried about him. Something's eating at him and I don't know what to do about it."

Gabby made a move to rise and the two headed for the exit. As they passed through the bar area Gabby noted the big screen TV was showing an image of Michael inset on the television screen.

"Oh great," Gabby intoned. "It's Barnum. Do you want to stay?"

Jeremiah Barnum sat, as usual, behind his large wooden desk, a massive American flag displayed prominently in the background. In the lower right hand corner of the screen in what looked like a box sat the image of Michael Neumann.

"I have to admit, until recently, I enjoyed listening to him", said Jules. "He's smart. I can't figure what he has against us.

77

We stood together on a number of issues, which I'm now sorry to admit. Let's stay for a few minutes."

Gabby and Jules sat at a low table facing the television screen. "I've been listening to him for a few years," Jules began. "At first I saw him as a replacement for Samsa's blogs when Michael stopped writing. Sometimes the guy makes sense, but lately, his rhetoric has put me off, he's become more strident. I think he's pandering to the lowest common denominator. I suppose it sells advertising but ever since he's taken off after us, I haven't the stomach for his rant. But perhaps we'll learn something to our benefit. He seems to speak for a lot of people."

"Or so he would have us think," Gabby countered.

Gabby and Jules turned their attention to the screen.

"They have infiltrated the very fabric of society. We must root them out and keep them from infecting the rest of us."

Barnum raised his left fist; in it, a sheaf of papers.

"The Samsamites and their collaborators hold influential positions in government, the military, and law enforcement. They walk the hallowed halls of academia and the corporate corridors of power. Well, people, what I hold here is only a partial list of those corrupting our culture. I have it on good authority the first task of Senator Gregory's Committee will be to discover the scope of their penetration as a prelude to rooting out their subversive influence.

"He will call authorities from the scientific and medical community to probe the threat this so-called Ulysses virus poses. He will call computer experts to explain how to control BRIDG technology without opening up our most sensitive networks to its insidious influence.

"He will call the leaders of this Administration; from Justice, from the FDA, and others to understand why they haven't done more to control the imminent threat BDT poses. Are the bureaucrats blinded by their ineptitude or are there more sinister reasons behind their inaction?

"There is one question every witness before the Committee should be asked and must answer. We need to know who to trust. We must know who's still human and who has become a soulless creature. We must root the Samsamites from our midst. They must not be allowed to attend our schools unsupervised, work in our factories unwatched or serve our country unguarded for they will only bring ruin upon us all. No people, we must identify them, control them, and prevent them from reproducing."

Gabby shook her head in amazement at the ignorance and fear she witnessed while Jules sat there, his hand covering his mouth, mystified.

A portly man in a well-tailored suit who had been sitting at the bar stood and made his way to the door. He looked down at Gabby and Jules and said, "Can you believe that guy? I have a friend who took the Ulysses Treatment; seems fine to me. Now, I'm not saying I'd go that way and I'm not saying I wouldn't but I don't get why he's making them out to be something they're not. I just don't get it." He waved dismissively at the TV as he walked out of the bar.

"Maybe we should hire a polling agency like Gallup to find out what people really think, mount a counter offensive," suggested Gabby.

"If we hire them the public will allege we bought the results. You've heard how questions are often asked by polling services. The answer is predetermined by the way they ask the question."

Barnum continued his rant, "We'll ask leaders of the major religions to confirm what we already know: that the

Samsamites are godless atheists bent on destroying the moral fabric of our society.

"The Committee will call the titans of industry to tell the world of the threat posed by the BRIDG. The liberals complained about the unconstitutional intrusions of the Patriot Act. Where are their objections to a technology that could realize the horror of Orwell's '1984'? Do you want Arthur Paulson to intrude on your private thoughts; to control whole economies, to become the real 'Big Brother'? He touts the benefits of the BRIDG and perhaps they can come to pass but not under his domination. He says he's offering the BRIDG at a nominal cost. Why is that?

"Why is a man whose reputation as a rapacious corporate schemer running one of the most successful businesses in the history of capitalism offering something for free? Because it isn't. He's selling technology with a built-in back door which can't be closed."

Jules turned to Gabby, "That's the same thing Cheryl said not ten minutes ago, verbatim."

Gabby nodded. "Makes sense. Barnum is probably in league with Senator Gregory. Gregory must be using him to build public support for the hearings; trying to sway the court of public opinion before the hearings begin. A dangerous strategy, don't you think?"

"It's a gamble, but I doubt he sees it that way," replied Jules. "They expect to stoke the fires of fear they've been fostering for a while now."

Gabby and Jules returned their attention to the television as they heard their names mentioned.

"When they testify we will come to know the depth of their conspiracy. We will hear from Arthur Paulson, Dr.

Gabriella Neumann and, most importantly, her husband: Michael Neumann."

"So, Jules, what's our strategy?" Gabby asked.

"Arthur thinks the Travelers should get together when Michael and I get back from Europe."

Gabby smiled at the mention of the 'Travelers' recalling fond memories. It had been almost four years. Gabby, Michael, Jules, and Peter had traveled to Jules' home in northern Wisconsin in an attempt to save Michael's life. The trip to the remote outpost had been necessary, in part, because they had to steal the viral specimens from under Arthur's nose and, in part, so that Gabby could administer the first Ulysses Treatment away from prying eyes.

Arthur figured out where they had gone and flown to the hideaway to confront them. At first, he tried to force Gabby to return to BDT to complete the Achilles project but instead decided to undergo the Transformation. He was the second. While there Jules told a tale entitled "The Traveler" about a man who chose to spend his life traveling but found, in the end, he could never return to the home he remembered fondly, a home he didn't realize he missed until it was too late.

The five traveled together back to BDT to stop General Scott from seizing the Achilles Virus and the Traveler name stuck. They coined the term "Voyager" for those who had undergone the Transformation to recognize the path they had chosen; one which would prevent them from going home but which offered the stimulation of exploring the full potential of the human race.

"And how can we identify these insurrectionists?" continued Barnum. "There is no obvious identifying mark, no look, no behavior. Instead the Senators will insist the conspirators produce lists of those who have undergone the treatment. They will be called to account. Our government will put a stop to further treatments and those who have been mutated will be watched to make sure they pose no further treasonous threat. While I hate the thought of quarantine, it would be for their own good.

"Public hostility is growing. Let's say many if not most of them are innocent dupes fooled into joining the movement. We need to protect them. They're so deluded they don't even know the risks they've taken."

Gabby looked at Jules. "What growing hostility?"

"He believes if he repeats it often enough others will get on the bandwagon."

"What will he do when they find out there is no 'list'? He just doesn't get it. We don't need one and purposely haven't kept one. They're so lost."

"Gabby, we're getting close."

"I know. It won't be long before genetic drift makes all their efforts irrelevant."

The two stood and walked toward the door. Outside on the sidewalk Gabby turned to her friend.

"Jules, promise me you will watch over Michael when you're in Rome. He's getting more reckless. He's got a family to think of."

"You know he's doing what he thinks he thinks he must. He would never do anything to jeopardize you or the kids. But I'll keep an eye on him just the same."

Gabby rested her hand on Jules arm. "Thanks. I hope you're able to get to the bottom of this. I fear what happened in Italy may have repercussions for us all."

Chapter 10

"But Peter, I don't understand," said Neil, one of BDT's senior system engineers. "How am I supposed to be in two places at once?"

"I'll help you," said Barb, another engineer. "Peter, I'll take this offline with Neil."

"Thank you, Barb", said Peter Keyes. "I guess that wraps it up. I'll bow out and let all of you get to it. I think we're done for today."

As the group dispersed Barb caught up to Peter.

"You seemed more distracted than usual," she said. "What's up?"

"Jules and Gabby were meeting with my ex. I had high hopes but I don't think it went well. I told Jules I was worried my history with her would color the discussions."

"I'm sure it wasn't your fault," said Barb.

"No, probably not," said Peter trying hard to convince himself.

Peter entered his office with a growing sense of unease. He could intuit from Gabby and Jules that the meeting had indeed gone badly and despite a deep desire to avoid the issue all together, he walked directly to his computer to see if he had a message from either. Sure enough, there were Jules' thoughts displayed on the screen.

"Could have gone better. She was very defensive. Despite her protestations, I think she still remembers you fondly. Big news is: she's a Natural. Did you suspect? She's a rejector and I worry she's close to the edge. We need to be careful, for her sake."

Rather than respond, Peter found his thoughts disconnected, jumbled. He stared at the screen. *Someday I won't have to use this monitor. It's so antiquated. I know I'm close. There's got to be a way to break down the barriers between electronic and biologic technology. The parallels are there.*

Among that initial group, the Travelers, Peter took most quickly to the technological side of their discovery. He knew that for centuries, mankind's relationship with tools and technology had been on a convergent evolutionary path. With the development of thinking machines in the twentieth century the dichotomy between mind and machine blurred even further. And with his creation of the BRIDG, the difference between the three pounds of jelly between his ears and this new processor became more difficult to distinguish. He felt himself on the edge of a breakthrough but hadn't come up with the right approach.

While he continued to ruminate on the problem a nagging thought in the back of his mind forced him to confront what he truly wanted to avoid. Since that day, the day he and Cheryl called it quits, he had done everything possible to distance himself from her, separate himself from his feelings for Cheryl. Now Jules and Gabby had to meddle.

Who am I kidding? I was curious. I wanted to know what happened. I've avoided thinking about her for all these years. Maybe it's time I finally deal with what I was totally incapable of confronting before. Analysis and logic were always my strengths. Emotions, another matter. Too much pain.

They'd been divorced six years.

§

"Peter we need to talk."

Peter sat staring at the computer screen in the small room they called a study. It was a Thursday evening. A cold dinner plate sat next to the computer, untouched. Rain spattered the lone window pane. Lightning crashed overhead, the sound of thunder shaking the house.

"Can it wait? I'm in the middle of something."

"No it can't."

"Fine", said Peter with more than a trace of irritation. "I'll just finish this."

Cheryl waited, tapping her foot. Finally Peter swiveled in his chair looked up into her face and said, "What is it?"

"Two days ago I told you I'd been offered that job in Washington with Congressman Wiley. You haven't said a word."

"What do you want me to say?

"You could find a job in Washington. They need computer experts."

"Computer experts? That's what you think I do? I'm a researcher. How easy do you think it would be for me to find something like what I have at BDT? They let me do what I want. I'm not leaving."

"I'm not staying."

Lightning crashed again. Close. This time the lights flickered and the power went out.

"Oh, hell," said Cheryl.

Peter's screen continued to glow sustained by his backup battery.

85

Illuminated only by the light from the monitor Cheryl continued, "So, does this mean we're breaking up?"

"What do you think?"

Cheryl stared at Peter, exasperation written across her features, her lips pursed, shaking her head.

"Well, I guess that's it then. I suppose this has been coming for a while. Peter, I just don't get you. You used to be so much fun to be with. Now you're just a lump blowing me off."

Peter, still sitting in his chair, his face an inscrutable mask in the back lit darkness said, "What do you want me to say?"

"If you don't know, I can't tell you."

She had seen something in him when they first met, a fire, a passion for discovery, and that dry sense of humor. She knew he was destined for greatness. But now all she saw was someone she barely knew. They had hardly spoken since she told him about the job.

"I guess this was a mistake," said Cheryl. "We just don't have that much in common anymore."

"You knew what I was like when you married me. I'm not an emotional guy. I don't get all tied up in my feelings like you do. A waste of time."

"I've been a waste of time?"

"That wasn't what I was saying, and you know it. We're just very different. I understand if you want to leave."

Cheryl found her way to the door in the darkness, hesitated then quickly turned to face him.

"I thought, in you, I found someone who got me; who let me be who I am, quirks and all. Someone who would encourage me, support me. Someone who matched my own need for independence. Together we could have gone so far."

A slight rueful chuckle escaped from her throat.

86

"But now I see I was wrong. I was so tied up in my own world, my own aspirations I didn't see you for who you are, or maybe more accurately, who you aren't.

"You say you don't get tied up in your feelings but you're wrong. You feel like everyone else, you just don't want or know how to express it. You don't like dealing with the mess. But life is messy. I feel sorry for you. You may not know pain, but as a result you'll never know joy."

Cheryl stopped talking. To Peter it appeared as though she was parsing her words carefully now.

"Peter, someday someone will pierce your bubble. It will come out of the blue when you least expect it. I hope, for your sake, you take advantage of it."

The lights came back on. Peter saw Cheryl rubbing her temples. She always did that when she had one of her headaches. She sighed and in words leaden with exhaustion said, "I'll start packing. I'll contact a lawyer. She can draw up the papers; a simple division of property. Good luck, Peter."

Cheryl walked down the stairs leaving Peter alone with his computer. He turned in his chair and stared at the monitor. He reflexively raised his hands placing his fingers on the keyboard. But they refused to move, his mind blank.

He felt an emptiness rise in his chest, past his heart, to his throat where it seemed to lodge in the back of his mouth. The emptiness expanded, emptying him of all thought.

He knew that familiar hollow feeling. Peter first felt it after his parents died when he was only six. He had been so successful at keeping it at bay, the lurking lion restrained in its cage. He dare not release it. The chaos would overwhelm him.

Despite all his effort, the tears came.

§

Peter stared at the monitor.

I was such a mess. Couldn't blame her for leaving. One more piece of baggage I thought I didn't need. So clueless.

But, a Natural?

Peter leaned back in his chair, his hands clasped behind his head.

She was always so intuitive. And those headaches. Hmmmmm.

Jules's right. I'll have to be careful. But I'm not sure I can trust myself. What'll I do when I see her? What if those feelings I kept bottled up over all those years come spilling out? Can't let that happen. Gotta find a way to help her. I owe her that much.

Peter leaned forward in his chair. Watching the screen he let his mind wander the web, searching for clues to the path he should take.

Chapter 11

The nondescript bank sat on a nondescript corner in the heart of Rome. Jules and Michael had entered through an unmarked portal. The financial institution, an affiliate of a Swiss bank, offered a secure entrance on a side street, away from the main thoroughfare affording access for its more discreet clients.

The two arrived via taxi from their quiet, out-of-the-way hotel not far from the Via Veneto. Even though it was past eight o'clock in the evening their cab zipped in and out among the speeding cars and scooters. Descending from the Quirinal Hill onto what had been the Campus Martius, the training ground for the Roman legions, their car fought the evening traffic through the winding narrow streets.

Dropping them off a block from the bank, they walked the short distance to the building and Jules punched in the security code which had been given to him three hours prior. The door opened and the two entered. Instead of turning to the right to access banking services, they walked straight ahead, down the hall coming to a row of identical doors. The third door on the left was marked by a number 5 etched onto a brass plate and centered at eye level. Jules punched the same code into the keypad to the left of the door, turned the handle, and stepped into the meeting space.

A wood conference table trimmed in chrome dominated the room. Off to one side Michael saw a buffet in the same design as the table. It held a pitcher with ice water along with a coffee and tea service. The bank officer had asked Jules if he would like wine or spirits but Jules declined. The subdued indirect lighting reinforced the clandestine atmosphere.

Eight well-cushioned black leather arm chairs, new enough to emit their characteristic odor, surrounded the conference table. In one sat a balding man in his late 40's dressed in a well-tailored gray sport coat and open necked black shirt. Angelo Famiglia stood, towering over both his guests and introduced himself.

"Buona sera and welcome to Rome," he intoned in a deep baritone accented by an Italian inflection Michael found welcoming. "It is a pleasure to finally meet both of you. I wish our first visit could have occurred better circumstances."

"As do we," responded Jules.

Michael turned to a sharply dressed women sitting across from Famiglia. "Gerta, so good to see you again. How are the children?"

Gerta Weiss led the NextAge Coordinating Council activities on the European continent. There were nine Coordinating Councils in all, covering roughly North America, South America, Europe, Africa, West and Central Asia, South and Southeast Asia (though India and China each had their own councils owing to their sizable populations), and Australia with the islands of the Pacific. Roughly because the designations didn't necessarily follow traditional geographic boundaries with Mexico included in South America and North Africa included in the West and Central Asia designation. Arthur Paulson, utilizing similar strategies to those he employed as CEO of BDT, had recommended the designations based on similarity of culture and economic development thinking the strategies for deploying the BRIDG, overseeing the induction of the Ulysses virus, and dealing with governmental and other institutional issues would find unique and related solutions in each.

"My children are well, Michael, though they are hardly children. My oldest will go to University in the fall and the youngest isn't far behind. How are the twins and Gabby?"

"All doing well. The twins are keeping us on our toes. I often find myself at a loss." Michael was shaking his head. "We're finding it difficult to stay ahead of them. I suspect it isn't easy keeping up with children who haven't been born with the Ulysses capabilities but in our case . . . well let's just say Gabby and I are discovering how little we understand them. They will lead us into a whole new world, one we couldn't have anticipated a decade ago. They can frighten me with their depth."

"Michael, how could you say that?" Jules chided. "They are the sweetest things; a little precocious perhaps."

"'A little precocious'? Jules, last week I found Kerry posting on the internet. But, enough about family. We are here to understand what may have happened to the Voyagers who were lost and to see if this may signal a broader threat. Angelo, what can you tell us?"

The man paused before speaking, collecting his thoughts, clearly struggling with the affair. "All six lived in and around Rome. They disappeared Sunday night April 17th. We suspect they were taken at night when most of us were asleep possibly so we wouldn't sense their distress immediately. It's possible they were drugged so they wouldn't send out an alarm but if so, we don't know how it was done. The next morning as the day began those who knew them became immediately alarmed. The mother of Gina, one of the women, who has also gone through the Transformation, called me in a very

91

agitated state to report her daughter missing and that she appeared to be in a desperate way. We suspect her daughter was being tortured. Gina appeared be holding up as well as might be expected, given the circumstances.

"Her mother was able to maintain the connection with her daughter throughout the ordeal. She thinks her daughter may have been able to draw strength from her and held fast to hope; but it was all in vain. Shortly after sunset Gina's mother felt the Break and she knew. Though she was sad, she took some comfort in being able to maintain the connection with her daughter until the bitter end. As she finished her story, she said something odd to me. She said 'Do not been too sad for me. She is not lost.'"

Famiglia paused.

"We contacted the authorities in the morning to report the kidnappings but they took little notice as our fellow Voyagers had not been missing long. Whether or not they trust our abilities is difficult to say but they definitely thought we were overreacting. However there is one police captain, a Voyager like us, who quietly intervened on our behalf and worked with other Voyagers in the police department. He had to be circumspect so as not to call his judgment into question.

"However, once we knew they died we were able to convince the powers that be to launch a full investigation, albeit grudgingly. They could not easily dismiss the simultaneous disappearance of six individuals. As they dug deeper it became apparent to them there had been foul play but, as of yet, have found nothing. There is no meaningful evidence and no one is talking. The trail appears to be cold. I am not confident they will learn any more."

"Angelo, we are all so sorry," said Michael. "Please convey our condolences to their families and the Voyager community. This is a grave loss for all of us. But we must now give attention what may have happened and what it might mean. Any idea how they were targeted?"

"We suspect whoever did this monitored the comings and goings at our induction center," responded Angelo. "They then selected those who lived alone so as not to arouse suspicion.

Jules turned to Gerta Weiss.

"Gerta, we have been following developments in Europe. There have been demonstrations and reports of harassment. We have heard of growing anxiety on the left and the right. In the States we've seen footage of neo-Nazis' and the far left publically protesting. How widespread is the threat?"

"I don't believe they pose any immediate danger," Weiss responded. "The left portrays the NextAge movement as just more encroachment by American capitalists on the rest of the world. The right, well, anything that doesn't fit neatly within their reactionist ideology must be evil. But we don't think this attack originates from within either movement."

"Why is that?" Jules asked.

"Gerta and I have spoken about this," said Famiglia

Weiss nodded for him to proceed.

"The police found little forensic evidence and no leads," said Famiglia. "The Voyagers were taken at a time when the kidnappers knew we wouldn't be able to detect them. And there is no trace of their remains. Our contacts among the police assure us this was the work of professionals; which only raises more questions."

"What were they attempting to achieve, were they successful, and, ultimately, who is behind this?" asked Gerta.

"Until we answer those questions, none of us is safe. We are all on alert."

As if in on cue, a red light flashed three times above the door grabbing everyone's attention. The signal indicated someone else had punched the security code in the outer entry.

Michael turned to his hosts. "Did you give the code to someone else?"

"I apologize for not telling you," said Gerta. "We weren't sure he would come and you will learn shortly why utter secrecy has been necessary."

"What could possibly have been so secret you couldn't have informed us ahead of time? How do you know these aren't the same people who took down your countrymen?"

Before they could answer Michael heard the digital tones as the visitor punched them on the keypad outside room 5.

The door opened to reveal a man in his mid 30's dressed in conservative slacks and a dark t-shirt under a dark brown leather jacket. He was a short 5'5" with a grave smile and a slight stoop for someone of his young years. Michael sensed they were in the presence of another Voyager and so dropped his guard.

"I apologize for arriving late," the stranger intoned in a gentle Spanish accent. "I had to be certain I wasn't followed."

He held out his hand in greeting. "It is a pleasure to meet you both. My name is Juan DeLeon. You may call me 'Father Juan'."

Chapter 12

Father Juan entered the room, shook hands and took his seat as Michael and Jules studied this new Voyager uncertain what to make of his revelation.

"This may sound like a stupid question," said Jules. "You're an ordained Catholic priest?

"Yes."

Michael asked, "When did you undergo the Transformation?"

"Two and a half weeks ago, here in Rome, under Angelo's direction and discretion."

"And does the Vatican know?" Jules continued.

"That is what I am here to discuss."

Turning to Angelo, Jules asked, "This is quite a development. Why didn't you say anything?"

"I thought it more important that we discuss this in person. It is vital that this information be kept to a select few."

"Before you explain the reason for all this secrecy, Father, I'd like to know more about you," Michael said.

"Claro, there is not much to tell. I was born in Spain not too far from Granada. I entered the priesthood at eighteen. The Church educated me first at the Universidad Complutense de Madrid. They then sent me to Notre Dame to study biological and cultural anthropology where I received my doctorate. I taught there while I continuing my research.

A few years ago one of my papers came to the attention of the Holy See and so I was brought to Rome. At the time I was not sure whether I was summoned because I had stepped over some line or if in fact some were intrigued by my studies."

"And what have you been studying?" Jules asked.

"Whether there is, in fact, a biological component to spiritual or mystical experience."

"An intriguing line of inquiry," observed Michael.

"Think about it. Our fascination with the miracle of human life reaches its apex in that most enigmatic of our internal organs, the brain. For so long the operating mind has embodied our greatest material mystery, and yet I saw in that mystery a gateway to understanding our connection to our Creator. As you may be aware, much of what we know about brain function is a result of studying the effects of injuries to various parts of the brain. Of course there is the much celebrated case of Phineas Gage who survived an accident in which an iron pole passed completely through his skull destroying a part of the left hemisphere of his brain and altering his personality. In the First World War we learned much about brain function from lesions suffered in battle.

"A few years ago, studies at the University of Udine here in Italy documented how lesions from surgery localized in the frontal and parietal regions altered personal perceptions of spiritual transcendence. My own area of interest led me to investigate the use of transcranial magnetic stimulation as a means to arouse the spiritual experience thinking it could be used as a form of therapy for those who feel cut off from God. I was on the verge of publishing my initial results when I was summoned to the Vatican.

"There were some here in Rome who knew of my research. What I didn't know at the time was that those same people were looking into NextAge Movement and, more specifically, the Ulysses Treatment. I have been here for almost a year.

"With all the research that has come to the fore in the past few years, a covert Commission had been formed to look into the connection between the brain, the mind, and the soul. It doesn't have a name and reports to a Cardinal who shall remain nameless, at least for now.

"To answer your unspoken question, there are those within the Holy See who see your tampering with the human mind as blatant heresy. But there are others who see your good works as evidence of God's hand in this. The Commission could find nothing specific in the Gospels which might condemn your efforts. The more I studied, the more I became convinced the Ulysses Treatment might hold the key to a fundamental understanding of the connection between the mind and the soul. Unknown to me other members of the Commission had reached the same conclusion.

"Quietly, carefully considering the implications, we came to believe that the only way to understand what you were experiencing was for one of us to undergo the Transformation. I was the natural choice given my background, my studies, and the direction of my research. By mutual agreement I was given special dispensation to undergo the Transformation, given the potential threat to my mortal soul."

"That 'special dispensation' could only have come from one source", observed Jules.

"Perhaps. The past two weeks have been a revelation. I am already convinced your discovery of the Ulysses Treatment opens new horizons for us all. The Lord has truly blessed you and created a means to bring all of us closer to Him; a means only open to a few before now", said the Father.

"What do you mean? God didn't create the Ulysses virus, my wife did," countered Michael.

"Yes, and who created your wife?"

Michael smiled. "Her parents, but I see where you're going. Gabby might agree with you. It really doesn't matter. Not to me. But I'm curious. What did you mean when you said the Ulysses Treatment offered 'a means open only to a few before'?"

"In my studies I have come across ample evidence pointing me to one conclusion: the effects of the Ulysses Treatment are not unique to our time and place; that others have had the same or similar experiences throughout history. I suspect many of the prophets, Daniel as a clear example, and, more recently, mystics have possessed latent abilities which you are now able to imbue in anyone. Let's take the case of Joan of Arc. Some, of course, have thought her visions a form of mental illness, epilepsy or the like. But those have largely been rejected based on what evidence we have of her behavior. How could she have successfully lead the French army of she was so debilitated?

"Then there is the story of Rabbi Jochanan ben Zakkai. During the siege of Jerusalem by the Romans in 70 AD no one was allowed in or out of the city except to bury the dead. The esteemed Rabbi was secreted out in a coffin and presented to General Vespasian. When confronted by the General ben Zakkai recounted a dream in which he saw the General becoming Emperor. Somehow the rabbi convinced the general of the truth of his predictions, which, in fact, did come to pass. Ben Zakkai was allowed to create an academy in Yavneh where, centuries later, other rabbis sealed the canon of the Jewish books of the Old Testament.

"Study the mystics. You see many shared the same understanding of mankind and the nature of our interconnectedness and how we are obligated to help each other. They also saw the necessary consequences of our foolish behaviors and as a result often accurately predicted what the future would hold. They may have used the theological language and paradigms of the day, but they were Voyagers nonetheless. Like us they spoke to their societies from a vantage point both within and without."

"Your thinking corresponds with our analysis at the Institute for Future Studies," observed Jules.

"I have heard you are organizing an Institute. What is its purpose?"

"Are you familiar with Foundation series by Isaac Asimov? Jules asked.

"Certainly," Father Juan responded.

Jules smiled. "Ah, another Sci-Fi aficionado. We'll have to talk more when we have time."

Michael rolled his eyes while Angelo and Gerta simply smiled.

"In a similar vein we're organizing academics and other Voyagers into a virtual institute for the purpose of creating predictive models and thus to formulate solutions to actual and anticipated economic, environmental and social challenges. We start with raw data on everything from population growth and distribution to economic and environmental trends, and biological development. We are creating algorithms to process the data to predict future roadblocks."

"In addition we also pursue subjects of more narrow notice. One of particular interest to me is the subject of Naturals, or as you call them, prophets and mystics."

"I am interested in discussing this topic with you," said the priest. "Perhaps we can pool our efforts."

"Maybe another time," said Michael. "Father, why are you here?"

"I took it upon myself to reach out to you. My superiors do not know I am here. I think it important for us to coordinate efforts. The Church cannot show overt support for the NextAge movement. However, I want to assure you we do not work at cross purposes. When the time is right I believe the Church must come forward. Perhaps your Future Studies Institute will enable us to envision that day, Jules."

Barely concealing his impatience, Michael asked, "Why isn't 'that day' now? We are facing resistance on many fronts and for the public to know the Church takes us seriously and sees the potential in the Ulysses Treatment would meaningfully help our cause."

"We cannot."

Michael's frustration would have been visible even to those who had not undergone the Transformation.

"I have heard you are an impatient man. This came through in your writings as Samsa, so I will try and explain. Though we are guided by the Holy Spirit, the Church is a human institution. And like all human institutions we must contend with our human frailties. Acceptance will not come easily."

"That is true," offered Gerta. "This is Europe. We don't tolerate change well. It is an arrogance borne of long tradition. I know it is difficult for Americans to understand. The founding of your country was a reaction to so much you found distasteful in European society: the entrenched class barriers and the constant wars over land and religion. But is America all that different today? The NextAge movement is forced to operate underground both here and across the Atlantic.

"With little exception we are forced to offer the treatment in secret with the help of BDT's facilities here in Europe and around the globe. Some persecute us, few understand what we're trying to achieve."

"All the more reason for the Vatican to come forward," responded Michael. "I'm not asking for an endorsement but if there were some sign that the Church saw the potential for merit that would certainly help."

Father Juan leaned toward Michael; his hands clasped together, forearms resting on the table. He looked into Michael's eyes. "Subjects like this are never discussed outside the Holy City but there is much debate. We are an institution founded in the highest human aspirations and basest fears. The Holy Father has not yet taken a position. When he does we can come forward. He has been moved by the recent deaths here in Italy. Though we may aspire to a higher moral code we don't dare risk greater instability. We must take the long term view. It is the same policy we followed during World War II toward German aggression and the Holocaust.

"And look how well that turned out," Michael observed. He paused choosing his words.

"Father I don't mean to put you on the defensive. You risked much in coming here and we are happy to have you as a fellow Voyager.

"Despite your cautious stance, the time for revelation will come soon, and not necessarily when the Church is ready. This is a new day. You feel the yearning all around you. The people don't trust public institutions. The failures of the entrenched power structures whether religious, governmental, or commercial to reduce suffering is propelling people to find new answers. You think my Samsa blogs were prescient? I wrote those before undergoing the Transformation. I was tapping into a universal frustration.

"Momentum is increasing. Make no mistake; the NextAge Movement is not the latest solution. It is only a vehicle for change. Plans and timetables will fall, swept up in an unassailable flow. I know you see this."

Father Juan smiled knowingly. "I do. And yet I am steeped in an ancient culture. I am still learning to see. I ask your forbearance as I navigate these treacherous waters."

Jules noticed the cleric appeared to be studying Michael unsure whether to speak.

"I have heard you are different and I sense in you something more than I sense in other Voyagers. I hesitate to ask but my curiosity . . . I have heard a rumor . . ."

Jules shook his head, "Don't go there."

Michael held up his hand. "Jules, it's okay."

Michael turned back to the priest. "It's true. You spoke of 'ancient cultures'. We estimate the universe to be 14 billion years old. The earth has only been here for 4 billion years. The first generation of stars was created what, half a million years after the Big Bang? That first group fused their hydrogen into helium and then into heavier elements: iron, carbon, oxygen. They died almost as quickly as they formed. And when they died they broadcast those heavier elements across the universe, the stuff of planets. Throughout this process the universe continued to expand, more stars were born. Time was different then, starting to slow down, but still very fast by our reckoning. Many generations of stars formed and died long before our sun came into existence. What is the chance that we are the first planet with intelligent life?"

"Wait a minute," interjected Angelo. "Are you saying the pace of time changed?"

"How do we measure time?" Jules asked rhetorically. "A year is a revolution around the sun; a minute one thirty-six hundredth of the time it takes the earth to rotate once on its axis. Our measure of time is arbitrary.

"Perhaps, said Angelo, but it is consistent."

"Here on earth, yes," responded Jules. "But at the turn of the 20th century physicists theorized that time would appear to slow down to an outside observer as we approach the speed of light. It's called time dilation. In 1971 scientists confirmed the theory by measuring the passage of time with the help of atomic clocks placed on two airplanes traveling in opposite directions. Atomic clocks are extremely accurate and the measurements precisely confirmed predictions made close to a century earlier. In fact, today's GPS systems utilize the same equations to accurately measure global position."

"I believe it was Einstein who said 'We need time so that everything doesn't happen at once'," said Jules. It's an artificial construct."

"Jules, thank you for the physics lesson," laughed Michael. "Can you see, Father, how it would have been possible for intelligent life to have existed in our universe evolving over billions of years? And wouldn't it be possible that those same life forms would evolve and possess a capability similar to what we have achieved with the Ulysses Treatment?"

"I have heard these arguments before," interrupted Father Juan. "While they may be eminently logical, they prove nothing."

"No they don't but it's the truth nonetheless." countered Michael.

"And you know this because . . ?" interrupted Gerta.

"You have the ability to sense truth. Do you doubt your senses?"

"No but, where is the evidence?"

"Peter may be brilliant, but he didn't come up with the initial circuit design for the BRIDG on his own. It's too far beyond anything we've developed. It was transmitted to me in the course of my first, and only, exchange or Encounter. Gabby and I were huddled outside under the stars. I had gone through the Transformation only two days before. I learned much and they helped prepare me for what is to come. To answer your original observation more directly, Father, the experience 'stretched' me as it were."

"Who are they and have you had any additional contact?" Angelo asked.

"I really don't know who they are and I have avoided reaching out to them again. I don't believe we're ready for more than what I have already become aware of.

"In addition to learning how to construct the BRIDG I began to understand the challenges we would face. But I also became aware that where there is good, there is also evil. There is the banal form we see in the resistance to what we must accomplish. But there are more insidious forces at play."

The three guests looked quizzically at Michael.

"You know the Ulysses Treatment is based on a retrovirus transfer. But you don't know that at the same time Gabby was developing the Ulysses retrovirus she was working on another treatment, named for Achilles, the Greek demi-god and soldier-hero of the Trojan War. This virus worked on the more primitive centers of the brain, like the cerebellum, for the purpose of creating soldiers with advanced physical coordination and agility: "super warriors" so to speak.

"But there were problems. Gabby dropped the project when it became evident the some of the lab animals did not adapt well to the treatment. Some had balance problems, but more concerning was the development of highly aggressive behaviors. A rogue general had sponsored the project and attempted to take the Achilles viral specimens by force. We had to stop him and destroy the samples. We could not allow him to unleash the Achilles virus. While we eliminated the immediate threat, Jules and I believe the Achilles Treatment is in development again and those same forces may be behind the murders here.

"How is this connected to your otherworldly contact?" asked the cleric. "I must confess it all seems too fantastic."

"Father, your church believes in miracles no more fantastic. After what you have already experienced do you really believe it isn't possible? Tell me you haven't experienced your connection with those across the globe. I am experiencing my connection with Gabby and the kids half a world away. This link we feel is independent of distance. Is it really so farfetched?"

Juan DeLeon shrugged. "Has anyone else experienced this contact?"

"Not yet," replied Michael. "Others have tried. I believe they only spoke to me because it was necessary to prepare us for what's to come. If we know too much we might be overwhelmed. I don't recommend the experience. Too much knowledge creates a problem of its own."

"So, I repeat my original question, how is this Achilles treatment connected to your Encounter?"

"Evolutionary biologists study fossils and species variance to understand how plants and animals evolved," explained Jules. "At the Institute for Future Studies we are trying to

105

predict how we will evolve from here. Think of the two primary evolutionary trees here on Earth. Man is the culmination of one branch, the vertebrates. Insects are one of the most advanced forms of invertebrates."

"Imagine splitting human beings into two new evolutionary trees. The first augments the higher functions as Gabby did with the Ulysses Treatment, the other our more primitive, reptilian brain. Can you see the potential for conflict not to mention where it leaves everyone in between?"

"You are describing a classic battle between good and evil, no?" questioned Angelo.

"It appears so," responded Michael. "What kind of world do we want? One where we recognize our connection to each other and work for the common good of humanity or one dominated by those who are physically the strongest, serving only their primeval needs. It's the age old question of freedom versus security. But I don't believe you can have one without the other. The Transformation has shown me that. We shall see who prevails. In either event we are still dealing with survival of the fittest. The only question is who will prove to be most fit.

Father DeLeon nodded. "To cast your description in more theological terms, it is our higher nature at war with our animal instincts. And God has promised that we shall emerge victorious. But God placed Man on Earth to fight this battle. Ultimately the Church must come down on the side of right. Unfortunately, they don't yet see this evil lurking among us. They see it as a question of whether the Voyagers possess some Truth that the rest of humanity does not. They are not aware of the true challenge we face. When will the nature of our common enemy become apparent?"

"No one can say for sure, but I believe it will come soon," said Michael. "That path is still cloudy."

Michael sat back in his chair seemingly lost in thought.

Reluctant to interrupt Michael in his reverie but mindful of the primary reason they had come together, Gerta said, "We are no further along in our understanding of who was behind the murders. What shall we do? I fear others may be spirited away by these nameless phantoms."

Michael sat forward. "They're close. They must know we're somewhere in the vicinity. Somehow they have learned of our meeting though I suspect they know only of our presence."

The others reached out with their heightened senses. "I perceive their malice," said Father DeLeon. "Should we call the police?"

"I can reach out to my contacts and arrange safe passage for all of us," said Angelo.

"But I cannot let anyone know I am here. All the good I can do will be undone," observed the priest.

Michael shook his head. "The surest means to discover what these stalkers are up to will be to confront them directly. Jules and I will draw them away from here. Once you sense they're gone the three of you can leave by another route."

"Michael, I want to know what's going on as badly as you, but do you think confronting them is the right way to go? I really don't want to be kidnapped or worse." said Jules.

"I think we can handle ourselves. And how else will we uncover what they're up to?"

Michael stood. "The three of you can wait until you feel it's safe."

Michael reached across the table and took the priest's hand.

"Father, it's good to have you with us. We'll need to communicate periodically. You can reach us with the BRIDG but how will be contact you? I'd like to get you a Communicator."

"I have seen photographs of the device. It is somewhat bulky and I wouldn't want it to be discovered in my quarters."

"Peter has developed a more compact prototype that looks like a cell phone", said Jules. "We'll get one to Angelo."

DeLeon nodded in agreement.

"Father, do you have access to the Vatican Archives?" asked Jules.

"Yes, why?"

"We are engaged in some lines of research which you may be able to assist. Are you interested?"

"Absolutely."

Jules and Michael shook hands with Gerta and Angelo. "Be careful, you two," said Gerta.

"Go with God," added DeLeon.

As they walked down the corridor toward the exit Jules said, "I hope you know what you're doing. If Gabby were here she would not be happy."

"And if she is sensing you right now, she'll know anyway. We'll call her when this is done."

"You're being very optimistic. These people play for keeps."

"So do we," said as Michael as they stepped through the portal to the waiting darkness beyond.

Chapter 13

Jules and Michael walked deliberately down the winding street trying to remain inconspicuous. Jules stepped off the curb but stepped back quickly as a fast moving motorcycle almost clipped him; its horn screaming as the rider passed in the distance. As they continued north the hustle and bustle of the late evening tourists and revelers filling the streets of the ancient capital gave way to quiet back ways.

"I sense them but they aren't yet close. They're more apt to confront us if we stay off the beaten path," said Michael.

Jules turned to his right and pointed. "Let's head off this way towards the river. Once they're close we can lure them into a more public area."

Three blocks later the two emerged from a side street in the Piazza di Ponte Sant'Angelo directly across the river from the Castello Sant'Angelo.

"There's a footbridge across the Tiber and it looks like there are plenty of people over there," said Jules and they headed to the bridge.

Michael looked over his shoulder and saw two men following them dressed in dark clothing and walking purposefully while keeping a safe distance.

"I see them. They're following us," said Michael.

"They're also coming towards us," and Jules nodded toward the Castle.

Four men approached from the other side. At this hour foot traffic on the bridge was light. About 100 feet away the two men behind Michael and Jules stopped; positioning themselves to prevent curious bystanders from interfering.

The men approaching from the direction of the Castle executed a similar maneuver with two remaining behind as the remaining two approached Michael and Jules.

"Maybe they just want to talk," said Jules.

"Follow my lead," responded Michael.

Michael stepped two paces back so that the railing of the bridge which stood chest high was close behind him.

The lamps on the bridge shed little light on the scene; intended more for the illumination of the stone-carved statues of angels. The men approached. From their movements Michael determined they weren't dealing with amateurs. Their confidence identified them as trained operatives. The first calmly approached Michael with his colleague hanging back a few paces.

He was a large man unremarkable in appearance except for his eyes. Even in the low light Michael saw iris's black as the blackest night.

"It's a beautiful evening isn't it?" the Nameless Man asked.

"A nice evening for a walk. What do you want?" asked Michael.

"Just to talk. I know a place, not too far from here."

"You're American," observed Jules.

The Man nodded. "Let's have a drink. As fellow Americans I'm sure we can sit across a table from each other and come to an accommodation, don't you think?"

"You murdered six people in cold blood. Is that the kind of 'accommodation' you seek?" challenged Jules.

Michael placed a restraining hand on Jules. "You'll understand my friend's reluctance to go with you. Why is this in our interest?"

"I represent an individual who sees the benefit of your movement and would like to collaborate with you. He is great man with great plans. He sees a way to make this world better, stronger. He understands the possibilities inherent in the BRIDG technology and believes there is potential for mutual benefit."

"The technology is available to everyone and is not expensive," said Jules. "Have him contact BioDigiTech and I'm sure we can produce processors for you. But you already know that and, I suspect, money is not an issue here."

"You are correct. It isn't quite that simple. We seek the use of the technology but don't wish to undergo the Treatment. Perhaps we can reach an accommodation where you supply both the technology and the individuals to use it. Why don't we find somewhere we can sit and negotiate in private?"

"Who's this individual you refer to?" asked Michael. "Perhaps we can meet with him in a neutral location when we get back to the States?"

The Man appeared to be considering his options and then pulled a semi-automatic pistol from beneath his jacket aiming it directly at Michael's chest. His partner pulled his gun and aimed it at Jules. Out of the corner of his eye Michael saw a white, unmarked van pull up to the curb at the side of the bridge from which they had come.

"Please come with us. I don't want to kill the two of you. Your Movement would be irreparably harmed."

Michael's eyebrows rose. "None of us is essential. The Movement has a life of its own born of biology and need."

Both men took a step forward.

Rather than back up Michael reached up, grabbed his shirt, and ripped it open, the buttons flying in every direction.

"Do you really think you can hurt me?" Michael cried. "Others have tried. Take a look."

Even in the dim light the Man could see the scar in the upper left quadrant of Michael's chest. It pulsed an angry crimson.

Michael, sensing the Man's brief indecision moved with a speed borne of the changes wrought by the Ulysses Treatment grabbing the Man's gun and tossing it into the river below. Only a millisecond later Jules did the same. As he tossed the gun into the Tiber with his left hand, Michael pivoted to his left placing his hands on the stone railing and leaped with ease over the balustrade into the flowing river below. Jules joined him while their assailants stood in shock and their associates came running.

They dove deep, their strong strokes propelling them for over a minute, their physical abilities making possible extended time underwater. Once they surfaced, the two swam rapidly for what seemed a long time until they heard the sound of rushing water.   Turning to the right and around the center pylon of the Garibaldi Bridge Jules and Michael swam only a little further before climbed up steps leading to the quay on south side of what appeared to be an island. The barkers' stalls had already closed for the night. Jules and Michael secreted themselves with their backs to the ancient wall smelling of dirty water and fatigue.

As his breathing slowed Michael asked, "Where are we?"

"We're on Tiber Island. There's a legend which says the Romans threw the body of the tyrant, Tarquinius Suberbus, into the river where it settled and over time formed this

112

island. For a long time the worst criminals or contagiously ill were condemned here. We fit right in, don't you think?"

Michael looked at his friend and smiled, "I learn so much when I'm with you. You are truly a fount of useless facts but I enjoy them nonetheless. Unfortunately your interests seem to be rubbing off on Alex."

"Then you will appreciate this next bit of essential trivia. Did you know that the term "swimming the Tiber" refers to one making the decision to convert to Catholicism?"

"I suppose that refers to the Vatican being across the river from Rome," observed Michael, "and I imagine Father DeLeon would appreciate our exploits this evening in that light. At least we learned a little more. For just a moment I considered taking their guns and turning those guys in to the Italian police, but what would we say? 'I think these are the people who murdered our friends?' We need to find out who they're working for. Any ideas?"

"We know more than we did an hour ago," said Jules. "The man with black eyes is clearly a sociopath. I sensed no empathy. I'm glad you asked about his leader. I couldn't tell much but I sensed he was more deranged than that whack job. I sensed he was more of a strategic thinker, not a tactician like this guy. I'll notify Harrison. Perhaps he can do some digging with the little we know. I sensed something when that brute was talking, an exhilaration when he spoke of the 'great man'. Something like a messianic vision. In any event, why don't you contact Gabby and let her know we're all right?"

Michael turned his head to face the river, resting it again on the wall. After a few moments Jules asked, "How's she doing?"

"She's calmed down but she's not too happy with me at the moment. Why don't we sit here for a while and dry off so we won't draw too much attention to ourselves when we go back to the hotel."

They sat motionless until Jules broke the silence.

"That was a nice trick with your scar." He paused, "Gabby thinks you're getting reckless and I'm tempted to agree."

Jules turned to look at him. "Michael, for the past several weeks you have been more on edge than usual."

"Than usual?"

Jules ignored the question. "On the flight over here I asked you about your dream. Gabby told me it's really eating at you. You put me off then, but I want to know what's got you all tied up. Why won't you let me in?"

"Because if I talk about it, I'm afraid it'll come true. Not exactly rational, huh?"

Jules said nothing, waiting.

"Believe it or not, I miss the days when I dreamed about the accident. It was so much simpler back then. People think I'm leading this whole thing but I feel like a puppet; events manipulating me, forcing me along paths that scare the crap out of me."

Michael paused, staring ahead at nothing.

"I'm in a room filled with people. You're there along with Gabby, Peter, and Arthur. In front of us is a dais with multiple thrones, maybe a dozen, I don't know.

"On each throne sits a king or queen. Dressed in red robes each wears a different crown. Their grave faces stress the seriousness of our situation. The crowns are made of gold and studded with jewels. Each crown is different but the one on the man in the center is larger than the others. I figure he's the lead. We're being questioned."

"Sounds like the upcoming senate hearings," interrupted Jules.

"My guess, too." Michael paused considering what to say next.

"The king in the middle raises his left hand slowly, ever so slowly, in a pointing gesture. The look in his eyes, vacant but full of malice at the same time, like he's possessed. He's all I can see. Suddenly I feel fear. Not just fear but terror. You know, when you're in the middle of a dream and you start to feel real emotions, it's almost as if you become semi-conscious?"

Jules nodded.

"The fear grows and I look up to where he's pointing. A curtain parts above his head and behind the dais and I see Kerry and Alex."

Looking in Michael's eyes Jules sees no recognition of his presence, seeming to have gone to some other-worldly realm.

"They are encased in black boxes, like coffins, and before my eyes the lids slowly close. The scene dissolves and I'm in some kind of dungeon. It's dark, dirty, and smells of death.

"The kids are there but I can't find them because there are these people in the way milling about like zombies. I am trying to get through them but they block my way. And then, somehow, in this subterranean world the sun shines and I become a zombie like the rest but I don't feel like one." Michael paused. "I know that doesn't make sense."

"Then I'm above ground out in the open and I hear the kids doing that 'I know something you don't know' thing in that sing song voice that drives me crazy. Then there is a great noise like an explosion and fire everywhere. But it's not really fire and there's this total, unthinkable devastation. And then I wake up.

"I don't know what to tell you, my friend. I can't fathom what it means. But I can see why you don't want you to testify."

"If I don't, maybe, the kids will be okay."

Michael inched closer to Jules. "But there may be another explanation. I haven't said this to anyone, not even Gabby.

"Jules, am I losing my reason? Look at what I did tonight with those thugs. I walked right into their trap; I did that silly thing with my scar, then jumped over the railing. I put you in harm's way. And for what? Scraps of information that will lead nowhere? Was I just looking for trouble?"

"We don't know where it will lead, Michael. Let's wait to see what Harrison comes up with."

"You said before that you and Gabby think I'm getting reckless. I haven't admitted this to Gabby but I can't help but wonder if the effects of the Treatment aren't more than I can handle. What if it's making all of us crazy? Are the kids in the coffins because of me? I couldn't live with that."

"Michael, you may get overly emotional from time to time but your actions tonight have been anything but crazy. You created a plan based on the best information you had. You executed it well. You may be desperate but you're not crazy. If anyone is going off the deep end, it's me."

"Jules, I sense your sincerity but you may be the most rational person I know. Why would you think that?"

Michael sat up, crossed his legs and waited.

"Like you I haven't said anything to anyone. But I need to confide in someone and I would really value your perspective. About a month ago I was at home. I was cleaning out a closet."

"Wait a minute; you rich people have to clean out your own closets, too?"

"Thanks for trying to improve my mood. As I was saying, I was reaching for a scarf hanging off the shelf. When I pulled on it a box fell and the contents spilled out. I got down on my hands and knees. I found photos and old letters from Vicki.

"I'd forgotten about the box. We were apart a lot before we were married. I was in grad school in Boston and she was in Washington. She would send me letters. Remember, those were the days before email. She always included a photograph so I wouldn't forget her. She called them her 'reminders'. I kept all the letters and pictures in a box, a kind of treasure chest. I hadn't looked in it since we were married and over time forgot all about it.

"As I sat on the floor rifling through the papers, one photo really struck me. I remember the first time I saw it. I'd just come back from class. It was a typical cold, gray winter day in Boston. When I got up to my room, I opened the letter and the picture slipped out of the envelope and fell to the floor. I bent over to pick it up." Jules looked wistfully at nothing in particular. "She must have used a tripod and timer. She was lying on her bed, her head on a pillow. On the pillow next to hers was a photo of me from our college days. She had her arm around the pillow like she was snuggling with me.

"The first time I saw the picture it made me laugh. Not this time. I started crying like a baby. It brought so many memories and how sorely I miss her. That appalling ache came back. It's been almost thirty years since I lost her but it was like it happened yesterday.

"As I was recovering my composure, wiping my eyes, I sensed something." Jules pursed his lips. "You know how we sense each other, feel that connection?"

Michael nodded.

"Well, I felt Vicki. Oh, it was faint, ever so faint. But it was her. I sat there in wonder, not wanting to let the feeling go. I can feel it still. Now, tell me I'm not crazy."

Michael sat lost in thought. When he responded he spoke deliberately. "Remember, back at the bank; Angelo was talking about Gina and her mother? He said something very curious. Her mother said 'Do not be too sad for me. She is not lost'. I wonder what she meant."

"Now my friend the atheist, you're not suggesting there's life after death, are you?"

"You mean, is there a world up in the clouds where we all go when we die? No, not that. You know me too well. But who knows what's possible now. The more we learn the less we know.

"Our world has shifted on its axis. You know as well as I, since going through the Transformation, nothing is the same. Maybe we think we're out of touch with reality because we see everything now from a different vantage point. Maybe crazy isn't so crazy after all."

Michael and Jules stood.

"We're not going to sort this out tonight," said Jules. "Let's get back to the hotel, change into some clean clothes and go home. We've got a lot of work to do."

As the two climbed the medieval stone stairway to the streets above Michael said, "I haven't seen the kids in way too long. By the way, did I tell you I found a nanny?"

"I know how hard you've been looking for just the right person. How did you find her?"

"You wouldn't believe it if I told you."

Chapter 14

Senator Paul Gregory stood in front of the mirror deftly straightening his tie. He struck an imposing figure; the kind of presence people couldn't help but admire. His jacket lay on the unmade hotel bed bathed in the morning sun streaming through the open drapes.

Cheryl Keyes stepped out of the bathroom dressed only in a partially buttoned blouse and slip, her strawberry blonde hair spilling over her narrow shoulders. She walked to the dresser where the senator stood. Stepping impossibly close she looked up in his eyes.

"Paul, I'm hardly dressed. Please close the drapes," she asked demurely.

Gregory took her arms in his hands pulling her closer and smelling the mix of expensive bath gel and shampoo.

"What are you afraid of, that someone will see how beautiful you are?"

Cheryl smiled coyly. "No, but if the press is outside it wouldn't do for me to be discovered with you. You may be separated but you aren't yet divorced. The country expects its elected representatives to behave discreetly. I wish it weren't necessary but it is, for now."

Gregory released Cheryl, walked over to the bed and grabbed his jacket. "I chose this hotel for its discretion. We're out in the middle of nowhere and no one knows we're here. But just to be sure, I'll go downstairs. You finish getting dressed and I'll meet you with the car out back. Please try and hurry." Gregory walked over and kissed Cheryl. "Our little diversion this morning has made us late."

Gregory turned and left the room.

Cheryl walked over to the closet and grabbed her skirt. As she sat on the bed putting on her shoes she wondered how she should pursue the subject he so conveniently and routinely avoided.

"I'm good at reading people", she thought. *"I know he loves me. He may not have said it in so many words, but I can sense it. He's just waiting for the right time. That bitch he was married to is making the divorce so difficult. I'll just have to accept sneaking moments of his time when I can."*

Cheryl checked herself in the mirror, walked to the door and exited the suite. Their bags would come later.

Both spent most of their time during the drive to the compound on their laptops and cell phones conducting business ignoring the verdant, hilly countryside as spring bloomed all around. As the car passed a sign advising: Private Property, No Trespassing; the Senator shut off his laptop and cell phone and instructed his aide to do the same.

"Cheryl, we're about to enter a Peacemaker compound. This may not be a government installation but for all intents and purposes you should treat it as such."

"Paul, I have accompanied you to military installations before. I've seen soldiers training in the field. I can't imagine this is so different. But, since you bring it up, why are we here anyway?"

"Do you remember General Scott? He's been to my office."

"Sure." Cheryl recalled a powerful man who walked with a slight limp; a man she found daunting despite his short stature.

"He's leading a new program for the Peacekeepers: one that will provide us with an even greater military advantage but one which also must remain entirely secret, for now."

Gregory turned in his seat to face her. He looked as though he were struggling with what to say next.

"Cheryl, you know the Senate is just a stepping stone for me."

She reached over and squeezed his hand. "Yes, Paul, I know. I've watched you for years. Your strategies have proven flawless; your every move well-orchestrated. You've been remarkably effective in building your powerbase and courting public opinion. You will be President and not in some distant future, but in just three years."

Gregory remained intent. "But you understand, this isn't politics as usual? I have a vision for this country and its place in the world. We have been decadent and divided for too long. It is not my intent to be just another name in a long list of failed administrations. I will not be that kind of President.

"Americans have become soft, pampered by excess. If we are to counter the economic threats posed by China and India, or the military threats from every tinhorn dictatorship, not to mention the organized terrorists bent on anarchy; we must steel ourselves. We must forge this nation anew, make a new beginning. The alliances I make now will position us for that new beginning.

"We're going straight to the top and more quickly than you can even imagine. My position as Senate pro tem assures that. But I need to know you are with me. I need to know you share my vision, see the wisdom in my strategies."

121

"Paul, I would hope, at this point, you wouldn't have any doubt. I share your vision and am fully committed to being a part of it."

As the car pulled up in front of a vintage southern mansion Paul Gregory said, "And I want you by my side."

Cheryl couldn't help but wonder whether he meant as a political operative or his wife. She wanted to ask him but Gregory reached for the door handle and stepped into the open air before she could get the question out.

She felt increasingly uneasy as she exited the car. Cheryl ascribed her anxiety to the clash between her fondest desire and his unwillingness to commit. But deep down, below her conscious awareness she knew she was stepping into a world from which there could be no safe escape.

The service jeep in which they now rode had just passed through another checkpoint; this one more secure than the last. They had ridden for fifteen minutes through the outer limits of the compound. General Scott sat in back with Gregory while Cheryl rode in front with the driver.

She turned in her seat, "General, how many of these facilities are there?"

"We have two others in this country: one in Idaho and another in the Nevada desert. Overseas we have camps in Nicaragua and Siberia. Perhaps you will have the chance to visit others in time."

Maybe I'm just being paranoid, but when he looks at me like that. . .

After passing through the final gate, the jeep pulled to a stop.

As they climbed out of the vehicle Scott said, "This is the Achilles training facility."

To Cheryl it looked more like a bunker than any kind of school she'd ever seen. The stark gray concrete structure with windows surrounding only the second story, displayed no sign to indicate its purpose. To her left Cheryl saw a large unoccupied, concrete surface. To her right and around the back of the building she saw what appeared to be a typical training ground. An electrified fence prevented access to the training area surprising Cheryl. *Why would they need such a high level of security so deep in the complex?*

She caught a quick glimpse of soldiers running the course. *Nothing unusual in that*, she thought.

The three approached a metal door with a security camera mounted overhead. The general uttered one word, "Scott" and the door slid seamlessly open.

They stepped into a cramped vestibule. Before them and behind a screen she saw two armed soldiers; one standing, the other at a computer console. There were two identical metal doors, one on each side of the guard station. No furniture adorned the space and Cheryl thought it would be difficult for more than half a dozen people to be in the room at any one time.

Scott stepped up to a retinal scanner allowing it to identify him.

The soldier at the computer console asked, "General, please identify your guests, for the record."

"Senator Paul Gregory and his aide Cheryl Keyes."

"Thank you sir, you may proceed."

Scott walked to his left as the door swung open; his guests following.

The contrast between the lobby and the lab stuck Cheryl immediately. They walked down a corridor between multiple laboratories, glass partitions on all and biohazard signs everywhere. She saw white coated lab technicians engaged in multiple activities, some attentive to their microscopes, some utilizing equipment and chemicals at their workstations, while others worked with test animals living in small cages mounted in the walls at the back of the labs.

As they rounded a corner they arrived at a glass door with the label "Simon Meyerhoff, MD, PhD. Director of Research" displayed prominently on the door. Scott opened the door and ushered his guests into the suite.

Meyerhoff looked up from his computer, rose, and walked over to the Senator taking his outstretched hand. He looked to Cheryl to be in his late sixties with thinning, gray hair.

"Senator, I am so glad you finally found time for a visit. I have much to show you. And who is this lovely lady?"

"I'd like you to meet Cheryl Keyes, my aide."

Cheryl stepped forward holding out her hand. "A pleasure to meet you. You have an impressive operation"

"Ah, but the pleasure is all mine, my dear. I am anxious to show such a bright and charming person around. It was kind of the Senator to brighten my world."

Meyerhoff winked.

"Come let me show you the latest," he said. The researcher held the door as they exited the suite. He turned to his left leading them down another hallway and into a very conventional looking medical treatment room. A magnetic resonance scanner stood in the center of the floor.

Cheryl gazed into the bore of the magnet and saw what looked to be a sleeping monkey, wires running from the animal's scalp to a junction box.

"Come see what we have here." Meyerhoff led them into a control room.

Looking at the screen Cheryl saw a cross sectional image of the monkey's brain. The cerebellum, the small portion of the brain directly above the spinal cord glowed brightly.

"Do you see the neural tendrils extending into the limbic system here? We now believe this is responsible for the emotional control problems our subjects have experienced. Having isolated the cause we can now mount a more effective method of control."

"How certain are you that you have found the proximate cause?" asked the Senator.

"Let me show you." Meyerhoff walked over to another console.

"The electrodes we have installed in the brain of the monkey are used both to control its sedation and to short circuit it's anger. The dial here on the left controls sleep and the one on the right controls its limbic response."

Meyerhoff reduced the voltage on left hand dial and the monkey stirred. As he reduced the voltage on the right hand dial the monkey began to thrash violently. Meyerhoff turned the right hand dial back and the monkey calmed down. Finally he moved the left hand dial halfway around, back to sleep mode.

"As you can see we have a temporary solution here until we come up with a biological one."

"Have you tried this new solution on any human subjects yet?" asked Scott.

"We are preparing to do just that. It's actually a simple procedure. We will implant the electrodes and wire them to a subcutaneous chip in the shoulder." Meyerhoff placed his right hand on his left shoulder to demonstrate the location.

The director continued, "The chip also contains a wireless circuit which can be manipulated by a controller."

"What's the range of the chip?" asked Scott.

"At this point, about five miles."

"And the balance problems?" asked Scott. It was clear to Cheryl that Scott knew the answers to the questions but instead voiced them for Gregory's benefit.

"Largely resolved. At this point they only occur in 1 to 2% of the subjects."

"So when can you begin the next stage of induction?" asked Gregory.

Cheryl listened intently for the answer though she found herself increasingly uncomfortable with the direction of the discussion.

"Achilles stage two should begin next week. All five of the subjects from stage one have been released. Would you like to see the training area?"

As they walked out of the treatment room Meyerhoff absently turned the amplitude on the sleep dial up all the way. Cheryl saw two techs enter the room from the other side as they exited. The techs pulled the limp monkey from the scanner and placed the dead creature on a cart going back through the door through which they had entered. Cheryl concentrated in an effort to hide her revulsion.

Chapter 15

As they crossed the courtyard to the other side of the complex Meyerhoff explained, "We have left the laboratory building and will enter the other wing which houses the training facility."

Cheryl turned her head in response to what sounded like bleating animals. She saw a small pen containing what looked to be five goats.

"Excuse me Dr. Meyerhoff," she said. "Are those goats?"

"After a fashion my dear; they're spider goats."

"Spider goats?"

"They've been genetically altered so that the milk they produce is actually the same fluid spiders use to spin their webs."

"You're kidding, right?"

"Spider webs," explained Meyerhoff, "are ten times stronger than steel. By infusing skin cells with the web fluid effectively replacing the keratin, we can make soldiers bullet-proof."

The doctor held the door as they entered the training facility unaware of Cheryl's visceral disgust. "We have a gymnasium and outdoor training field, housing, and other amenities for the recruits along with medical facilities."

"How many troops are in the next wave?" Gregory asked.

"Five, as in the last. We must be judicious. I'm sure you understand. Once testing is completed we plan to induce ten each week."

Cheryl found herself puzzled by the oblique references but kept her counsel not wishing to kick the hornet's nest.

As they walked past an elevator Meyerhoff continued, "Housing is located on the second floor."

Cheryl noticed that the elevator required a security card for access. As they rounded a corner behind the elevator she saw the stairway access and noticed the stairs also required a security swipe.

They passed a small but well-appointed cafeteria. The smell of Italian food enticed her nostrils but they kept walking. Cheryl noticed the lack of windows anywhere in the building.

As they rounded the next corner Cheryl heard the unmistakable sound of a bouncing basketball. They walked into the gym and saw a group of six men; magnificent physical specimens all, clothed in shorts, gym shoes, wearing T-shirts of various colors and styles engaged in a vigorous three-on-three game of basketball.

"These men form our next class," explained Meyerhoff.

The man with the ball stopped dribbling when he saw the inspection party and stared in their direction. The others stopped running and turned their heads as well. He was the largest of the six and stood there bouncing the ball, his eyes narrowed as if trying to determine the solution to a problem.

As Cheryl looked closer she realized she knew him.

Her obvious recognition caused Gregory ask in a subdued voice, "Cheryl, what is it?"

"I think I know him"

"Really? From where?"

"We went to high school together."

Scott heard the exchange, considered his next course of action and then said, "Talbot, come over here."

The recruit stopped bouncing the ball, handed it to a red headed player and walked toward the group.

The tall, well-muscled athlete stood directly in front of Cheryl, that same look of confusion on his face.

"You're Tommy Talbot."

"You look familiar. Do I know you?"

"Cheryl Cooper. Well, I was Cheryl Cooper. We went to Franklin together. I think we were lab partners in Biology."

A half smile illuminated Talbot's face. "Yeah, I remember."

Cheryl smiled broadly and Scott saw his chance.

"Why don't we leave you two alone to catch up," said Scott. "Doctor, would you be so kind as to show us the medical facilities?"

The three walked off.

"What have you been up to?" she asked. "I remember you said you were joining the military. You talked about finding direction, a purpose."

As Cheryl spoke she felt her anxiety rise uncontrollably. She tamped it down reflexively while wondering, *what's happening to me?*

"I joined the Navy and became a Seal."

"But you're here. Are you still with the Navy?"

"Nah, I joined the Peacemakers a few weeks ago and I'm stationed here for now."

Hearing an opening Cheryl asked, "What's your assignment?"

"I shouldn't say anything, top secret stuff and all."

Cheryl nodded, unsurprised in his response.

"But Cheryl, what brings you to this neck of the woods? We don't get too many visitors."

"The guy I'm with, that's Senator Gregory. I'm his aide." Tommy seemed impressed as she had hoped. But try as she might she couldn't shake a feeling of impending doom as she spoke with him sensing more to their connection than she could fathom.

"Do you ever talk to anyone from the old days?" he asked.

Meyerhoff, Scott, and Gregory descended in the elevator to the basement.

Meyerhoff was explaining, "These are the induction rooms. The subjects will be placed in a coma and the virus will be induced. At the same time we will perform a minor neurosurgical procedure and implant the controller chip. We anticipate the entire procedure will take twenty-four to forty-eight hours.

"When will you begin with this next batch?" Gregory asked.

"Within the next couple of weeks," responded Meyerhoff.

A lab tech entered the room. "Dr. Meyerhoff, could you come with me? We need your help."

"Gentlemen, will you excuse me?" and Meyerhoff left the room.

Scott turned to Gregory. "Paul, I'm not sure it was a good idea to bring her here. Events are about to be set in motion from which there can be no turning back. We cannot afford a leak. She was married to Peter Keyes. I have to know that you can enforce absolute discipline in your ranks. We cannot tolerate a breach of any kind. Do I make myself clear?"

Gregory leaned forward, his eyes narrowed. "Do you doubt my commitment?"

He held Scott's gaze for what seemed like an eternity and then leaned back. "You have no need to worry. She's with us. I haven't told her anything but when the time comes she will be on board. And if not. . ." Gregory shrugged dismissively.

"Jim, I have plans for her. We can use her to our advantage. I'm sending her into the lion's den. I'll see what she does. If she plays it well; great. If not, she won't be the first congressional aide to meet with an accident."

Scott nodded. "I'm pleased to hear that. I want to make sure you're not thinking with your johnson."

Meyerhoff returned and said, "Well, gentleman, if that's all let's go find that pretty young thing and send you on your way unless Mr. Talbot has taken her to his quarters."

They returned to the gym to find the two still talking.

"Are you finished reminiscing?" asked Gregory.

"I'd better go," said Cheryl. "It was good to see you, Tommy. I hope this works out for you."

Talbot watched as the visitors left. *She doesn't remember,* he thought. *Or she doesn't want to admit what happened.* As he considered the last time he saw her he felt a chill. Seeing her reawakened an old foreboding. Her predictions were coming true. And he felt powerless against the flow.

Meyerhoff walked with Gregory while Scott hung back with Cheryl. "What do you think?" asked Scott.

"A very impressive operation. It appears you're breaking new ground. I'm anxious to learn more."

"All in due time my dear; all in due time. Paul says you can be trusted. I'm glad you are with us but we are playing for very high stakes. We wouldn't want to call your bluff if you know what I mean."

"I know what you mean, General. I'm committed to Paul and his cause. You have no need to worry. But perhaps you should share your concerns with the Senator."

"I already have."

In the car on the way to the airfield Cheryl said, "I don't like him."

"Who? General Scott?" Gregory asked absently.

"He gives me the creeps. I don't think you can trust him."

"I'm well aware of the General's shortcomings but we need him for now. Once he's fulfilled his purpose we can jettison him if need be. What was the deal with that Talbot fella? Was he coming on to you?"

"Oh, Paul. I knew him in high school."

"I just don't want you to get any ideas; he's quite a hunk."

"Are you jealous?"

"No," Gregory protested, "but I don't want you communicating with those recruits. Do you understand?"

Cheryl looked him in the eye and he turned away. After several minutes Gregory spoke.

"I need you to do something for me. It won't be easy. I want you to go to BDT and have a talk with your ex." Gregory took her hand looking deeply into her eyes, "I need to understand what they're up to. I won't have them getting in the way.

"Learn as much as you can. I want to understand how the BRIDG works and how we can turn it for our purposes rather than for whatever God forsaken uses they're putting it to.

"Cheryl, I'm where I am today in part due to your phenomenal insight with people. Your caution and guidance has helped me avoid many traps which might have felled a lesser man. Use your considerable skills to get under Peter's skin. See if you can find anything we can use to undermine their Movement. Feign support if you have to. Hell, tell him you still have feelings for him and want to get back together, if necessary."

"Paul, I don't know. We may be divorced but Peter's not a bad person. He got swept up with the wrong crowd."

"Good, go with that. Help him to see the error of his ways. Bring him over to our side if you can; if we have a plant in the inner sanctum, so much the better. See, I knew I could count on you."

Reluctantly Cheryl nodded her assent. "When do you want me to go?"

"There'll be a plane waiting for you at the airport. I had the office arrange for a car and notified Arthur Paulson's office of your visit."

"So suddenly?" What's the rush?"

"As I said, events are in motion. When you get back to Washington, I'll be hosting a meeting of my most trusted advisors, movers and shakers some of whom you haven't met. I want you there to present your findings."

"What if he won't see me?" Cheryl suspected she would have no trouble getting to Peter, especially after her run in with Jules and that Dr. Neumann. But she didn't want to let Gregory know she had met with them.

Why am I being so secretive? There's no reason I can't tell him. And yet Cheryl's intuition, now running full tilt, cautioned her to remain silent.

"Paulson will persuade Peter to see you in the event he's reluctant. I've billed it as a friendly fact-finding visit. What choice does he have?"

Cheryl laughed to herself. *Arthur will persuade Peter to see me? Boy, Paul doesn't know Peter.* She knew once Peter set his mind to something there was not a force in the universe that could make him change course.

"Paul, I'll do anything you want. You know that. But Peter can be quite obstinate. I can't promise I'll get results."

"You'll find a way. Do whatever you have to," he said as he patted her knee.

As she sat in the terminal waiting to board the plane Cheryl couldn't shake her growing anxiety, her thoughts disjointed bouncing between memory and immediate perception. She felt as though she was in some kind of fugue state. *Something isn't right. I know I'm nervous about seeing Peter, but I've had this feeling ever since I entered that damn compound. What's Paul up to? I don't trust the people he's working with. Maybe that's why I'm all nervous.*

And seeing Tommy didn't help. What's happening to me?

Chapter 16

He paused on the sidewalk in the dark gazing up at the three story brownstone standing shoulder to shoulder with other homes in one of the tonier areas of Georgetown. The first story windows shone with welcoming light, welcoming to all but him.

Dammit, I didn't expect her to be here.

Nevertheless he climbed the thirteen steps to the front door and tried the handle: locked. He reached into his pocket and pulled out the key hoping it would still work. Sure enough, she hadn't yet changed the locks.

How will she ever survive? thought Paul Gregory as he closed the door.

"Who's there?" he heard her call from the back of the house.

He cringed at the clack-clack of her heels on the hard wood floor, the sound coming toward him.

Gail Gregory stepped cautiously into the foyer.

"Oh, it's you. What are you doing here?"

She was still a handsome woman. She'd been the perfect politician's wife, attractive, quiet, and loaded.

"You should get the locks changed."

"The locksmith's coming tomorrow. What are you doing here?"

"I left papers in the library. I won't be long."

She had been the ideal mate until her sister, Susan, died. The poor thing succumbed to inflammatory breast cancer. Gail nursed her through the illness and emerged a different person. In her earlier life she'd done her obligatory charity work, been the right face with the right people, hosted dinner parties with the right movers and shakers; friends of her father.

She'd married well according to her parents. They saw her as a weak copy of her older sister. No more. Gail now worked with the underprivileged in Washington. Which could have worked to Gregory's political advantage had she not developed a political sense diametrically opposed to his. She could have cared less about politics before, ideal arm candy. Now she was nothing but a liability; with assets he no longer required.

"Where's your whore?"

"You're ugly when you're bitter."

"We have an agreement. You're not supposed to come over here without prior consent."

"The ink's hardly dry on the contract. I'll be out of your hair shortly."

Without waiting for a response, Gregory turned and walked to the library, closed the door, stepped to the sideboard and poured himself a Longrow in a fine crystal tumbler. He took a long drink, filled the glass again, and sat heavily in the brass studded, black leather wingback chair.

The sooner I put this whole divorce thing behind me, the better. I don't need the distraction, not with what's to come.

Halfway through his drink he rose and walked to the maple bookcase. He squatted and opened the cabinet door. Long ago he installed the safe to hold his most confidential records. Gregory thought he had removed everything when

136

he moved out but found he had missed an important list. He input the combination, opened the safe, and pulled out a sheaf of papers. He rifled through them and removed what he needed.

As he knelt to replace the rest of the material, she walked in on him. Like a small child with his hand in the cookie jar he jumped up though he tried to appear non-plussed.

With a wry smile she asked, "Did I startle you?"

"I'll be gone in a minute."

He knelt back down closed the safe, rose and walked to his briefcase depositing the files.

"What's that; a list of illicit campaign contributions or porn? Though I suppose there isn't much difference."

As he straightened up clutching his briefcase Gregory looked directly at her. "You've become quite witty."

"You're ugly when you're bitter."

"Me, bitter? What have I got to be bitter about?" He chuckled.

She walked to the side board and poured herself a drink, turned to face him.

"Oh, you put on a good show: the man in command. But I know you for who you really are. I know your secret fears. I know what gnaws at you in the small hours of the morning."

"Be careful, woman. Don't try to impede me."

Gail took a sip from her drink. "Don't misunderstand me. I know full well what you're capable of. But in the end, you're just like your father."

"I'm nothing like him. He was nothing but a failure."

"He did everything he could provide for you. You call that a failure? To me that's the true measure of a man."

"But then he was laid off. Lost his spark. He became a shadow of who he was. I made sure that would never happen to me."

"Are you still fifteen years old, even now reliving that trauma? By resolving that it would never happen to you, you're still living his life, can't you see that?"

"What do you know?"

His mind tried to coax his body to leave but he stood fast, somewhere deep in his soul he wanted to hear her answer.

"What do *I* know? When we first came to Washington, you wanted to make things better in this country. Wanted make sure the working man had a fair shot, a chance to get ahead. You thought you had a handle on the American Dream, but you saw only a part of it.

"You went to a good school, studied hard, worked as an investment banker, made good money, and married well if I do say so myself."

She took another sip.

"But you want to create an America where only those like you prosper. You believe the old Protestant saw that God smiles on the rich and powerful. In your heart of hearts, liberty and democracy belong only to those who can earn it. The poor, the middle class, they exist to serve the elite."

"You understand me so poorly."

"I understand you all too well. Anyone who disagrees, who gets in your way, you have no compunction about rolling over them as if they weren't even there."

"We've suffered too long under weak leadership," replied Gregory. "The people have grown soft under a welfare state that provides for every need and tells them all they need is self-esteem. No, I don't hold any truck with that lie. America has lost its way. We can put it right again. We can be back on top."

"We or you, Paul?" She took a step toward him. "I admit it. I've been a pure, blind fool," she continued. "I watched you claw your way to the top. I watched as you took your noble intentions and ground them into fodder to your power. You were popular from the start. Your colleagues loved you. You've done a great job galvanizing your allies and demonizing the opposition whether in the other party or your own. And, you have a knack for fundraising and let's face it, that's the job of a legislator these days. You were on the forefront of the demise of this democracy. And you haven't cared who you stepped on to get here."

"You're right, you are a fool," he responded. "Your misplaced idealism is what's dooming this country. We can only compete as a nation when we return to our roots. And that won't happen under leadership which seeks only to compromise. I'm nothing if not principled and I will not sacrifice my principles on the altar of political expediency."

"I believe I've heard that speech before and I'm tired of it."

She walked to the door and then turned to face him.

"You know, you would have been better off to ally yourself with Arthur Paulson when he came to you all those years ago, but instead you got in bed with that psychopath Gates because he was freer with his checkbook."

"You don't know what you're talking about. You . . ."

The glass slid through his fingers. The fine crystal should have shattered into a million pieces but instead bounced off the Persian carpet spilling its amber contents.

"You, you're one of them. You're a Samasamite."

She languidly strolled to stand directly in front of him, looking him in the eye.

"I hate that word. It sounds so, so cultish."

"I should have known." Gregory smiled. "You've made my job easier. Now I can blame the divorce on you. I suppose I should say thank you."

She continued to stare into his eyes.

"No need, Paul." She reached up slightly on her toes, closed her eyes and gently kissed his cheek.

Gregory stepped back; confusion written across his face.

"What was that for?"

Gail sighed.

"One last kiss for the man I married. You think you have it made. You think you're on the verge of a great triumph. And perhaps you are, but in the end you face nothing but ruin. And despite all that's gone between us, it makes me sad. For you, for me, for what we had."

She turned and walked toward the door.

"You'd better watch yourself."

Without turning to face him she said, "Paul, as I said before, I know what you're capable of. You needn't worry about me. Make sure you lock the door when you leave."

Chapter 17

Cheryl sat pensively in the back of the Lincoln Town Car; her eyes closed while she massaged her scalp just above her temples with the tips of her fingers. Nothing fit. Images of the events of the past few days flew around her mind seemingly possessing a life of their own, colliding into one another and breaking off again. She tried to make the noise stop, make the headache go away. She felt sick to her stomach.

For as long as she could remember, she had the headaches but they grew worse in college. Assuming they were migraines, or worse, a brain tumor, she went from specialist to specialist attempting to discover the source and, in so doing, stop the pain. But the best neurologists couldn't find a cause despite all their tests. They made little of the images which accompanied her headaches telling her they were probably random firings of neurons, a form of seizure disorder. She tried several medications but found the side effects to be worse than the treatment. In desperation she sought relief in alternative medicine.

She found a therapist who helped her see that the floating images as icons of stress brought on by the demands of college and her maturing mind and body. She accepted the explanation and, using relaxation and concentration techniques he taught, she found ways to blot out the unwanted images which, in turn, eliminated the headaches.

She found that by breathing deliberately and rubbing the sides of her head in a circular motion she could regain control over the images and the pain would subside.

Over the years, the headaches had receded. She chalked it up to maturity and hadn't thought about them until they began again following her lunch with Jules.

Cheryl sat forward in her seat and opened her eyes. *Did seeing Jules bring this on? Am I really that stressed to see Peter? That must be it. Why did I agree to see him? Maybe I'm feeling stuck between Paul's request and my anxiety. But why am I anxious?*

As if in response to the question the images came fast and furious. Out of morbid curiosity Cheryl closed her eyes and focused on the visions. Icons of Paul and Peter danced around each other with images of Scott fading in and out. Between them Tom Talbot rose on a column of water. Sweeping them all together she saw a clenched fist, black as night and somehow she knew it for an obscenity, a deep abiding evil. Fire emerged from the fist engulfing everything. And for the first time in a long while Cheryl experienced gut wrenching fear.

She felt as though she were walking a path with chaos on either side. She knew if she were drawn into the chaos she would never emerge; that way lay madness. She imagined walls on either side of her path, building them with her mind to contain the assault.

She forced her eyes open dispelling the hallucinations. The headache was gone but in its place her heart hammered, her breath coming in short gasps. She slowed her breathing consciously attempting to block out the lingering visions.

Her heartbeat decelerated, control returning. *I'd better get it together; Peter can't see me like this.*

Cheryl checked herself in the backseat mirror. Nothing looked out of place. *I'll be fine. This moment's been coming for a while now. I didn't realize how anxious I'd be. He's just my ex.*

Cheryl waited in the well-furnished outer room of the Chairman's office. Groupings of overstuffed chairs and sofas were placed strategically around the room. The back wall held two wooden doors that Cheryl guessed led to Arthur's inner offices.

After entering the rolling hills of BDT's campus, the driver told her that he had been instructed to drop her off at building A. She'd been met at the car and escorted to the fifth floor. She wondered what kind of conditions Arthur Paulson would place on her visit. She figured he would arrange a meeting room nearby for her to see Peter. *He'll probably have one of his attorneys present,* she thought. *I'll have to find a way to get Peter alone.*

Startling her out of her speculation, Arthur strode energetically into the room. She rose, holding out her hand in greeting but Arthur, ignoring the gesture, embraced her.

Stepping back he said, "Cheryl, how long has it been? I don't think I've seen you since the wedding."

Cheryl eyed him cautiously. Arthur, in business with Jules ever since college, had attended her wedding. The man before her was not the stiff, preoccupied man she recalled.

"I believe you're right."

Arthur motioned for her to sit while he took his seat across from her.

"I wanted to see you before you went over to meet with Peter. I'm told you're on a fact-finding mission and so thought you might have some questions for me."

143

"Arthur, I hadn't expected to see you but I appreciate that you took time out of your schedule to see me. I'll take this as an opportunity to get answers to some questions which have been gnawing at me. As you know the Committee will be looking into your operations here. I thought I could gather firsthand information to help the senators in their deliberations. I imagine Jules told you that you'll be called to testify."

Arthur nodded. "That won't be a problem. How can I help you today?"

"Before we get started, I'd like to know what ground rules you have for my visit.

"No rules. You can see whatever you like, speak to whomever you like. When we're done here I'll escort you over to Peter's building."

"I have to confess I'm surprised. I didn't expect you to be so forthcoming. Aren't you afraid of what I'll find?"

"We have nothing to hide. I'll admit that some of our areas are off limits to outsiders as we are bound by confidentiality agreements with many of our customers. But you can go anywhere you like if I can count on your discretion."

Arthur raised his eyebrows waiting for her response.

"I'm only here to learn more about the BRIDG, hence my desire to see Peter. This visit is strictly business. But speaking of business, and since you offered, I have reviewed your corporate tax returns."

"Are you worried we aren't paying our fair share of taxes? We try to be scrupulous in our filings."

"That's just it. For years, BDT paid little in taxes sheltering income in the way many successful corporations do. But in the past several years, your tax burden has increased. It's

144

evident the business is still profitable, but why have you elected to terminate several of your shelters? It would appear self-defeating."

"We undertook a thorough review of our finances three years ago and the Board determined some of the shelters were not the best place to put our assets, and we wanted to be seen as good corporate citizens, contributing our fair share."

Cheryl frowned.

"Speaking of the Board, two of your outside directors have resigned. Why?"

"You're wondering whether they were forced out. In fact, I tried everything I could to persuade them to stay. But we made some changes in the direction of company which they felt to be against corporate interest."

"What changes?"

"As you know BDT has been closely held since its inception. While I made use of venture capital early in our history, I was able to build the company without going public and so maintain the kind of freedom and agility I felt was necessary."

Arthur chuckled to himself.

"And I suppose my need for control prevented me from succumbing to Wall Street scrutiny. Though in retrospect, I still believe it to have been the right decision. In any event, we decided to sell the company to our employees. Their shares vest based on their contributions and the profits are now returned to them; it helps them focus on the right things, don't you think? It took us a while to fully implement the plan because we wanted to structure the deal equitably to avoid any unintended consequences. Since the program went live a little over a year ago productivity has soared."

"I imagine you and Jules held a majority of the shares, am I right?"

"You're close."

"Then that means you gave up income that had been coming to you."

"And your point?"

"Arthur, that behavior runs counter to everything I ever knew about you. Has the Ulysses Treatment so warped your thinking that you've given up all you've achieved for this cockamamie movement?"

"Do you really believe that's what's going on here?"

Cheryl stared back at Arthur enjoying the fact she had put him on the defensive.

"I have to confess I'm a little disappointed in you, Cheryl. Is it your assumption that people can't change, can't improve?

"Improve? You were at the top of the heap."

"If you're referring to wealth and power, perhaps you're right. But for you to think that's the end game betrays a superficiality which I hadn't known you possessed. Sounds like you've changed, too."

"Oh, come on. I'm not some head in the clouds idealist."

"You used to be."

"And I've grown up."

Arthur nodded. "Let's start over. I admit I've changed and I'll also admit it's a result of the Transformation. But don't assume you know me. All you know is indirect by way of reputation and rumor. Think back. Are you the same person you were back in high school?"

"Of course not; who would want to be?"

"And why did you change?"

"I grew up."

"That's not an answer."

"All right, I made choices. I learned things in college and at work which made me realize what was important to me; and you can stop trying to psychoanalyze me. I'm asking the questions here," Cheryl replied her anger growing.

"You asked a question and I'm attempting to answer it. It's a matter of perspective. Before the Transformation, my life was defined as a series of conquests; endless battles against others for dominance or against my own limitations. I found my greatest joy in the win and I was so good at it I was rewarded handsomely. But it wasn't about the money; it was never about the money.

"I was under contract with the Pentagon to deliver a top secret project. We had deadlines to meet and I pushed. The researcher leading the effort refused to do as I instructed and so I fired her, Dr. Gabriella Neumann. Unfortunately the woman chosen to replace her was totally out of her depth and we found ourselves even further behind.

"I figured out that Dr. Neumann had left the state and was holed up with Jules. I didn't know what they were up to and didn't care.

"You know that Jules and I were roommates in college. You also know that we started BDT together. What you don't know and what I never wanted to admit is that I resented his intrusion. Not that he didn't add value, but I didn't want him meddling in my affairs. I saw my chance to take him down and so traveled to his retreat in the Wisconsin Northwoods. Little did I know that Michael Neumann had undergone the Transformation only days before.

"Despite all my success, I couldn't get enough, caught in a spiral of self-loathing. I never felt as though I was smart enough, quick enough to match my ambition. When I met Michael and understood the effects of the Treatment I had to

147

have it. It was my ticket. I know it sounds insane in retrospect, why with everything I'd accomplished would I take such a risk? But I was blinded by my own need for dominance. Just before I went under, Michael told me I would change but I refused to believe him.

"I awoke from the induced coma with new insight. From your perspective you might say I saw the commercial potential in the BRIDG and the Ulysses Treatment. But there was more to it, much more.

"Would you accept the proposition that we're products of our biology? That our society reflects both the best and worst in human nature?"

"Arthur, I'm not looking for some obtuse philosophical argument. I want to understand the reasons for the changes in BDT."

"Obtuse philosophy? Hardly. You may be familiar with the writings of Paul Lawrence, a Harvard Business School professor. He posited four drives or motives: the need to acquire, defend, comprehend, and bond. Empirical research supports his theory and creates a blueprint for a more productive workforce. You don't get any more capitalist than the B-School at Harvard."

Arthur continued, "Why do you think capitalism works so well? It's because it's the product of our innate greed and ambition. But it also leaves individuals free to create their own value. By harnessing our inborn aggressiveness with our creative force we've created more wealth per capita than mankind has ever seen.

"But there's a problem. With the exception of the lesser developed world, we've eliminated hunger and everyone has a place to live, correct?"

"That's not entirely true," she admitted.

"And that's my point. The post-World War II economy took off fueled by the fundamental economic and technological changes begun the 40's. In the 1950's and '60's we saw a dramatic rise in the middle class but it's numbers have been shrinking ever since the 80's with wealth concentrated in fewer and fewer individuals. And that concentration conflicts with our higher nature.

"Supreme Court Justice Louis Brandies said, 'We may have democracy, we may have wealth concentrated in the hands of a few, but we cannot have both.'

"We've done a fair job pricing goods and services: food housing, and computers as examples. But we struggle to capture the worth of other vital values: education, health, and our natural resources. These are the longer term investments which get lost in the push for short term profits. The system must evolve to recognize the value in those commodities just as capitalism has evolved to recognize the growing complexity of modern society.

"Arthur, are you arguing for government control, for a socialist state?"

"Of course not. Nor am I for radical decentralization. The excesses which led to the recent recession are based in human nature; too much self-serving greed. The solution is in joint evolution. That sounded like a slogan didn't it?"

Cheryl nodded surprised by Arthurs passion coupled with his self-deprecating manner.

"Look, every year the BDT human resources people would come to me with a new program to boost morale. Some were more successful than others but at the end of the day, the people who work here too often felt like drones stuck in meaningless jobs. But teaming and morale programs don't build self-worth. That comes from harnessing the creative force in each of us. Ever since we sold the company to the employees and structured individual jobs to encourage free-thinking and participation, morale has soared. We're transforming the company in line with the insights gained from the Ulysses treatment coupled with the BRIDG technology. There's great long term potential here. To that end we're talking with a number of fund managers on Wall Street. Historically their focus has been on quarterly profits. We're looking to see if it makes sense to sell stock in the company to investors who value long term appreciation and not just dividends."

Cheryl rolled her eyes but before she could give voice to her protest Arthur interrupted.

"And before you say it, only about a fifth of the employees have gone through the Transformation. It's not a prerequisite for success. Our plans are moving at a pace that all our employees can embrace. If we move too quickly some will be left behind, not only here, but the other companies we do business with. We have a terrific competitive advantage but if we get too far ahead we'd descend into chaos. But enough about BDT, you've come to see Peter."

Chapter 18

Arthur led Cheryl out of the suite, down the elevator and across the campus. As they walked, Arthur continued, "I'm taking you over to Building F. It's our newest building and the hub for BRIDG development."

A gentle breeze wafted across the rolling hills of the BDT campus carrying the scents of spring. The sun shone brightly in a cobalt blue sky dotted with small, puffy clouds. Cheryl couldn't help but feel at ease walking through the pastoral setting. But as she felt herself succumb to the allure she checked her feelings. She was here to get information and not to be lulled by Arthur Paulson's enlightened words and the beautiful day. *I have to be strong,* she resolved.

"You must feel as though you're Daniel walking into the lion's den", said Arthur. "Don't worry; we won't bite."

Cheryl halted in her tracks. "Stop it!"

Arthur turned to face her, his face impassive.

"You're not going to win me over with gentle words or dime store philosophy. And I don't like you reading my mind. It's an invasion of my privacy."

Arthur continued walking and Cheryl caught up with him.

"I don't need to read minds to know what's going on in there. Have you always been so hostile? You don't have to answer. It's a lousy way to live. Take it from one with far more experience."

"I have a job to do."

But what job? Arthur reflected. *You've been less than honest with me. But if I challenge you further, I could do damage. Best to let you come to realization for yourself.*

They rounded a stand of trees when Cheryl stopped and gasped.

"Beautiful isn't it?"

"It's breathtaking."

Arthur's broad smile betrayed his pride. "We call it the Collaborative."

Glistening like a many faceted jewel, Building F sat nestled against the hillside its angled panes of glass reflecting the green leaves on the trees surrounding it. A stream ran the length of the building like a medieval moat. A glistening bridge crossed over the water leading to the main entrance.

"Peter insisted on the bridge. I'm sure you recall his sense of humor and the rest of us didn't see much of an alternative."

Cheryl smiled in spite of herself. As she crossed the span she sensed she was leaving the world she knew behind, entering a realm as foreign to her as the compound in Virginia.

Walking into the building Arthur explained, "BRIDG computing can be found throughout the campus but the Collaborative houses servers more powerful than anything on the planet buried deep into the hillside. And don't let the glass fool you, this LEED certified building is impregnable. A direct hit with a blockbuster bomb wouldn't even dent the glass. It's based on a silicon-titanium crystalline formulation we've developed.

Once inside Cheryl noticed the lobby occupied a two story atrium with no offices apparent.

"Most of the facility sits underground; its' more energy efficient and easier to protect. We channel natural light using ambient concentrators here in the lobby and situated on the hillside."

"Why all the security? Are you all that worried someone's going to try and break in?" Cheryl asked as they descended in an elevator.

"We're not concerned with the lone individual. It's the organized resistance whether a terrorist bomb or government takeover. I'm sure you can appreciate our predicament", Arthur added caustically.

They rode the elevator down to level B5 and exited into a brightly-lit, high-ceilinged corridor. Cheryl saw people working in offices through the glass and chrome walls. She noticed that some of the walls were opaque and seemed to move. She saw conference rooms filled with people who appeared to be animatedly discussing their work. She couldn't help but recognize the positive energy all around her but said nothing.

They passed through two sets of sliding glass doors and came to a wall which looked into what appeared to be a large aquarium. Multi-colored fish glided past the glass oblivious to her presence. Coral and sea anemone swayed with the gentle currents. She watched as a moray eel poked its head out from its hiding place in a well-concealed cave. As she peered more closely at the glass a sea turtle seemed to swim out of nowhere causing her to take a step back.

"I'll leave you here, Cheryl. Peter should be along shortly. Enjoy the view. I hope you have a productive visit."

Arthur smiled, turned on his heel, and retraced his steps back toward the elevator.

A device, vaguely human in shape, glided down the hall toward her. It moved on two sets of wheels which self-balanced like the vehicles policemen and security guards ride on sidewalks and in the mall. Above the wheels sat a box and on either side was affixed a mechanical arm ending with a simulated three fingered hand. Instinctively Cheryl looked to the thing's head. At first glance it appeared white in color but as it moved closer the white gave way to shifting colors. And as it pulled up to her the face took on Peter's visage.

"Hello Cheryl," said the mechanical voice emanating from a very human looking mouth. "I'm just finishing something up. Would you like to watch?"

She nodded tentatively.

As the doppelganger turned to face the aquarium the ocean scene seemed to lose focus and then disappeared altogether. Cheryl looked down into a cavernous space descending fifteen feet behind the glass of what had been the aquarium. The wall opposite where she stood held three video screens. The one in the middle stood over ten feet in height with smaller screens to its left and right. A man in a white lab coat stood in front of the screen to her left while a woman in similar attire stood before the screen on the right. In the center of the room, below Cheryl and directly in front of the largest screen, stood Peter.

But what she saw on the screens attracted her attention as a flame to a moth. Around the periphery of the screens she saw faces, all of whom seemed to be participating in whatever was going on. The center of Peter's display showed what seemed to be multiple DNA molecules and rapidly reformulating chemical equations. As the equations stopped shifting and settled, pieces of the DNA molecules shifted out of their current location on the strands while other molecules floated in to take their place.

In the center of it all she watched Peter gesticulating grandly as though conducting an orchestra. In fact, she thought she could hear dramatic music faintly through the glass.

"I'll be done in another 5 minutes," said Peter's simulacrum. "You are watching a BRIDG Collaboration among biochemists and cell biologists in Berkeley, Paris, Nairobi, Tel Aviv, Bangalore, and Shanghai.

"Some diseases can be traced to a single allele, a single spot on a strand of DNA, but others, like diabetes, are the product of multiple alleles. We are simulating DNA changes and mapping the protein interactions in an effort to find a treatment while minimizing side effects. When we're confident we've isolated the correct genes we will start simulation exercises before testing with lab animals to make sure we haven't missed anything. We find this approach minimizes the damage to the animals and as a result is much more efficient."

Cheryl surprised herself by asking the robot, "I can hear music through the glass. Is that part of the process?"

"Our left brain generates the linear and logical part of our thought process. But good science also requires creativity which resides more in the right hemisphere. We've found that music helps to bridge (no pun intended, or maybe intended) both sides of the brain, another dimension to the collaboration, if you will."

"I'm glad to hear you haven't lost your lousy sense of humor."

Cheryl paused and looked at the robot.

"What am I doing? I'm carrying on a conversation with a machine."

"Not really. I'm speaking to you through the machine."

"At the same time you're working down there?"

"Sure, why not? Don't tell me you haven't worked on your computer while talking on the phone. Follow me and I'll take you to my corporeal self."

She rode another elevator down one floor with Peter's robot. As they approached a frosted glass panel it slid aside and Cheryl walked into the lab as the music ended and the screens went blank.

Peter walked over to where she stood, a smile spreading across his face. He stopped a few feet from her.

"Before I give you the tour I have a few things I want to show you. First, though, I want you to meet Karen and Edgar."

Peter's assistants stepped forward and shook hands with Cheryl.

"These two worked in Gabby's old lab and were instrumental in developing the Ulysses retrovirus. Karen, could you make sure Gabby sees the footage of what we just did? In particular, I want her opinion on steps 11 and 114.

As Peter led Cheryl through a door in the back of the lab and down a corridor she asked, "So Dr. Neumann didn't develop the virus on her own?"

"She did," Peter responded. "At the time she led a project for the Pentagon and they were assisting her. She began the development of the Ulysses retrovirus while still on the faculty at the med school in an attempt to heal Michael's brain injury. The school was starting to ask uncomfortable questions about her research. Coincidentally, she was recruited by BDT to work on the Pentagon project. While no one here was aware why she was developing the Ulysses treatment, Arthur wanted to use Gabby's techniques to construct another virus which would enhance physical capabilities for the military. They dubbed the project 'Achilles'."

"Achilles?" she asked. Cheryl tried to appear nonchalant having heard that name the day prior during her visit to the Virginia compound.

"While the Ulysses treatment increases the density of cerebral tissue, the thinking part of our brains; the Achilles treatment targeted the cerebellum, the center of coordination and muscle control. The idea was to create super soldiers. It sounds like the plot from some comic book, doesn't it?"

Cheryl's unease swelled. She knew Peter must be sensing what she was feeling but couldn't help asking, "Was it ever tried on anyone?"

"Gabby's testing made it as far as animal trials. A number of the rats exhibited balance problems and, more troubling, hyper-aggression."

"Who was her handler at the Pentagon?" she asked already having guessed the answer.

"General James Scott. He quietly retired in disgrace after trying to steal the viral specimens."

Cheryl felt her headache returning. To try and calm her seething apprehension she asked, "How did you get involved?"

"Gabby ran into some roadblocks so Arthur asked me to step in. I ran simulations which helped match the DNA and RNA sequencing. Then, when Scott increased the pressure on Arthur to deliver, Arthur fired Gabby because she was unwilling to fast-track Achilles, afraid the side effects would prove catastrophic. At the same time, Michael's paralysis was spreading so I hooked Gabby up with Jules and the rest is history; though it's really mystory. Get it? His-story, my-story?"

Cheryl looked up at Peter feeling a long-lost fondness. No, it was more than fondness. There was a comfort there, a peace. And something more?

They now stood in front of a glass wall, nothing but darkness beyond.

"I'm really excited to show you this", said Peter as the room beyond began to brighten.

While the past few days had been filled with new discoveries, Cheryl could barely comprehend what she saw before her. As far as she could see, in front of her and below, bathed in subdued illumination, hummed banks of computer servers.

"It's massive. What is it?"

"When we began this project Gabby had what she referred to as her Garden. Those were the tanks where she grew the Ulysses and Achilles retroviruses. Her Garden has expanded by leaps and bounds to grow modified organic molecules, and cell cultures. I can show them to you later if you like.

"To complement Gabby's Garden is the Farm. This server farm is the largest on the planet by a factor of seven the next largest being Intel with 100,000 servers."

"What's it for?"

"The Farm fulfills multiple purposes. As I'm sure you're aware, we're able to link our minds with a BRIDG processor without the need for a physical connection and independent of distance. That one capability has increased the demand for computing power over a thousand fold. As more people undergo the Transformation the need for connection increases. Also, we're using the power of these processors to solve problems at greater orders of complexity than ever before. For example, under contract with the FBI and the NSA, we've developed de-encryption algorithms which we're using to monitor internet and wireless traffic for signs of terrorist threats anywhere in the world."

"Sounds like Big Brother, to me. Are you listening in to my conversations, Senator Gregory, the President?"

"Come on, don't you think the government's been doing that all along? And what about all the places you go online who record your preferences in order to sell you more stuff? We lost our privacy years ago. As computer technology has evolved, we've struggled to keep up. But now with the Treatment we're better able to partner in that evolution and, in effect, exercise more control. It's kind of like 'Multivac'."

"Multivac?"

"You never did read Asimov, did you?"

"So this Farm is connected to the internet?"

"Even though we don't need it for the connectivity, I developed a web gateway so that we can hook in through more traditional means. Most of the businesses we work with still require internet connectivity."

"Peter, this is all very impressive but can't you see where it's leading? I can help you get out; put your talents to real use. I know you think you're doing some good here, and maybe you are. But you've leapt too far ahead. They're not going to allow you to continue. They're going to take all this away and you'll end up in prison."

Peter shook his head. "When we were married we shared our dreams with each other. You're living yours. Can't you see I'm living mine? How could I leave what we've built? I know you can sense how happy I am. I used to be so cynical, disconnected, rebelling against any threat to my isolation, to my singular world view.

"I get it. There are a lot of people out there threatened by what we're doing here. Many coming from the same isolation I used to know so well. At the same time how do we quit, with so much at stake?

"The very nature of our world forces change on us from the moment we're born 'til the day we die. The future doesn't belong to the strongest or the smartest, but to the most adaptable. Help us get the message out, tell the world we offer real progress, not just hope."

Cheryl took a step back shaking her head, denying the truth of what she heard.

Peter took a step toward her.

"I've stopped lying to myself. Now it's time for you to stop, too. I pushed us apart wallowing in my own cynicism. You've never seen this sincerity coming from me before."

Cheryl backed up again.

"No, and it scares me to death. What have you become? You're not, you're not you."

Cheryl's balled fists shook with frustration.

Peter took another step toward her.

"You couldn't be more wrong. I'm not the person you were married to. I've been able to uncover what I really am under all the crap I piled on myself, from my parents' death in the airplane crash, to Jules' absentee parenting, to God knows what else."

"Peter, I don't want to see you hurt," Cheryl pleaded through her tears. "I couldn't bear that."

Peter took one more step and took her in his arms.

"I said before you were living your dream. But you aren't, are you?" Peter asked.

"You've made compromises, reconciling yourself to your impotence hoping to create something good despite all the politics."

Peter took half a step back holding her arms and looking deeply into her eyes.

"You can't deny who you are any longer. The headaches are back."

Cheryl nodded. She brushed a strand of hair back over her ear. "The stress is really getting to me. I guess I care more about what happens to you than I thought."

"I don't think that's it."

"What do you mean?"

"Do you find it odd you're working for Gregory?"

The mention of the senator's name sobered Cheryl. As she wiped her eyes she said, "No, he's the most powerful man in the Senate, a great leader. Working for him is my ticket, don't you see?"

"He sent you to see me, to trade on our history for some advantage. No, don't protest. You should know what I'm capable of by now. The problem is: you don't see the whole picture. Gregory will try and bring us down but it's already a lost cause. Do you think it mere coincidence that you work for him?"

"Are you saying he hired me only because of my connection to you?"

"Don't be insulted. You know better than I how things work in Washington. Didn't you tell me you went to work for him because it gave you an advantage? Is it really so different? We're not what we say but what we do. We're defined by our choices. Those choices form a pattern tied to the patterns of those around us.

"You used to be the positive one, the optimist, but in your quest for success you've lost that. The time is coming soon. You'll have to make a choice, a life or death kind of choice; and the outcome will depend on whether you can accept who you really are and what's truly important to you."

"Peter, don't be so melodramatic. Are you afraid of us?"

"You? You would never intentionally hurt me. But the people you work for: Gregory, General Scott; these are not good people and you're just a tool to them."

"You think so little of me?" Cheryl spat.

"Just the opposite. They're not worthy of you, of your intelligence, of your drive, or of your heart."

Cheryl pulled away nodding; "Now this all makes sense. You figured out I'm involved with Paul. I fooled myself thinking I could have hid it from you. But I was right about one thing: there's no way I can sway you from your path. You're too stubborn. Peter, I loved you once but that was over a long time ago. You can't manipulate me with your vaunted skills into coming back to you. Our marriage is over. I may still harbor some feeling for you but we'll never get back together. I'm going to take you down."

"Listen to yourself. Can you even hear your paranoia?"

"I'd like to leave now."

As she uttered the words the mechanical Peter approached. This time there was no face to the device.

"Think about what I said. You don't have much time."

Peter stared after her as the robot escorted her away.

Chapter 19

An unnatural glow from the computer monitors cast the only light on the lone figure. Peter reclined in a large cushioned chair, eyes open. He minimally furnished his sanctuary to avoid unwanted distractions. Located in a corner deep in the Collaborative, Peter was the only person with access to the sound-proof space. Conventional disturbances, like phone, were absent. On most occasions one might find him, day or night, prowling one of his labs, supervising the many projects underway, tinkering quietly with a new piece of technology he had developed, or meeting with a team of system architects and software developers. But there were times when Peter needed a concentrated stretch to reflect or brood undisturbed.

He hadn't seen her in years, not since she left for Washington. As he expected, her presence opened old wounds and older memories to clash with his new-found understanding. When they had been together, there had been no way for him to have known she was a Natural. Now the realization shed new light on their past. He understood how the denial of her nascent abilities had become a technique she used to avoid unpleasant truths constructing instead an imagined reality which only reflected truth at the surface as one might look into a pond and, seeing their image, ignore all the activity below.

They had been married less than five years. Their mutual attraction grew from their complementary personalities: his technical brilliance and offbeat humor contrasted her ambition and easy social skills. At the same time, Peter struggled with intimacy owing to the death of his parents in an airplane crash when just a child. Cheryl's inability to consciously confront their problems, instead hoping against hope that they would go away, doomed their marriage from the start. By the time both understood the source of their conflict it was too late to do anything about it; Peter oblivious to their deeper connection, Cheryl unaware of how she contributed to their downfall and unwilling to accept her deeper feelings for him.

She'd thrown him for a loss. The Transformation connected Peter to an inner life he'd never known existed. And with those awakened emotions he couldn't help but wonder if there was still some spark there. *Why else had she remained single all these years*, he wondered. The revelation that she was seeing Gregory surprised him but he sensed all was not right; a connection of convenience, one which enabled her to live out her fantasy.

He worried for her. The walls she built around her soul had grown taller, thicker. But he could sense the dam cracking. His gentle probing revealed someone unaware and unwilling to confront her own demons not to mention the demons around her.

What did Jules call her? A rejector? I could have pushed harder but the results might have been disastrous. Without knowing it, she sits at the nexus of the conflict. There's got to be another way. She won't be able to hold back the deluge for long. If the dam breaks there'll be no saving her. She sees

164

shades of gray, a means to an end, but there is evil in the world and its consuming her. I wonder what they're up to?

He knew something was afoot but struggled to identify the source or scope despite all the resources at his disposal. Gregory might be at the heart of the conflict. At the same time Peter sensed there was more to his agenda than the BRIDG or the Ulysses Treatment.

But what?

Peter closed his eyes, breathed deeply and attempted to release the tension. He decided to explore a curious sensation he'd discovered during his last solitary session. Most who used the BRIDG circuit accessed it to communicate or to augment their own thought processes with its computing power. It served well as a vehicle to solve analytic problems permitting multiple researchers to interact simultaneously with a computer affording the capability to consider multiple variables simultaneously. The collaborations had led to breakthroughs in the fields of chemistry, biology, physics, and medicine. Advancements in social sciences, such as economics, had proven more complex owing to the number of factors to consider. And the social sciences didn't offer the closed systems which made the hard sciences, where one could presumably control for all the variables, easier to model.

Initially, some balked at the collaborations. Using the BRIDG as the connection had a mechanical feel to it. Exposing their thoughts to the BRIDG processor caused some to fear they would lose their individual identity in a machine world which might easily overtake them. At the same time, the experience of connecting with the circuit brought on a feeling not unlike a subtle intoxication. They found that to have one's mind unfettered by biology and to coexist within cyberspace at times had the feel of standing on a Plexiglas platform extended out hundreds of feet over a chasm. Others found linking with the ruminations of fellow Voyagers made for an uncomfortable and unfamiliar intimacy. The mind reading that some believed the Voyagers possessed only came close to reality in cyberspace.

But, over time, as the collaborators accustomed themselves to the novel experience, most came to realize it was really no different than learning any new skill whether riding a bicycle or learning to play a new video game. As comfort grew, so did enthusiasm and skill, such that Peter found most collaborators eventually eager to throw themselves into their work.

He expected the upcoming venture with Jules and his Institute for Future Studies would raise them to the next plane of complexity. The plan, as Jules laid out, was to take a relatively complex social issue such as homelessness and explore the societal effects of various interventions over the next hundred years. But as intriguing as these projects were, Peter wanted more.

From the time Peter first connected with the BRIDG, following closely on the heels of Michael's and Arthur's Transformation, he discovered a natural affinity with the circuit. While the Ulysses Treatment may have opened his eyes to a world of personal intimacy which had gone unnoticed before, his fundamental personality hadn't changed: he found the world of electronics so much cleaner, so much less complicated than the world of human interaction; a world where immutable principles applied, unencumbered by messy emotions.

But with experience came wisdom and with wisdom he'd come to understand that those 'messy emotions' while often responsible for some of mankind's greatest failures, also lay behind mankind's greatest achievements. It was Gabby's fear of losing Michael which fueled her passion resulting in the Ulysses retrovirus.

Sitting there in his sanctuary, confronted head on with his unresolved feelings for Cheryl, Peter began to wonder, *if the BRIDG processor simulates the connections in the human brain, could there be some way to program it to encompass emotion as well? And what if I could establish rules, like Asimov's Three Laws of Robotics, so that these emotions could serve reason rather than corrupt it? Could I exist as a thinking, feeling individual in both this body and in the network? Kurzweil may be right, but his timing was a bit off. Then again he didn't count on Gabby, or me.*

The thought of Gabby recalled for him a conversation with the doctor just prior to undergoing the Transformation.

§

Peter lounged on a couch in the living room at Gabby and Michael's house. The Travelers had returned from Northern Wisconsin just two weeks before. At that time Gabby and Michael still lived in a two bedroom wood-frame bungalow. Gabby outfitted the spare bedroom as a treatment room. Jules had undergone the Transformation three days prior.

"Peter, I'm ready." Gabby stood in the doorway looking down at him.

"Sorry. I was just thinking," said Peter as he started to rise.

Michael standing behind Gabby said, "Peter, you don't have to do this."

Gabby and Michael stepped into the room.

167

"You're a jumble of emotions," said Michael. "Tell us what's going on."

"I don't know what to think," admitted Peter. "I'm excited with all the potential. I couldn't develop the BRIDG and not be able to use it. But, all the same, I'm terrified. I've learned to trust my mind. It's gotten me this far. Now I feel like I'm jumping off a cliff with no safety net. I don't know what to think and I can't stop my mind from telling me all the things which might go wrong.

"Peter, I didn't have a choice. It was the Ulysses Treatment or die."

"I know that. But the chance for discovery . . . I see what you can do. I want that, too."

"Peter, the Treatment is safe," said Gabby. "Jules, Arthur, Michael, its gone perfectly with everyone so far. I understand if you don't want go forward but don't let your mind trick you into an irrational decision.

"What do you mean?"

"Remember the story I told when we were away, about what I was feeling when I was stuck there on the floor of your car?

Peter nodded.

"I was in college, terrified to take a risk; one that I knew couldn't end badly. All the while my mind chattered at me like some wild monkey, filling my head with unsubstantiated fear. Don't' listen to the monkey."

"Easier said than done."

"My mother taught me a lesson a long time ago", continued Gabby. "I was in middle school at the time. We were in gym class playing basketball. I had always been something of a bookworm, not one of the popular girls. One of the mean girls caught me staring at a boy across the gym and threw the ball at my head; totally nailed me."

"Wait a minute," interrupted Michael. "You were interested in some guy before me?"

Gabby turned to Michael and patted him gently on the cheek. "Yes, dear. You were not my first, but you will definitely be my last. . . . if you behave yourself."

Gabby turned back to Peter. "I turned to face her. She and her pack walked over to me and told me how I could never catch such a cute guy. Said I was too much of a nerd.

"I waited until I got home. As I walked in the front door, I broke down in tears. My mother asked me what was wrong and I told her everything. She took me into the living room, left and came back with a mirror, and held it up to my face.

"What do you see?" she asked.

"I looked at my tear-stained face and said 'a loser'."

"Look deeper," she said.

"At first I didn't know what she was talking about. And then it dawned on me. I nodded as I handed the mirror back to her."

"'We see only what we want to see,' I told her."

"That's part of it," she replied. "Some people have built in mirrors. By that I mean they can clearly see their strengths and limitations. Most have cloudy mirrors and only see themselves indistinctly; others have no mirror at all. You can't be responsible for other's mirrors, but you can cultivate your own. I know it looks like those girls are something special. But if you keep working on yourself, become stronger, more self-aware, there's nothing you can't accomplish.'"

"I guess she was right," smiled Gabby.

§

"I'll create a virtual mirror," reflected Peter.

Peter allowed his awareness to enter the BRIDG Network partitioning a sector on one particular server. With his mind, he then created a process to echo back whatever it saw into a structured repository to determine where content should reside using what Gabby taught him about how the brain works; locations for memories, sense perception, emotion, motor control.

He took a deep breath.

Peter concentrated and cautiously allowed his collected memories to touch the simulated mirror. As he did so, the virtual mind he created on the server stored those memories. The process seemed to be working well so Peter relaxed and allowed the BRIDG to probe more deeply letting the experience wash over him like a wave. He felt the mirror now reflecting his thoughts, his feelings, and his perceptions creating a virtual Peter within the infinite confines of the computer network.

Cautiously he allowed his mind to enter the server and found himself looking back. The image was dizzying like standing between two mirrors and seeing the echo of one's image in infinite succession.

Peter pulled back. *I'll build another virtual mirror around my digital self. I'll make it half-silvered like the mirrors used in lasers only allowing my presence in while permitting me to see out from my twin self. That should make it hacker proof. If a hacker finds me he'll only see what looks like everything else around him. It's as though I'll be invisible.*

Peter tied off the programming.

I can now move it into the Cloud. I'll exist simultaneously everywhere and nowhere. Also, now that my virtual self also exists I can see if I can improve on the original design. Maybe that way I won't be ruled by my own irrational perceptions. I'll create new modes of thought. And only I can access myself.

Okay, that sounds way too strange. I'll have to come up with a new vocabulary to describe this Convergence. Can't wait to tell the rest of the Travelers.

Chapter 20

"It's a nice house," said Dawn as the car pulled to a stop in the driveway of a late model French Colonial. Michael got out and walked around to the trunk to get their luggage. He had notified Dawn an airplane ticket was reserved in her name, circumstances forcing him to meet her at the local airport, their flights arriving less than half an hour apart.

Dawn came around to the trunk and grabbed a large duffel bag holding her remaining possessions.

"Now remember," said Michael, "no matter what you see or hear they're really just kids."

Dawn walked behind him, taking in the surroundings and wondering just what was behind his caution. As he entered the house she heard from inside an enthusiastic 'Dad' which seemed to come from two voices at once.

Stepping into the foyer, a space lit warmly by the light spilling in from multiple windows, she watched as Michael dropped his luggage to embrace the children who held on to each of his legs. Dawn noticed a third, older child hanging back in the shadows.

A woman, whom Dawn assumed to be Michael's wife, walked in from another room wiping her hands with a towel. Gabby stepped up to her husband and kissed him. "Welcome home, dear."

Turning to Dawn she added, "You must be Dawn. We're so glad you decided to join us. Come. Meet the kids."

The twins stepped back from their father and appeared to be studying Dawn. They looked to each, smiled and chanted in unison, "We know something you don't know."

"This is Alex and Kerry, and over there is Bobby. Bobby, please come over here and meet Dawn," said Gabby.

Bobby stepped forward, looked up at her face and said, "Hello."

Dawn responded with a crooked smile, "Hello, Bobby." A chill shot down her spine.

The twins giggled.

"Enough, you two, go get ready for dinner."

The three children ran from the room.

"I thought you only had two kids," said Dawn. Two kids would be hard enough.

"Bobby's mother had been our previous nanny. She died two months ago in a car accident," said Michael. "We've been appointed as his legal guardians."

"I appreciate everything you're both doing for me but I'm not sure I'm the person you need. I don't know if I can handle one much less three kids," admitted Dawn.

"You'll do just fine," said Gabby with a broad smile. "I have a feeling about you. Why don't you take a seat in the dining room while Michael helps me in the kitchen?"

Gabby poked Michael in the ribs with her elbow.

"Ow!"

"Don't you complain; you're always telling me how you love my bony elbows."

Gabby locked Michael's arm in hers. Dawn couldn't help but hear her utter as she led Michael away, "well done, dear. You never cease to surprise me."

She thought she heard Michael respond, "I'm not sure what it is," as they walked into the kitchen.

Who are these people, she wondered as she stood waiting in the dining room.

Dinner had been a pleasant if uneventful affair. Dawn couldn't remember the last time she sat around a table with a family for a home cooked meal. After cleaning up Michael took the kids for playtime and to get them ready for bed.

"Would you like to join me in the den?" asked Gabby. "We can drink a little wine, get to know each other".

"Sure," said Dawn.

Gabby sat on a couch facing Dawn while Dawn sat with her back to the cushion gazing across the room.

"I'm glad you chose to take the job," Gabby began. "It's not easy finding the right person."

"And you're sure I'm the one?"

"I guess we'll see. You were pretty quiet at dinner."

"I felt awkward. We've just met and I'm trying to understand how I fit in."

"It won't be easy, as you saw," said Gabby.

"The twins, they . . . I don't know . . . they . . . I don't know what I can do with them. They seem so self-confident and at the same time like kids. And they're so smart."

During dinner Kerry and Alex bantered easily with their father probing behind his stories to uncover the grim truth concerning his trip to Italy.

"The Ulysses Treatment transforms the DNA in every cell," began Gabby. "If either parent has gone through the Transformation any children they have will be born with the Ulysses capabilities. For good or ill, I underwent the Treatment while newly pregnant. Who knows what that might have done? Anyway, Alex and Kerry grew to full consciousness in utero. I became aware of them in my sixth month.

"I have no idea how long they were conscious before that. Evidently they could hear Michael and me talking and so we made a conscious effort to begin connecting with them before they were born, speaking to them often. Many parents do that, almost as a lark or to get them used to their voices, but we took the time to try and help them understand what was going on and especially about the birth process.

"I can't imagine how frightening that would be if you were conscious when that happened," observed Dawn.

"Michael's abilities are stronger than mine, than the rest of us. Soon after his Transformation he was pushed, after a fashion, and his capabilities grew. He was able to more directly touch the kids mentally, speaking and teaching them language. They were quick learners as you can imagine. And that's only accelerated since they were born."

"I don't see how I'll be any help," said Dawn. "They'll run rings around me."

"They sound more sure of themselves than they are. Much of what you heard comes from study, not experience. You can't think of them like any other child you've known. They're not better, just different.

"They see a natural order to everything around them. They see patterns where most people see chaos. Their abilities aren't any different from any other Voyager, but they've never known the world any other way.

"It's an imperfect analogy, but imagine you were born knowing how to ride a bicycle. You would understand how to get on the bike, move the pedals, steer, maintain balance, and brake safely. But as an infant, and even as a small child, you'd be too small to ride, to reach the pedals, to put your knowledge into practice. That's a source of great frustration for them and so they try to do more than they're prepared to handle.

"But that creates another problem. They assume everyone else knows how to ride a bike. They've always known how and it's difficult for them to comprehend that someone else wouldn't know something so obvious. It's just the way the world is. It should be apparent to everyone."

"Must be hard for them," Dawn responded.

"Most of humanity muddles about doing the best they can but it's a struggle. We strive to provide for ourselves and our families barely conscious to our shortcomings and drenched in denial that death waits around every corner. It's how we cope with the pain and uncertainty. That same struggle for survival pits man against man fighting for every scrap of bread, every piece of ground.

"And that's the source of Alex and Kerry's other great frustration. They have always known the true unity of all mankind; the same way you know those curtains over there are blue. You and I grew to learn the pain of alienation and loneliness, even as children. Thank God they can't even comprehend it. They take our connectedness for granted.

"But don't think them naïve, not for a minute. They see the consequences of mankind's self-destructive behavior as clearly as any Voyager. They're already working to get the message out any way they can. They developed a software program and use it to build their portion of the pattern."

"How do you and Michael parent them?" asked Dawn.

"We do the best we can, like any parent," responded Gabby. "There are no manuals. We talk a lot."

"You two seem really close."

"We started out that way but after Michael's accident we started to drift apart. We each built a moat around our hearts for protection telling ourselves it was to shield the other but we were only deluding ourselves."

"How did you fix it?"

"We hit rock bottom. We didn't understand it at the time but I think the pain of potential separation was greater than either of us could bear. I don't know how I can make you understand but, we really are physically connected with one another."

"I'm sorry but that sounds like so much mystical bullshit to me."

Gabby nodded. "Neither Michael nor I are given to sloppy thinking. I was trained in the sciences and Michael's always been something of a cynic but our eyes were opened even before the Transformation.

"Michael'd been having a recurring dream about the car accident, the one where he was injured. It was so real to him that sometimes he would wake screaming. And then I started having the same dream. Eventually we saw each other in the dream. It was hard to deny something was going on no matter how hard we tried. Once Michael had the Ulysses Treatment we came to understand the basis for the connection. I don't think we're any closer than we were before, but we certainly appreciate it more."

Dawn looked down into the deep red at the bottom of her wine glass. "You've got what I thought I had. I figured if I found the right guy I'd feel complete. All my dreams would come true. I thought I could have a fairy tale life; a man who would love me forever, kids, picket fences, the whole thing. But that's not real. I grew up believing in all that nonsense. Maybe it's true for some but not me."

Gently Gabby probed. "You're so young, about 24?"

Dawn nodded.

"Not to sound like a cliché but you still have your whole life ahead of you. At the same time, I can tell you have the weight of the world on your shoulders. What happened to you? What killed your dream?"

"You found your Prince Charming; mine was a jerk. We started dating towards the end of high school. Never did too well in school. Everything moved too fast for me and I fell further and further behind. I wasn't real interested in all that stuff anyway. I couldn't see why it mattered who did what to who when. It all seemed like a waste of time.

"I was looking to have fun and I knew that if I found the right guy I'd be set. I was kind of shy, didn't have a lot of friends, just had to have a boyfriend. Guys seemed to sense that. Got pregnant when I was sixteen. The father wanted nothing to do with me. I gave my son up for adoption."

Dawn paused, took a deep breath.

"Where was the rest of your family in all this?" Gabby asked.

"I had five brothers and sisters. My folks didn't seem to care that much. With six of us they scrambled just to keep food on the table. 'Cause I was pregnant they put me in a school for the misfits. I met a guy there. He swept me off my feet. Told me I was beautiful. We both felt like outsiders. We'd go down to the lake, talk about our life together. I knew he was the one.

"We figured we needed a fresh start away from everything. I thought we could run away from the past. Pretty stupid, huh? Took me a while to learn you can't hide from yourself. When I turned eighteen my folks kicked me out and we left town. Found a place. Sam, that was his name. Anyway, Sam found a job as a car mechanic. I got a waitressing job. What they don't tell you is that when two people live together, their relationship changes. Back home everything seemed magical, so full of promise. But then reality intruded."

Dawn stood. She walked to the picture window and stared into the black night still holding her wine glass.

"Sam worked days and I worked evenings so we didn't see much of each other. I'd be asleep when he left in the morning and he'd go out while I worked. A lot of times I'd get home before he would. I'd fall asleep in a chair waiting for him and he'd come in stinking of beer. We'd fight. He loved to fight when he was drunk.

"Anyway it just got worse and worse until one day I came home from work to find he'd cleaned out all his stuff. I thought 'good riddance' but when I checked our bank account in the morning he'd taken all our cash. We were behind as it was. I just kept getting in deeper and deeper."

"But now you can make a fresh start," suggested Gabby.

"Yeah, right. I'm still me. I'm damaged. I get anxious even thinking about the future afraid of what's coming next."

Dawn turned to face Gabby. "You seem to have a wonderful family and you've all been very nice. But being here just makes it harder. I don't see how I fit into any of this: the kids, this house, your crusade. The thought that you would choose me to be your nanny over anyone else, I just don't get it."

"Come here." Gabby patted the seat next to her and Dawn sat reluctantly.

"Dawn, we're all damaged. You've created this fairy tale in your mind and that's all it is, a fairy tale. Despite what you see in this house, there's no happily ever after. Every day is a struggle. There are times when I think I'm too damaged to continue. And I know Michael is." Gabby looked over her glasses with a wry smile, trying to get Dawn to relax.

"I wouldn't know where to begin."

"I won't suggest you undergo the Transformation. It's no cure, but it is a help. First you have to figure out what you really want."

"That's just it. I don't know any more. What I thought I wanted isn't real and everywhere I turn I ache."

She'd never unburdened herself like this before. She didn't know if it was the wine or an all-consuming need for release. Her tears belied her cynical words.

"It doesn't matter what I do. I should be grateful, but being here, with all of you, only fills me with pain when I see what I don't have, what I can't have. I don't see a way out. And even if I could. "

Dawn now sobbed uncontrollably.

She didn't want to say more, her anguish overwhelming, blocking out all thought, all sensation . . . all but the light touch of a small hand.

She turned and over her shoulder saw little Alex standing next to her, his face drawn in pain, his eyes filled with unshed tears.

His little hand rubbed her back gently.

"I'm gwad you're here," he said in a small, tentative voice. "Maybe you didn't come here to take care of us. Maybe we can take care of you."

"Alex, that's very sweet," said Gabby. "But it's time to go to bed. I'm sure your father's looking for you."

The little boy nodded somberly and left the room.

"He's very sensitive," said Gabby. "But he means well. He feels too much for a three year old but I don't know how to protect him."

180

"You could send me away. I'm obviously not good for him."

"Stop it! You're dead wrong. Leaving isn't the answer. I'm sure we can help."

"You don't get it. I don't deserve to be 'helped'." Dawn spat that last word. "Haven't you been listening? I'm a screw up and always will be. I gave away my own flesh and blood, damn it! I'm not worth your pity."

"No one in this house feels pity for you. Pity's a waste. But you've got to see yourself deserving of love."

"I'm *not* worth it, don't you see?" she begged plaintively. "My dream confirms it."

Gabby sat up.

"What dream?"

"It's nothing."

"Let me be the judge. Start at the beginning. Is it a recurring dream and how often do you have it?"

"They're pretty much the same. I have it almost every other night now. It's nothing."

Gabby waited.

"OK. Sometimes I'm in an open field, but most of the time I'm staring out a window. It's getting dark outside, very dark but it's the middle of the day. There are black clouds all around. They're growing and moving like something's boiling over, spreading and blotting out the whole sky. I feel like they're closing in on me. There's no lightning, no thunder, no rain."

Dawn stared straight ahead. "I'm getting real scared; like something horrible is about to happen. I think in the back of my mind a tornado's coming. Then I look to my right and there's a boy standing there. He's reaching out with his arms like some kinda zombie."

"What do you mean?"

Gabby noticed Dawn's breathing getting shallow.

"His face, it's like, he's got this vacant look. His eyes, they just stare at me, accusing me. And his arms, they're straight out like you see in a zombie movie. I know he comes from the storm and despite how he looks I want to help him.

"But then I look out the window and this tornado's coming right for us. I want to protect the boy from the storm. As the tornado gets closer I feel the darkness closing in."

Dawn stared straight ahead, her eyes unfocused.

"I'm not in the room anymore. I'm not anywhere and the darkness surrounds me. There's this figure, like a dark cloaked man but with no face. As he glides closer the boy moves away and I'm gasping for air and I feel a terrible pain in my stomach."

As if in response to her description, Dawn doubled over in pain.

"What is it?" ask Gabby.

"The pain, it's getting worse."

"Describe it."

"It's in my stomach."

"Here?" Gabby pointed at Dawn's stomach.

"No, lower."

"On a scale of one to ten with ten being unbearable how would you rate your pain?

"An eight sometimes?" said Dawn as she sat up, the pain subsiding.

"That seals it, I'm taking you to my doctor."

"Fine, but I'll only stay until you find another nanny."

"You're that uncomfortable being with us?"

"Don't you see? My dream's coming true."

"Why? Because of the pain?"

182

"Because the boy in the dream; he looks just like Bobby."

Chapter 21

"Today's the day."

Tom Talbot sat on a bench in the locker room just off the gym. He'd finished a strenuous workout with one of the other program participants. Colin Simms had just voiced the obvious.

"Yeah, I know," said Talbot.

"Are you scared?" asked Simms.

"A little," admitted Talbot. "But I'm not backing out now. Nowhere else to go anyway."

"I know what you mean. You get the feeling we were selected because we wouldn't be missed?"

Tom nodded, staring straight ahead. "My mother's dead. Dad wants nothing to do with me."

The recruits rarely talked about their lives before reaching the compound. They had been encouraged to focus on their mission and not clutter their minds with a past lost to them. But now with induction day upon them, Tom felt an inexplicable need to remember.

"How'd your mom die?"

"I killed her."

"What?"

"May as well have. I was responsible for my brother's death. She loved him so much. Couldn't bear it without him, couldn't forgive me for what I did. In the end she just gave up."

§

The mid-afternoon sun shone brightly as summer suns do on twelve year olds. Tommy Talbot, his tanned body already showing signs of the man he would become stood on a raft in the middle of the lake; across from him stood his brother, Billy. Despite the three year age difference Tommy was already exceeding his older brother, physically. Competitive to a fault as brothers can be they also shared a deep and abiding love though never giving it voice.

The Talbot family rented a cabin on a lake for a family getaway.   Dad went off fishing and after lunch the boys ran down to the beach and spent an hour tanning and looking at the girls. But tiring of the boredom (and lack of results) they had just finished a race to the raft. Billy climbed out of the water first, barely beating his brother.

As they sat on the raft catching their breath, Tommy said, "OK, you won that one but I've got another game. Let's play 'king of the raft'. Whoever gets pushed off first loses."

"Fine, but you can't win this one," taunted Billy.

"We'll see about that."

The boys stood and faced each other, bracing themselves.

The smell of gasoline and the whine of outboard motors permeated the air as speed boats careened across the lake. Skiers traced behind the boats creating crystalline curtains of water as they cut the wake.

The boys circled each other until Tommy, seeing an opening, rushed Billy. The older boy easily stepped aside letting Tommy fall on his face while Billy laughed.

"Come on, big man. You can do better than that."

Tommy sprang to his feet and rushed Billy again. This time Tommy's mouth found Billy's elbow splitting his lip.

As Tommy wiped blood from his mouth, Billy taunted again, "ready to declare me the winner?"

"No way."

"Come on. Mom's gonna be pissed I split your lip. I can hear her. 'Now boys, quit it before someone ends up in tears'. Give up before it gets worse."

"No way."

Tommy rushed him again.

As Billy stepped aside his foot slipped on a slimy patch of water and he fell backwards into the water. Tommy laughed realizing he won but before he could gloat, the unthinkable happened.

A slalom skier cut the wake intending to splash the boys playing on the raft. But a bump from the wake of another boat caused her to lose control.

The skier flipped out of her ski flying through the air and into the water beyond Billy. The ski, with a life of its own, struck Billy's bobbing head.

Tommy saw his brother's inert form face down in the water. Without a thought he dove in and, with a strength he didn't know he had, pulled his brother up on the raft.

The skier had climbed on the raft, too.

"Do something," pleaded Tommy. "He isn't breathing."

The woman knew CPR and began chest compressions but by the time the lifeguard reached the raft it was too late.

Tommy's mother heard the commotion from the cabin and rushed down to the beach. Tommy heard her scream and saw her collapse in the sand in undisguised anguish as the life guard stood shaking his head.

Another lifeguard rowed a boat out to the raft and brought both boys to shore. Sitting on the beach, his mother cradled Billy's head; her keening cry throwing Tommy into oblivion.

§

"My mother never got over it. She just seemed to waste away. My dad never said but I think she OD'd on her meds my last semester in high school. He was so lost. Never talked to me after I joined the Navy. I don't know if he resents me for what happened to my brother and my mom or if he checked out, too. I guess it doesn't matter."

"That's quite a load you're carryin'," said Simms.

Looking down at his feet, Talbot said, "There're some things you just can't fix. So I figured making the most of my God given talents was the best way for me to make up for what I've done. Maybe this is it."

"Maybe. We got half an hour before we have to report to the Induction Center," said Simms. "I'm gonna go hang in my room for a few. See you there."

"You bet."

The five recruits, clothed only in hospital gowns waited on their beds in the Induction Center, a medically-equipped ward with white tile walls, linoleum flooring, and bright florescent lights. No curtains separating the beds.

Harold Helvey, their commanding officer, stood in the center of the room addressing the men. Meyerhoff waited in

187

the shadows with his nurse. An array of syringes rested on a Mayo stand at his elbow.

"Men," Helvey began. "The time has come for you to fulfill your promise. You will each be given an injection to make you sleep. This is necessary as the transformation you will undergo will be dramatic and it will be best for you to wake up after it's complete. The electrodes attached to your chest will measure your heart rate. Those attached to your head will measure brain activity. In your case, Fester," he said looking at one of the recruits, "the current tracing reflects your lack of mental activity." The other recruits laughed as Fester gullibly turned his head to look at the monitor.

"What are you laughing at Frank? Look at your heart monitor. Tells me you have no heart."

The other recruits laughed, Fester hardest of all. Frank leaned back against his pillow, arms folded, his face perpetually frozen under a sour expression.

Helvey smiled to himself confident in his ability to put the men at ease. "We have a veritable Wizard of Oz situation going here: no brain, no heart." Helvey paused. "But no lack of courage among any of you; no siree. I salute you for that.

"Once you are asleep Dr. Meyerhoff, with assistance from the lovely Nurse Vicki, will administer the Achilles virus. You will not get an infection. This is a specially engineered virus designed to enhance mental function. You will wake up stronger, faster, and we hope, especially in your case Fester, smarter."

Even Fester laughed at that one silently hoping the prediction would prove true.

"While you sleep Dr. Meyerhoff will administer the spider milk combining it with the keratin in your skin making you bullet-proof. I know this has all been explained to you before but does anyone have any final questions?"

No one raised a hand.

"Good. Men, we salute you for your dedication and your bravery. You are the forerunners of a whole new breed of soldier. God be with you."

As Meyerhoff moved to the first bed Tom felt his heart begin to race. Involuntarily he thought of the victims at Auschwitz being led to the showers for delousing only to be gassed en mass to a hideous end.

"*Stop it*", he told himself. "*They're not trying to kill me. That's just fear talking. This will make me into one of the greatest soldiers who ever lived. This must be the purpose Cheryl spoke of all those years ago,*" Tom felt with newfound excitement. "*Odd I would see her right before this happened. Must have been fate.*"

But there are fates worse than death.

Chapter 22

She found him right where the twins said he'd be.

The Neumann's home sat on a little over an acre far enough out of town to avoid close neighbors. It's not that they weren't sociable; it's just that they figured their lives were enough out of the mainstream that they wanted to avoid upsetting those around them with all their comings and goings. In purchasing the house and property Gabby and Michael took into account their own experiences in their first home.

In that first house, purchased when Michael worked for the hospital and Gabby held a position on the medical school faculty they had neighbors living close on both sides. On one side lived a family, the Fry's, who owned a German Shepard. Gabby and Michael had been friendly with the couple and their young daughter but didn't know them well. The Fry's kept the dog chained up in the back yard, no dog house, rain or shine. It wasn't unusual for the dog to bark at all hours of the night often waking the Neumann's.

Gabby and Michael were becoming increasingly exasperated and were planning to talk with the Fry's. One afternoon, after Michael's accident but before the Transformation, while Gabby was working at BDT, the doorbell rang. Michael wheeled to the door and when he opened it he saw Fry's daughter, Angela, dressed in her Brownie uniform.

"What can I do for you, Angela?" he asked.

"I'm selling Girl Scout cookies. Would you like to buy some?"

"Sure. Gabby loves Thin Mints. We'll take three boxes."

"Great. Give me just a second. I have to write down your order."

Michael watched as she tried to record the order without anything firm to write on. Finally he interrupted. "We have a table here inside the entry. Why don't you use that?"

"Thanks."

She stepped inside as Michael moved his chair out of her way. He noticed she yawned as she wrote.

"Not getting enough sleep?" he asked.

"Maxie keeps waking me up at night."

"I understand. Happens to me, too."

The next night, as the dog barked at around 2 am, Gabby jumped out of bed, threw on her robe and marched over the Fry's. A bleary-eyed Cameron Fry answered the door and when Gabby confronted him he said, "What barking? I don't hear any barking."

"Your daughter's complained about it."

"News to me."

Gabby turned heel and stormed away. When she got back into bed she said to Michael, "I can't take this anymore. You're going to have to talk to the city."

"I'll take care of it in the morning."

Michael contacted a city mediator who scheduled a face-to-face meeting. When presented with the details the mediator turned the Fry's and without asking their side said, "So what are you going to do about it?"

Michael and Gabby didn't want to be those kinds of neighbors.

Mature trees shielded the house from the road. The back side of the property sloped gently downward and was bordered by a stream flowing along the property line. Trees grew on both sides of the stream whose banks sloped down about three feet from the tree line.

That's where she found him. She saw him jump up as she approached. Dawn stepped carefully down the bank to avoid losing her footing and saw Bobby, now sitting on the other side of the stream; digging in the sandy dirt with a stick. Dawn sat on the bank facing him. He didn't acknowledge her presence. Dawn didn't say anything either. Finally, Bobby spoke.

"Go away."

"Why don't you come back to the house," she began. "I'll make you some brownies."

Bobby didn't reply, stared at nothing, continuing to dig with his stick.

"It's going to take you an awfully long time to get to China at the rate you're going." She thought she saw a hint of a smile.

"Look Bobby, I don't like you hanging down here by yourself. And I can't leave the twins up there by themselves."

"Why not?"

"They're not even four years old."

Bobby looked at Dawn out of the corner of his eye, with an expression, too mature for his age, which said, 'are you kidding me?'

"Well, yeah, maybe you're right. They seem to be able to take care of themselves pretty well."

Dawn thought for a moment. "Don't you like them?"

"They're okay."

"They seem to like you."

"We're like friends and stuff but, I don't know, I just. . ."

Bobby continued digging in the dirt.

"The Neumann's seem nice," said Dawn.

"Everybody's nice. That's not it."

"You miss your mother. Do you want to talk about her?"

"No."

"I've found that sometimes it helps to talk about your feelings. It can make you feel better."

Bobby continued digging in the dirt.

"I don't want to talk about her. What do you care, anyway?"

"Well, first, I hate to see you so sad, and," Dawn looked off into the distance, "I'm something of an orphan too."

Bobby stopped digging and looked up at Dawn.

"What do you mean? Are your parents dead, too?"

"No. But they may as well be. They want nothing to do with me. I haven't talked to them in years."

"That's horrible. If my Mom was still alive . . ."

Dawn thought she saw a tear trickle down Bobby's cheek.

"Maybe we can look out for each other," said Dawn.

"What do you care? You just met me."

"I know but I feel a kind of connection with you. Maybe it's because we're both missing something." Dawn didn't tell him about her dream. If it didn't make sense to her, it certainly wouldn't make sense to him.

"What do you mean?"

"You know, orphans?"

"Why won't your mom and dad talk to you?"

"I've done some really stupid things."

"Like what?" He was now looking at her.

"Doesn't matter."

"Must have been pretty bad," said Bobby. "I've done some stupid things but my mom never stayed mad at me for long."

"That's what a real mother would do. She must've been a pretty special person."

"I guess." Bobby was digging in the sand again.

"Look, I won't try and kid you. I don't have all the answers, heck, I don't know if I have any answers. But one thing I do know is that it's easier to get through the tough stuff if you have someone to go through it with."

Dawn craned her neck to try and look Bobby in the eye.

"Sometimes Alex and Kerry are lots of fun, but sometimes when I'm with them I feel like I don't have any clothes on," Bobby admitted.

"I get it. I've only been here a few days but I already can tell it's not easy living with them: Gabby, Michael, the twins," said Dawn. "They're all so intense, always on edge. But that's not the hardest part. I feel like they can see right through me. I can't have any secrets from them and so it makes it harder for me to hide from my bad feelings."

Bobby leaned back using his arms to support his upper body while he sat cross legged facing her. "Don't get me wrong," said Bobby. "I know Gabby and Michael like having me around. They try real hard to make me feel like I belong. And the twins told me they really like you."

"But you still feel like you don't fit in?"

Bobby nodded.

Despite her cynicism and self-doubt Dawn found herself caring for this boy. *He seems so lost. I can't imagine what it would have been like if I lost my mother. He must think there's no hope.*

Perhaps it was sympathy for Bobby's situation, perhaps it was insight into her own dilemmas but for just a moment the

194

thought crossed Dawn's mind almost as a reflex, *there's always hope.* Though the thought left her mind as quickly as it arrived swallowed by her self-imposed isolation, she knew what she had to do.

Dawn stood and walked down to the side of the stream.

"Bobby, we're in this together. We'll figure out a way to help each other, okay?"

Dawn reached out with her right hand. "C'mon back to the house with me. I can't imagine you'll turn down brownies.

Bobby looked up at Dawn. He stood, walked down to the side of the fast flowing stream. He stared into her eyes with a look which said, '*Maybe it's worth a try.*'

He stepped out onto a rock to cross taking Dawn's hand for balance. The rock proved slipperier than he expected. His right foot went out from under him and he fell. Dawn didn't let go and they both found themselves sitting in the cold, flowing water.

"You're soaked!" said Bobby with a giggle.

"You are, too," laughed Dawn. "Together?"

"Together."

Chapter 23

Cheryl talked into her telephone head set as she scanned her computer screen all the while searching for a manila file folder among so many cluttering her desk.

"Cheryl," her assistant shouted.

Cheryl looked up from what she was doing, a quizzical look crossing her features. Her assistant mimed removing the headset and Cheryl took the cue.

"He's ready for you."

Cheryl grabbed her notebook along with the found file and headed out of Senator Gregory's suite in the Senate office building and down the hall to the multimedia conference room. She knocked softly on the door and quietly entered.

Senator Gregory sat with his back to shaded windows facing a large plasma screen. No one else occupied the room but on the screen, in different windows, she saw two people she recognized. And one she didn't.

She took a chair and sat quietly while they finished their conversation.

In the pane on the left she saw the full-faced Jeremiah Barnum, the most familiar of the three. She had heard Paul refer to him disdainfully as 'the Reverend'.

Occupying the right pane with short gray hair and hawk-like features, sat her recent acquaintance: General Scott.

In the middle of the screen sat the image of a man with graying blonde hair and piercing green eyes. He appeared to be sitting on a couch and behind him stood another man but she could see only from his waist to his shoulders, his face beyond the range of the camera.

"General, I'm glad to hear the next round of inductions has begun. We eagerly anticipate positive news, especially after the last round," said Gregory.

"Now to our next order of business," continued Gregory. "This is my chief of staff Cheryl Keyes. She will be organizing the upcoming hearings. Cheryl, you know Mr. Barnum and you met General Scott last week. This is Stanford Gates. You will recognize his name from the rolls of my campaign donors.

"Gentlemen, I asked Ms. Keyes here to brief you on her visit to BDT. Cheryl . . ."

As Cheryl relayed the results of her visit and attempted to answer their questions she couldn't help but wonder what the four men had in common. None were on her witness list for the hearings. The red light on the television console told her the transmission was encrypted. That was typically only used for clandestine national security briefings. *What's going on here that they're afraid someone would hear?* she wondered.

"It sounds like your visit, Ms. Keyes, was a failure," said Barnum.

"I wasn't able to turn Peter, if that's what you mean."

"I wouldn't call it a complete failure," said Scott. "You've given us marginally valuable information on their security and their technology set-up but nothing to help us with Operation Liberty."

"Let's switch gears and talk about the hearings," said Gregory.

Cheryl suspected Paul changed the subject to one where she could demonstrate greater mastery. *I don't need you to protect me*, she thought while at the same time finding the gesture charming.

"I have arranged for our media outlets to begin prepping the public for the testimony," Cheryl began. "Members of the Committee are appearing on the talk show circuit. We've enlisted seven prominent bloggers to fill in the gaps between shows."

"I have received your recommended scripts," said Barnum. "My staff has begun editing."

"The timing is important," said Cheryl. "The messages are laid out sequentially to capture the growing groundswell of attention and lead the public to an obvious conclusion."

For the first time Gates spoke. "And what conclusion is that Ms. Keyes?"

"First, that BDT is a threat to the economy and must not be allowed to function unfettered. Second, that the NextAge Movement and their leadership pose a threat to national security and must not be allowed to operate within our borders. Third, that the Committee should be granted extraordinary powers to control the threats."

"There is one more objective I would like you to consider," said Gates.

"What is that, sir?"

"The public must see Senator Gregory as their champion, a strong leader not afraid to take control, not afraid to do whatever is necessary to secure their future."

As he spoke Cheryl saw Gates raise his left hand for emphasis. While she expected to see him raise a finger as if lecturing; in its place she saw the obsidian hand.

Where have I seen that before?

While she agreed with Gates' assessment Cheryl sensed something in his voice: calm, control, but something else.

198

Somehow she sensed disagreement would bring severe consequences.

"Of course, sir. I will weave those thoughts into our scripts."

She turned to the Senator, "may I continue?"

Gregory nodded.

"Once we've completed opening statements members of the medical and scientific community will be called to testify."

"Do you have any concern they will voice support for the Samsamites?" asked Barnum.

"We will be asking opinions only from those we have prepared adequately ahead of time," said Gregory. "Others will only respond to questions covering potential threats posed by the Ulysses Treatment and the BRIDG processor. We have authorities lined up from Harvard, Cal Tech, MIT, IBM, and Berkeley.

Cheryl continued, "Slated next we have representatives from a cross section of the various religious communities."

"Any Muslims?" asked Scott.

"Yes sir," replied Cheryl. "We've targeted popular, conservative preachers from all major denominations. We want to show a united front irrespective of their individual beliefs. We expect them to strike a strong emotional chord with the public. They are there to set the stage before we call the NextAge leaders: primarily the Neumanns and Paulson."

"And what do you hope to gain by calling them?" asked Gates.

"We intend to use prior testimony as leverage to incriminate them publically. They're arrogant enough I have no doubt we can get them to admit to crimes sufficient to land them in prison."

"Would it help to get an indictment before they testify?" asked Barnum.

"What are you thinking?" asked Gregory.

"Based on Cheryl's description of her meeting with Paulson, I wonder if we can catch BDT in an SEC violation."

"Do not underestimate these people," interjected Gates. "They are smart and they are organized. You are not going to catch them in an obvious mistake. And I suspect they will be prepared for any question you might throw at them. We need another form of leverage if Operation Liberty is to succeed."

"Operation Liberty?" said Cheryl. It was the second time she heard the reference.

"Ms. Keyes, I want to thank you for your update," said Gates. "It appears as though you have done a very thorough job. It is now time for us to move on to other business."

The finality in Gates voice caused Cheryl to look at Gregory who, with a slight nod of his head toward the door affirmed that her presence was no longer required.

Cheryl stood, offered a demure "thank you, gentlemen" and quietly left the room.

If someone saw Cheryl striding back to her office they would have thought she was ready to commit murder.

Who in the hell do they think they are? I've orchestrated this whole thing to come off perfectly and they dismiss me out of hand. Why? 'Cause I'm a woman? Paul played along with it! And who does this Gates guy think he is?

Cheryl's anger hardly abated as she stormed into her office slamming the door behind her.

I'll show them. Exclude me from a meeting will they?

Three months prior, at Gregory's direction Cheryl installed a bug in the conference room as a means for him to listen in on any meeting that might take place. Cheryl plugged her headset into a jack, turned up the volume, and leaned back in her chair.

" . . . Are you're sure they're the ones publishing under the Dialogos banner?" Barnum's voice.

"Without a doubt," said Scott. "Our source in the NSA confirms it."

"Amazing," said Barnum.

"During the hearing we will send in an Achilles strike team and remove them to the Compound," said Scott. "They will provide us with the leverage we require."

"The hearings are vital to secure our position," said Gregory. "Arresting the Neumanns' collaborators may still prove necessary but this will give us the leverage to get what we need out of them."

"Very good." That sounded like Gates. "And are you prepared for Stage 2?"

"We've used multiple intermediaries," said Scott.

"And the President, the Speaker, and the Vice President will all be at Camp David?" asked Barnum.

"Yes. I will not be able to attend the retreat due to my commitments here in Washington."

"And your speech is prepared?" asked Gates.

"That's one speech I'll write myself," said Gregory.

Cheryl heard laughter.

I write all his speeches. What's going on?

As she mentally voiced the question a blinding pain struck Cheryl between the eyes. Gut wrenching nausea accompanied the agony filling her head. Cheryl bolted from her office, the listening device flying from her ear.

Cheryl sat on the floor in the bathroom stall, her head over the commode; the images retreating into her subconscious. They had come fast and furious, without control. She could make no sense of what she saw feeling as if she were in the middle of a dream. As she came out of the fugue, she could only recall the sound of crying children, a hot wind, and an odor unlike any she had smelled before.

She shifted so that her back was against the tile wall of the stall, her knees pulled up, head in her hands, the pain subsiding. Gently, other images captured her attention.

§

Cheryl sat opposite her best friend Margie. Each wore light jackets protecting them from the chill of early spring; Margie's a bright pink and Cheryl's a matching yellow. Cheryl's heart swelled with anticipation as she reveled in the smell of grass reborn and reawakened trees mixing with earth moistened by melting snow. Her hands felt chilled against the metal handle of the seesaw but held on nevertheless, enjoying the sunny day.

They had finished lunch in the school cafeteria and now watched as the boys and some of the girls in their second grade class chased each other in a spirited game of tag. Cheryl preferred quieter activities with her best friend and soul mate, Margie. They met three years before when Cheryl moved in across the street from Margie and the two had been close ever since.

"Margie, isn't this a beautiful day?" asked Cheryl in her sunniest voice.

"I guess."

Cheryl noticed her friend lost in thought.

"What's the matter?"

Cheryl was at the bottom of the cycle while Margie at the top only shrugged.

As she pushed up sending Margie down, Cheryl began to wonder what could be bothering her friend. For as long as she could remember Cheryl could tell when people were troubled. And if she really concentrated, images might come which would tell her a story.

Wishing to help her friend unload her burden Cheryl focused her thoughts and the images appeared. She saw Margie's parents. They were fighting. Not the disagreements she might witness from time to time between her mother and father. No, they were having a knock-down, drag-out argument.

Cheryl stopped, her feet on the ground while Margie sat suspended in mid-air.

"I'm sorry," said Cheryl as she thrust upward.

"About what?" responded Margie.

"That your parents are getting a divorce," replied Cheryl matter-of-factly, high in the air.

Margie stopped the seesaw motion, her feet on the ground, her face betraying a look of stricken recognition as though she now knew something that she should have suspected all along.

"No they're not!"

Margie jumped from her seat sending Cheryl plummeting uncontrollably.

As Margie ran for the safety of the school building, a muddy Cheryl ran after her, calling.

Cheryl cleaned up in the girl's restroom but when she got back to class Margie was nowhere to be found.

That evening Cheryl lay on the floor in her living room coloring a picture for one of her classes when she heard a knock at the door. Her mother walked to the door, twisted the knob and was confronted by Margie's mother.

"Well your little Cheryl's made a mess of everything."

At the mention of her name Cheryl looked up from her pink pony.

"What do you mean?" asked Cheryl's mother.

"Your daughter told Margie that Rick and I are getting a divorce."

Cheryl's mother's eyes narrowed. "I don't know how she would know that. Cheryl, come here."

Cheryl dutifully walked to stand next to her mother.

Cheryl's mother looked down at her. "Did you tell Margie that her parents were getting a divorce?"

"Yes."

"Why would you think that?"

"I just know it"

"I'm sorry Lois; I don't know where she gets such ideas."

"You haven't said anything to her?"

"It's true?"

"Yes. I wanted to be the one to tell Margie but Cheryl blurted it out on the playground. How did you know?"

Cheryl shrugged.

"Maybe she overheard you and Rick. Or Margie might have said something."

"I told you Margie didn't know anything." Lois looked down at Cheryl. "I don't want you coming by our house anymore. Margie is too upset. We'll be moving soon anyway."

Lois turned heel and stalked away.

Cheryl's mother thoughtfully closed the front door. She took Cheryl by the hand and led her to the sofa.

As they sat she asked, "What were you thinking?"

Cheryl shrugged.

"Cheryl that's not an answer. How did you know?"

Cheryl looked up at her mother, her large eyes brimming with tears. "Why can't I see Margie anymore?"

Cheryl's mom shook her head. "I'm sorry dear but Margie's moving away."

And as she trudged slowly to her bedroom Cheryl began to hate the pictures in her head.

§

"What's happening to me?" Cheryl asked in a quavering voice, her legs growing cold as a chill seeped through the tile floor.

Cheryl heard the bathroom door open. The head of her administrative assistant appeared below the stall door.

"Are you OK?" asked Helen.

"Just having a bad day. Don't worry about me. I'll be out shortly."

As she picked herself off the floor and straightened her skirt Cheryl thought to herself, *"I'm falling apart and I have no one to turn to. Maybe Peter's right. I may not have much time before I lose it completely."*

Chapter 24

"I'm worried about her," said Peter. "She's caught in events and whether she knows it or not, she doesn't have the strength to swim against the current."

"She's struggling," said Jules. "What do you think it is?"

"Too many competing agendas," replied Peter. "She was always good at multitasking but never could handle emotional complications. She's torn between me, Senator Gregory, her ambitions, and her fears. She still denies who she is and the shell she built around her true self is cracking."

The Travelers gathered as they could, the demands of their harried schedules sending them in different directions more often than not. Peter and Jules were catching up while waiting for everyone to take their seats. Harrison Gage, Deputy Director for the FBI, had arrived at the BDT conference room only a few minutes before. While he was not considered a part of the original quintet, his early involvement and key position in the government not to mention a long association with Arthur and Jules commanded his attendance as the agenda permitted. Today there were multiple imperatives to discuss.

As Michael entered Gabby pulled him off to the side.

"We got the results back from Dawn's scans."

"And?"

"Ovarian cancer, probably stage 3 or 4."

"Wow. So what do we do now?"

"It doesn't look good. Let's talk more after this."

Michael and Gabby took their seats as Arthur entered.

"Arthur, Peter was just filling me in on Cheryl's visit," said Jules.

"She's going to be a problem," said Arthur shaking his head. "She didn't get what she came for and so is going to be even more difficult. I was hoping to sway her to a more moderate point of view but her paranoia is only increasing."

"I agree," responded Peter. "There's a serious possibility she's going to crack under the pressure."

"I'm not so sure," said Gabby. "She may surprise us all."

"Let's get this meeting underway," said Arthur as he sat. "We have four meaty agenda items as I see it: first, our quarterly update on BDT activities, second an update from Jules on progress with the Institute for Future Studies; third, the Contingency Project, and fourth, preparation for our Senate testimony. Does anyone have anything else?"

"Just one thing," said Peter. "I've created a virtual Peter in the Cloud."

"A what?" said Gabby.

"A virtual me, with all my senses, emotions, and memories."

"This is the Convergence Project you've been talking about, right?" said Arthur.

Peter nodded.

"What will you do with it?" asked Jules.

"I'm still working on that. I've made the initial breakthrough. Now I have to start thinking with it to figure out what it's good for."

"I don't know if we can handle another one of you," said Michael.

"Yeah, I am pretty special. I worried that I might overwhelm all of you but then I figured you'd all be glad there's more of me to love." Peter paused. "I'm sorry. I have to apologize. I have really been struggling to come up with a pun here but I got nothing."

In unison Gabby, Arthur, Michael, and Jules applauded.

Gabby marveled. Just four years before they'd all been working at cross purposes: Gabby and Michael's marriage foundering on the shoals of their divergent obsessions; Peter unable to see anything but his own self interest; and Jules and Arthur battling for control of the company with Gabby, Peter, and Michael in the middle. *How far we've come,* she thought. *I only hope we can hold on to what we have.*

"Thanks a lot," laughed Peter. "Let me get some more experience with this new self and we'll see where it goes from there. Maybe I can get a portion of its consciousness dedicated to feeding me puns."

"Perfect," said Arthur with more than a hint of sarcasm in his voice. "Let's begin."

Arthur called on the members in turn discussing progress on key projects. Gabby summarized progress with her various genetic engineering endeavors focusing on treatments for three complex diseases in various stages of development from lab simulations to human trials.

"Thanks, Gabby," said Arthur. It sounds as though you're close to a number of breakthroughs. Let's revisit in a month. I want to make sure we can get the manufacturing capacity online quickly."

"Arthur, we're a long way from production," said Gabby. "Once we're satisfied we have a viable product we still have to get FDA approval."

"That sounds like a discussion you and I had four years ago," said Arthur.

"A lifetime ago," said Gabby.

"You can bet the regulators won't rush to judgment," said Michael. "Every solution we offer going forward is going to be held up in the political arena. We have advocates on Capitol Hill but Gregory and his ilk will block whatever we propose. They're using us as pawns in their political game."

"That's why we have to court public opinion," said Arthur. "I'm using our public relations staff to leak our results to the media creating a tide of sentiment the politicians will find very difficult to resist."

"We'll see," said Michael staring down at the table.

Gabby, sitting next to Michael, looked sideways at him. Since his return from Italy he had grown increasingly sullen and withdrawn.

"Peter, how did your BRIDG Technology Summit go?" asked Jules.

"It was pretty wild, as secret meetings go. I found it funny that everyone publically declined to attend but we got the CTO's from IBM, Apple, and Microsoft along with academics from the MIT Media Lab and Cal Tech. They flew into different cities and came by different routes to your northern Wisconsin retreat, Jules; everyone wanting to fly below the radar. Hey, there's my pun. I haven't lost it."

"Peter, please stay on point," said Arthur.

"If nothing else, their curiosity has them ravenous to get their hands on the technology to see what they can do with it but they don't know how to do so without creating a political firestorm within their companies. There's no question they see the business and research potential but are searching for ways to control access and in so doing limit internal concerns.

"At first, they talked about how they might set up a firewall or somehow create components to prevent Voyagers from accessing the processor without authorization. The guy from IBM, who's had the Treatment, just laughed. We explained to them how disabling the any of the BRIDG's capabilities was like building an airplane but then removing the wings because they took up too much space.

"I used the Darwinian Postulate. I explained how survival of the fittest translates into the business and technological arena. I helped them see how the pace of technologic and biologic change brought about by the development of the BRIDG and the Ulysses Treatment accelerated the rate of co-development transforming evolution into revolution. I reminded them that we are also planning summits in Asia and Europe. They realize that if any of their competitors get access to the technology before they do they could be left out in the cold. The guy from Apple accused me of backing them into a corner. But his colleagues helped him realize the revolution is inevitable.

"After a while they all really got it. They see the potential beyond hardware upgrades and software development. They figured out what I'm really trying to do here. They know that when we find a way to implant our individual consciousness in a machine that the implications eclipse any of man's other inventions or discoveries. This was their first glimpse of the Convergence Project."

"They're going back to their respective companies to try and figure out how to get in bed with us without creating havoc. We're scheduled for a Collaborative next week."

"Let's move on," said Arthur. "Jules, why don't you brief us on the progress with the Institute for Future Studies," said Arthur.

"It's been a challenge, but we finally have agreement. We're endowing fellowships at Harvard, Berkeley, Princeton, the University of Chicago and the University of Wisconsin.

Harvard's proposal was most unique coupling the Sociology, History, Psychology, and Economics departments. There are several faculty members who have undergone the Transformation to act as advisors from other departments, too. The intent is to develop a new academic discipline a la Asimov's Foundation proposition.

"Asimov's Foundation proposition?" said Arthur.

Peter groaned. "Really, Arthur, and I thought you were an educated man."

"I don't recall covering it in business school," Arthur responded with a smile.

Everyone chuckled except Michael, who, Gabby noticed, didn't seem to be paying much attention.

"Arthur, and anyone else who is similarly ignorant," began Jules as he looked around the room preparing to lecture, "Isaac Asimov, in his Foundation series posited that the future could be predicted using the principles of 'mathematical sociology' which looked for macro patterns in human behavior to predict future events. We touched on this briefly during our meeting Rome.

"In a sense we're like prophets from the Old Testament," continued Jules. "The insight we gain from our ability to see patterns and anticipate consequences can be likened to the visions of those seers. It was a different time, a different context, different language. That's at the heart of what Father Juan is looking into.

"With the help of Peter's BRIDG technology we're attempting something similar: to forecast major trends in economics, politics, and social interactions pulling in the variables of technology development and population dynamics. As our methodologies develop we'll bring in Law and Business to understand how we can craft a more just and progressive society. Initially, we'll try and understand what effects the Ulysses Treatment might have on societal development in an effort to anticipate conflict and head it off. At the same time we'll determine how long it will take for genetic drift to make the outcome inevitable."

"Genetic drift?" asked Harrison.

"It's the basis for our inevitable triumph," said Gabby. "Think of it this way. Every parent who's had the Treatment passes their capabilities on to their children. Given that the Ulysses mutation exhibits as a dominant trait, it won't take long, either through those receiving the treatment or through their offspring before the majority of the population has the genetic characteristic. Our opponents know this and that's why they want to round us up and prevent us from having more kids."

Harrison nodded. "Your comments couldn't be timelier."

"That's putting it mildly," observed Michael.

"What do you mean?" said Gabby, growing increasingly irritated with Michael's mood.

"Events are overtaking us", said Michael. "I'm not sure we'll be able to stay ahead of the curve."

"Michael, we understand the risks," said Arthur. "Is there something else we're missing?"

"Mankind has never shown itself to embrace revolutionary change. The Church excommunicated Galileo. Even Einstein for all his brilliance and creativity could not accept the fundamental principles of quantum mechanics. Our traditions, our mental constructs limit our ability to accept the new and different. Hell, the prophets you mentioned earlier, Jules, weren't accepted in their own time. They saw too much and it scared the daylights out of everyone. I'm hoping for the best but I fear the worst."

"And that's why we're implementing the Contingency Project", said Harrison. "We've led people to believe that the Farm and Garden are only located here at BDT so we can maintain security and control. In truth we have completed installations of duplicate Farms around the globe in secure locations. We've meticulously sited secret locations for Gabby's Garden in places no one will find them. The locations are known to a select few Voyagers."

Gage continued, "Gregory and his followers are becoming desperate. You don't have to have our abilities to feel their fear."

Peter nodded. "I certainly sensed it with Cheryl. But are there that many people who are so violently against us? Everyone I met with last week seemed pretty excited to get on board."

"They don't need many," replied Michael. "Gregory, Barnum, and their allies overseas are whipping people into a frenzy. There's no telling what they can do. If enough people see a threat, real or imagined; they'll throw out our Constitutional protections without a second thought. We don't have to look further than the internment of American citizens of Japanese descent during World War II. Hell, just a few years ago we invaded another country with no legitimate justification. We don't need Jules' Future Studies Institute to see the possibilities."

"Michael, what do *you* think will happen?" asked Gabby.

"All our efforts could easily boomerang. Isaac Newton said 'For every action there is an equal and opposite reaction'. I think it's likely that governments around the world will assert power, limit personal freedom in the name of security for the populace but really in defense of their powerbase. I have no doubt they've figured out where we're heading. The more insecure among them will lash out. Look at Iran and Saudi Arabia. Both just enacted laws making it illegal to be a Voyager and banning the use of the BRIDG. Both offenses are punishable by death and imprisonment of the violators' families unless they come forward. They call us an abomination to Allah."

"Michael, those are extreme examples," objected Gabby. "There are plenty who see the benefit in what we're doing."

The others around the table looked from Gabby to Michael and back unwilling to interrupt the apparent power struggle; as if two angels wrestled for the minds and souls of mankind.

"Fine, let's look closer to home," responded Michael. "Peter, what did Cheryl say, 'we'll all end up in prison'?"

"More or less," responded Peter. "But, like Gabby, I'm hoping the public will see through the insanity."

Michael shook his head violently. "Maybe, but the public, as you call it, isn't in power. It's just as likely we're about to descend into darkness. Democracy and liberty have been failing for years in the face of political and religious extremism; long before we were on the scene.

"Michael!" chided Gabby who folded her arms and wouldn't look at him.

Michael shrugged in response.

"Which brings us to the upcoming Senate testimony," said Arthur attempting to divert the apparent conflict. "Gabby, Michael, and I have been subpoenaed. We're scheduled to testify next week. The three of us will be spending the next several days with our attorneys in preparation. Jules and Peter, you should join us. You may be called before the Committee at some point and we may as well do this just once.

"We'll be asked about our intentions, our goals. We will be asked to implicate others, anyone who's gone through the Transformation. They believe we've infiltrated every level of government and society. Michael isn't wrong. They'll probably try to use this as a first step to limit our civil rights.

"They're building their case to come after the three of us," continued Arthur. "Gabby, they'll come at you first. They've already set the stage portraying the Ulysses Treatment as a public health menace and since we still don't have FDA approval they'll use this as an opportunity to make the case to take away your medical license. You may not care, but it will be like pulling a thread on a sweater. One charge will lead to others. They believe we pose a very real danger and will make a case for such in painstaking detail. Your testimony will provide just one more building block enabling them to take control.

"But Arthur, isn't this a chance for us to turn the situation around in our favor?" asked Gabby. "They're televising the hearings. They think people all over the world will come out against us but I think they're missing the boat. They only hear opinions which support their cause."

Peter nodded and said, "There's growing movement in opposition. It's not affiliated with us but it's fueled by what Kerry and Alex have done. Their dialogues have tapped into latent resentment to the power structure just as your Samsa blogs did, Michael. I think we'll be surprised by the support we see."

"Which will only escalate the conflict", said Michael. "The greater the threat, the greater the backlash."

"In any event, Cheryl and Senator Gregory have done an impressive job painting us into a corner," said Jules. "Even though the witnesses have been biased and self-serving they're masterfully making their case.

"The business communities' testimony has been the most benign," said Arthur. "Interestingly enough there's been little damaging testimony, most of it coming from economists who caution that the BRIDG would create an unfair business advantage for BDT and the Voyagers. They've been smart by not attacking the technology but instead our connection to it. They say we'll be in absolute control of all data and computer processing and as a result control all of society.

"The testimony from religious leaders has gone about as expected. The extremists have said we're all made in God's image and that any change is borne of evil. The more moderate members of the Committee including the few who are more openly friendly to our cause have attempted to find opposing witnesses to try and moderate the tone, but I worry they haven't been as successful as we would have hoped. It would have been helpful if we could get some of the more positive religious leaders to come forward, but the Committee leadership wants to hear nothing from them."

"Father Juan would have been helpful," said Michael to no one in particular.

"The testimony from the scientific community has been the most damaging," said Jules. "There's speculation on side effects with no basis in fact but it's raising peoples' fears nonetheless. The more vehement ones have called us a 'plague' upon humanity but the Committee's been smart. Not wanting to appear too extreme, they have other voices calling for quarantine until the long term effects can be known. They recognize that this isn't spread like an infectious agent but instead either through infusion of the virus or to our children.

The plan will probably be to intern us, and to separate the men and women so we can't reproduce."

"So their plan is to take control of the BRIDG technology and put us in unisex concentration camps," said Gabby. "They're going to ask us to name names so that the Voyagers can be rooted out and isolated. How do we counter it?"

"There are several strategies we've already put in motion," said Arthur. "The Committee is attempting to try us in the court of public opinion. Human rights groups have been mobilizing to get our message out. They see the threat to personal liberty as more serious than the threat to national security. Some of the more liberal clergy have joined that movement. The scientific and academic communities are conflicted but our polling of media and public opinion indicates the Committee runs a real risk of running aground. And I have to agree that Kerry and Alex through Dialogos have played no small part in getting the real issues out there."

Michael smiled. "The apple doesn't fall far from the tree does it? And yet I'm worried for them. I have a sense they won't be able to keep their identities secret much longer. I'm terrified something bad is going to happen, very bad.

"I'm seeing patterns in the undercurrents which terrify me. I'm suffering under an anxiety that I'm having difficulty controlling. I can't shake the feeling we're heading for a trap with cataclysmic consequences."

"Michael, I see the possibilities, too," said Gabby. "I think the best course is to prepare our testimony. We can run rings around those goons and in the end we'll prevail. They're televising the hearings. I have no doubt we can use that to our advantage. Michael, do you agree? Michael?"

Michael looked at each of the others in the room weighing his words carefully.

"I've seen this coming for a while. I predicted these very events four years ago. Remember when we were flying back to BDT after Arthur and I went through the Transformation? I spoke about an upcoming battle for domination. It's going to get worse before it can get better, if it ever does, and I'm not going to contribute to it."

Gabby's eyes narrowed. "What do you mean?"

Michael looked directly into Gabby's eyes and calmly explained, "I'm not going to testify."

"Michael, you have to testify," said Jules.

Without turning his attention from Gabby Michael said, "No, I don't."

"Michael, don't do this," said Gabby. "You, more than anyone, can sway the Committee, convince those watching and listening that we pose no threat and that, in fact, we offer only solutions."

"Something is wrong," said Michael, his conflict readily apparent to all. "Something is very wrong. I don't know what it is. We stand on the edge of a precipice. Terrible things will happen if I testify. There's more here than meets the eye."

"So what are you going to do, run away?" said Gabby.

"That's about it. I won't be a party to this."

"They will hunt you down. They'll put you in prison."

"Not if they can't find me."

"So you're running out on us? That's no solution."

As Peter looked from Michael to Gabby he sensed a struggle of titanic proportions. A kind of glow enveloped them which he knew he could not pierce. As he looked from Jules, to Arthur, and then to Harrison he felt their strength but also saw their anxiety, their helplessness.

"Michael, you can't fix every problem", said Gabby.

"Then why are we here?"

"I need you to stay."

"And I'm telling you I can't. I will not be a part of what is about to occur."

"And just what is that? Your dream again?"

"Yes, that and more. As clear as my vision is, I feel blind."

Gabby took Michael's hand. "I know you think you're doing the right thing but can't you see the consequences? You'll give them an excuse to do the worst."

"They don't need an excuse. Arthur's lawyers won't be able to save us. It's not only about my dream about the kids or the specter of concentration camps. There's something else here. I wish I could be more specific. I won't be the cause of so much suffering. I have to find a way, an alternative path."

Michael stood. Gabby looked up at him still holding his hand.

"So, you've already decided."

"I'm leaving now. Don't try to find me. There's something I have to do."

"What do you have to do?" asked Gabby. "Whatever it is we can do it together."

"As much as I wish that were true," Michael shook his head, "I have to do this myself. I know I'm not making sense. Hell, I don't really know what I'm doing. I have this feeling and it's overwhelming my reason. I don't have a choice. Please trust me."

"Of course I trust you, but I don't see why you have to leave."

Michael released Gabby's hand.

"I'm going to mask my connection."

Michael couldn't help but see the stricken look in Gabby's eyes. "You'd do that to me?"

Michael squatted down next to Gabby.

"I'm sorry, my love. I'll be back when I figure this out." profound pain carried on every word. "I'm not worried about you. You were always the stronger one."

Michael rose, turned on his heel and left the room.

Chapter 25

Running.

Breath coming hard.

Heart laboring.

Moving so fast. Never been so fast. Fly like the wind.

A wall, taller than me. Plant my right foot.

Now sailing through the air easily clearing it. Falling forward. Catch myself with my hands and roll.

On my feet again. Running. Run forever. Only way to control the anger.

Everything looks different; a red hue.

Find an escape. A way out. There's got to be a way out.

See the wall. Electrified fence on top. Leap over. No, too tall.

Find a tree. Climb it. Get over the wall. Freedom. Run forever.

Muscles tighten. NO! Not again.

"Why do you think he's trying to escape?" asked General Scott.

Meyerhoff shook his head as they stared at the monitor. They watched as two handlers warily approach Tom Talbot, seemingly frozen in place.

Speaking into a microphone Meyerhoff said, "Let's get him back here. I want to know what he's experiencing."

Concrete walls. A locked door.
Pacing.
A window. Chair didn't break it.
Pacing, scanning.
Got to be a way out.
Clenching and unclenching hands. Feels crunchy. New skin. Don't like it.
A voice. Ignore it. Asshole.

"Mr. Talbot", the electrical voice called again from the speaker mounted above the observation window.

"Fuck you".

"Mr. Talbot we want to help you."

"You want to help me? C'mon in here. I'll show ya how to help me."

Meyerhoff didn't react. Instead he manipulated the slide controls on his console.

Nothing.

Meyerhoff readjusted the levels again and Talbot's pacing slowed. He looked at the window.

Leaning to the microphone, Meyerhoff said, "See, I can help you."

Tom stared back at him, hands clenching reflexively.

"You may sit if you like."

Tom glanced at the chair laying on its side in the corner and looked back at the window, every muscle in his body taught, begging for release.

"Can't sit."

"Very well. Mr. Talbot, what are you feeling?"

"You gotta be kidding me. How am I feeling? I'm fucking pissed off, that's how I'm feeling."

"What is making you angry?"

"Being locked in this cage, my goddamn skin, you."

"Are you angry all the time?"

Tommy pressed his fists against his temples. "Even in my dreams."

Meyerhoff placed the palm of his hand over the microphone and turned to Scott. "Now, watch this." His hands worked the settings again.

Tom felt his muscles relax, his breathing less frantic, his mind more lucid.

"You see? We can help you. Over the next several hours we will gradually lower your stress level. Soon you will be released from the 'cage', as you call it, to return to your quarters. Today and tomorrow you will rest."

Meyerhoff stood and motioned for a white coated lab assistant to fine tune Talbot's controls.

Tom Talbot looked through the window, his eyes narrowed in a feral gaze.

Fools. They have no clue what they've unleashed. They may control me for now but I will find a way to break their programming.

As he became more lucid he started to wonder: *What are they planning?*

As Tom Talbot's mind asked the question he noticed a totally new experience, something like a new sense, a new awareness. It was dim, faint, almost imperceptible; but real nonetheless. It was as though he could sense what Meyerhoff and Scott were feeling, could feel their detachment, their malice.

As his heart rate continued to slow Tom walked to the corner of the room righted the chair and sat, knees apart, elbows on his thighs, head in his hands.

Try as he might Tom could remember little prior to waking up in a hospital bed. He recalled being a soldier but little about his training, his missions; and before that . . . nothing.

With memory gone he could only feel his need. Dark and without form, passions emerged. He'd failed before, big failures. His inaccessible memories revealed an all-consuming need to make it right. He had a Purpose. He knew it. And someone, he knew her, couldn't remember her name but could almost see her face; she could reveal his Purpose.

Why do I remember only that?

Chapter 26

As Michael drove up to the house he noticed it looked different somehow. It had been his sanctuary these past few years, the place to find a small peace if only for an infrequent respite. It tore him apart to leave but he knew he couldn't take off without saying goodbye to Alex and Kerry.

They were waiting for him as he entered.

"Mom's upset with you," said Alex.

"Yes, I know."

"What did you do?" asked Kerry.

Bobby entered the room with Dawn in tow.

"Let's go into the living room," he said.

Michael sat on a couch with the twins on either side. Dawn sat in a chair across from them while Bobby stood in a corner near the fireplace.

"What have you two been up to?"

"Nothing much", they answered in unison.

"Have you been posting?"

"Yes," guiltily and in unison.

Michael smiled. "What's the latest?"

"Weww," said Kerry. "I was reading where Barry Goadwater said 'extremism in the defense of wiberty is no vice'?"

Michael nodded.

"Awex and I were talking about it", said Kerry. "It's often used as a rhetorical justification for extreme acts. The probwem occurs when that same extremism can deprive others of their wegitimate wibety.

"We used that as a basis for talking about how societies evowve which sets up a naturaw tension between tradition and innovation. Traditionaw institutions by their nature protect the status quo whyow innovation is brought about by individuaws with vision and drive.

"I took the part of defending tradition and Kerry took the part of the necessity of radicow innovation", said Alex. "I pointed out how, over time as pubwic sentiment grows in favor of new approaches, the institutions wike the courts and even churches can change with the times."

"Very good," said Michael. "But I'd like you to do me a favor. I want you to resist the urge to dialogue again for a while. Can you do that for me?"

"Sure," said Alex. "But why?"

"I'm worried you're making yourselves targets and I couldn't bear it if anything happened."

Michael looked from Kerry to Alex and back again. "Can I count on you?"

"Yes", again in unison.

"But why is Mom mad at you?" asked Kerry.

"I have to go away for a while. You know I'm one of those innovators you've been talking about? I'm afraid that anyone close to me could get hurt if things heat up. I'm hoping to diffuse the anger of the authorities if I drop out of sight until I can figure a way out of this. I masked my connection to your mother and I will mask my connection to you when I leave in a little while."

"That's not right," said Kerry.

"No, it's not right," responded Michael. "I hope it won't be for long. I have to pack. Then we'll say our goodbye's, for now."

Michael stood.

"Now, go play. I want to talk with Dawn. I'll find you before I go."

All three children walked sullenly out of the room.

"Dawn, I'm sorry we're putting you through all this. I wish things could have been different."

"It's okay. I seem to jump from one bad situation to another. The kids are wonderful, all three very loving. I worry about Bobby. He's sweet enough but there's something so lost about him. I wish I could help, but it looks like I won't be around much longer."

"You're talking about the cancer?"

"Everybody's used a lot of encouraging words but I'm not stupid; I can read between the lines. I don't have much time; maybe a year. When Gabby gets back I'm going to talk to her about finding another nanny."

"There's no need for that."

"Yes, there is. Kerry and Alex have already grown attached to me and I couldn't bear to put Bobby through something like that again. He's already lost his mother."

"That isn't everything, is it?" said Michael.

Dawn paused before continuing. "You've all been so good to me even though I've been a pain in the ass." Dawn paused again, thinking what to say next. "I've really grown attached to the little monsters. If I stay any longer I couldn't bear to leave and I won't let them watch me die."

Michael stood.

"You're missing something here. I wish everyone was right and I could see into the future. I wish I could tell you what's gonna happen next. At the same time, I don't think that's the way your story ends. I'm the last one to talk about false hope, but . . . I know you don't believe in fairy tale endings."

"Gabby told you."

"Of course. There may be no 'happily ever after', but that doesn't mean the worst is yet to come. Stick with us a little while longer. I still believe you have a role to play here. We're coming to . . ." Michael trailed off. "Now I've got to go pack some things or I'll lose my nerve."

Half an hour later Michael came downstairs carrying an overnight bag and called for the children.

Looking at the twins Michael said, "We have an agreement, right?"

"Yes", said both.

"Good. Now Bobby, I want you to keep an eye on them. No more Dialoguing for those two and I expect you to make sure they don't. I'm also expecting you to keep an eye on things around here. You're the oldest and I know you can be responsible."

Bobby, who was standing next to Dawn, moved closer to her as she reflexively pulled him near. "Don't worry, Michael," he said. "Dawn and I have a plan."

Michael smiled. "I bet you do. Dawn, Gabby's going to be testifying next week and we'll need you to hold down the fort. You may see some extra security around. Don't let it bother you."

"Come back soon. They need you," said Dawn.

"I'll try."

"Pardon me," said Dawn, "but that's not good enough. Look, I don't know much. Forget all this Ulysses crap. Sorry kids. But I know how important you are to them. They're the most amazing children I've ever met but they still need you. And they've never been cut off from you. I certainly don't understand what you're up against but you can't run away. Trust me, I've tried."

Michael looked at Dawn with newfound respect nodding almost imperceptibly.

"We know you have to go," said Kerry. "Come back soon."

Michael heard the tremor in her voice.

"I'll do my best. Now, come here. I need a hug."

All three ran to him and as they embraced Michael felt a vibration, deep and low.

He stood and took a step back, his eyes wide, attempting to catch his breath.

"Remember no posting," he said in a distracted tone.

The twins nodded in unison.

And there was no posting. But Michael had no way of knowing that his appeal had come too late.

Chapter 27

He had no destination in mind. He'd been driving for hours lost in reverie, trying to recall simpler times; times when the world didn't press on him so.

Something was wrong with his vision. *Probably tired.* He pulled into a parking spot on the outskirts of a park and began walking.

Ever since leaving the house his mind had been a jumble of thoughts and feelings. That thing with the kids, where he felt the vibration, seemed to knock him off balance. He didn't feel in his right mind. His thoughts, the world around him, seemed disjointed, disconnected.

He watched as a man ran after his dog shouting, "Don't run away."

Michael smiled to himself recalling Dawn's parting words and marveling in the coincidence.

Am I running away?

He continued along the sidewalk; the chill in the evening air beginning to seep through his jacket as dusk began its descent. The paved path led down an incline and into a tunnel formed by a footbridge overhead.

In the dim light he noticed someone sitting on a park bench under a burned-out street light. As he walked past he heard a voice say, "Excuse me, sir, do you have the time?"

Michael stopped and turned toward the voice. Despite the deepening darkness he could still make out her features. She was a small, white-haired lady. African-American as best he could tell. He bet if she stood up she'd barely come to his shoulder. As he looked at her eyes he noticed she wasn't looking at anything in particular: blind.

"Uh, sure. It's about 8:45. Are you all right?"

"I'm just waiting for someone."

As Michael turned to continue his walk she said, "You can't run away."

Michael turned back.

"Excuse me?"

"You can't run away."

"I heard you the first time."

"My, my, you sure are testy. You're the one who said 'excuse me'. I thought you wanted me to repeat myself."

"You got me there."

Michael saw something out of the corner of his eye but ignored it.

"Are you sure there's nothing I can do for you?" he asked.

"I'm just fine, but I suspect you're not," she replied.

She's pretty perceptive, must have heard something in my tone of voice, thought Michael.

Before he could turn away she said, "The world weighs on you. You're looking for a way out of a problem. The answer doesn't lie only with you. You are one part of a bridge. She is your other half, your support to the other side."

Without acknowledging the old woman's comment Michael turned into the tunnel.

Something's going on. Everything's moving so swiftly. I feel like I can't fight my fate, like I'm swept up heading to some kind of destiny I can't avoid. I should be with them. But what am I supposed to do? I couldn't stick around; too much risk for everyone.

231

As Michael emerged from the tunnel he saw that the full moon had risen over a tree covered hill, its glory muted in the mist. Again out of the corner of his eye, he thought he saw something move but when he turned to look there was nothing there.

He continued walking. It felt good to walk. There had been a time, not that long ago, when walking would have been impossible, his body failing him. Gabby rescued him, brought him back from certain oblivion.

She saved me and this is how I pay her back? I'm not running away but what am I running to? It feels odd not to feel her connection after all this time. It was like we're becoming one person. Not like it was before, drifting apart after the accident.

A memory of the accident intruded; accompanied by the terror and pain he'd thought he'd forgotten. *I've been moving forward so deliberately I haven't thought about the past in a long time; probably've been burying that memory.*

As if in response another memory encroached on his consciousness, this one from childhood, but more than a memory. It was though he was having the experience all over again but knowing it was just a memory.

And as quickly as the experience came, it departed.

He found himself trudging between two low lying hillocks. Again he thought he saw movement in his peripheral vision. As he turned, it disappeared.

He was standing in a hospital corridor. *Where am I?* He looked into a room, the door slightly ajar.

It's Gabby. I remember. It's the night the twins were born.

Joy and relief suffused him.

Must have been right after they were born.

He walked over a rise. *What's happening to me?*

He stopped next to a tree, his disorientation growing. Michael placed a hand on the trunk to steady himself. The bark seemed to move under his hand as if shifting in minute movements. He lifted his hand but saw nothing.

I'm hallucinating, losing control; unbidden memories making it difficult to distinguish between fact and fiction. But I know these hallucinations aren't real. They say if you think you might be crazy you aren't; small comfort.

Michael walked a little further before he sat down, his back against a large boulder. He tried to collect his thoughts, searching for stability in the shifting landscape.

I wish Gabby were here. She's the one who grounded me when I wanted to give up, inching each day closer to death. She never lost faith in me, in us. And this is how I pay her back, by running away. But is this the fate we all face, a slow descent into madness? If I can't figure this out, I'll have doomed her and the kids.

When did I last feel like myself, feel normal?

Again a memory intervened, so real, so immediate.

He was with Gabby. They were in Jules' cabin in the Northwoods. It had been a couple of days since he underwent the Transformation. He was only beginning to discover his capabilities. Now Arthur lay in that same hospital bed in that same room where Michael underwent the change; Michael reliving the moment as if it were happening all over again.

"How's he doing?" he asked.

"So far, so good", Gabby replied.

She looked less careworn than she did of late. *The kids, work, me, all of this weighs on her so.*

"How would you like to go for a walk outside?" he asked. "I won't take you away too long."

Gabby looked up at Michael and smiled. "Nothing would make me happier. It's been a long time since you and I went for a stroll together. Are you sure you're up for it?"

"I'm tired but I'll be fine for a little while. It's pretty cold, in the teens. You'll want your heavy coat. Let's go without a flashlight. I want to look at the stars."

If someone had walked past Michael with his back against the boulder they would have thought 'what an odd place to put a statue'.

Gabby and Michael walked arm in arm under a cloudless sky. The moon hadn't yet risen and their eyes adjusted slowly to the complete darkness.

Michael felt the still, cold autumn air on his face, could smell the rotting leaves of late fall in the Northwoods as if he were there, despite four intervening years.

"I don't think I've ever seen so many stars," Gabby observed. Tiny points of light filled the sky blotting out the darkness.

"Do you see that band of stars?" Michael asked. "It runs across the entire arc of the sky. That's the Milky Way galaxy."

"Oh look," Gabby exclaimed pointing north. There, not far above the horizon Michael saw what looked like faint, undulating waves like curtains.

"It's the aurora borealis," Gabby declared.

"I've never seen it," marveled Michael.

"Neither have I, except in photographs."

"You know, in the city you look up, see a few stars and think most of the night sky is black totally missing out on this beauty. Out here you realize the night sky is full of light.

"Poor Arthur, I hope he finds his light," Michael added.

Michael couldn't remember being more content. Here they were, just the two of them out in the middle of nowhere, their breath forming clouds in the air with nothing around but primeval forest and the night sky; the pain and stress of the past few years gone leaving only the two of them.

"Are you happy, Michael?" Gabby asked.

Pulling her close he looked down at her and replied softly, "very".

"Look, a shooting star," she cried as she pointed.

"Do you ever wonder if there is life out there?" he asked.

"I figure there must be. The chance life exists only here on Earth, with all the billions of planets out there; it's so unlikely we're the only ones."

The memory of the moment and its pleasure vanished in a flash, Michael's heart racing.

I had this feeling once before. Right before I . . .

Michael's eyes opened wide but to no avail. The movement he had seen out of the corner of his eye earlier was now all around him, through him. It was as though the very fabric of the space in which he sat moved with a life of its own. He couldn't help but recognize that he had this same feeling right before the Encounter when he had been stretched by an alien intelligence, learning the formulas and design for the BRIDG circuit and the struggle to come.

But now, as he sat there, his back to the boulder still, he realized he'd been wrong. There wasn't some bug-eyed alien out there instructing him. He had been locked into his conventional ideas of time and space. The memories; he was becoming unstuck in time because there was no time, not where he was now. And it wasn't an alien on some distant planet he encountered but an intelligence, no not an intelligence, but pure intelligence, right here, right now. Not intelligence in the IQ sense but intelligence in the form of pure consciousness, order suffusing everything. His limited brain latched on to the alien metaphor because that's all he could comprehend at the time.

Michael turned his attention back to the experience. His perceptions seemed to merge making it difficult to discern between sight, sound, smell, touch, and taste. His awareness existed simultaneously in his body and in this new dimension.

In the midst of this new experience Michael checked himself. *Is this just a hallucination? No, the BRIDG is real. This is real.*

In an attempt to better understand what he was feeling Michael tried to focus on particular angles of the experience as one would look at a map and focus on first a city and then a state to put geography in context.

As he did so he noticed multiple layers; dimensions within dimensions. He recalled an article he read once: something about how a two-dimensional being couldn't see a sphere but only a circle. It would lack the ability to perceive depth. Michael realized his eyes were only vehicles to transmit the corporeal experience of light. With his mind's eye he could see so much more.

Probing deeper, he pulled up short, his pulse racing. Fear clutched at his heart, adrenaline sending alarms to every tissue in his body.

Instinctively he knew there would be no going back. He knew if he took the next step he couldn't return to what he had been before, just as a spring, when stretched beyond normal limits will never go back to its original form.

But that same instinct told him he must move forward. Somehow he knew this was their only hope, for Gabby, for Kerry, for Alex, for everyone.

With grim determination Michael pushed deeper. As he did so he felt his body growing more distant. He experienced a lightness of being unencumbered by flesh. Deeper he plunged consumed in light, sound, pure being.

And with absolute clarity he realized the old woman had been right. He would anchor his side of the bridge.

Chapter 28

"The day for which we have prepared so diligently is upon us."

Gates stared at the screen in his study as he sat on his beige leather sofa, the Man standing behind him just out of camera range. Images of Senator Gregory, Jeremiah Barnum, and Jim Scott filled the screen.

"The Neumanns are in Washington", observed Gregory. "My sources have seen only the wife but I'm sure he's lurking around somewhere. He wouldn't dare defy the subpoena."

"What about Paulson and Allen?" asked Scott.

"They're here, too, along with Peter Keyes", replied Gregory. "The whole damn mess. I'll take pleasure in bringing them down. C-SPAN has been carrying the hearings so far but now all four major networks smell ratings and along with cable news are geared up to televise the hearings."

"And your aide, Ms. Keyes?" asked Scott.

"She's ready to go. Everything's been orchestrated to a tee. Though I have to confess, Jim, she's off her game of late. You may have been right. I may have to jettison her."

The image of Scott on the screen nodded.

"We're set to provide commentary during the breaks," said Barnum. "I have a panel of reactors set to expose their lies for what they are."

"And to support the strong stand Senator Gregory is taking?" interjected Gates.

"Yes, he will come off as the hero of the day."

"No. He must be seen as more than a tinhorn hero."

Gates raised his iron fist for emphasis.

"We've suffered too long under weak, ineffective leadership. Compromise has been the name of the game, but it is a failed game; all this petty bickering over meaningless drivel. 9/11 and the Great Recession have played right into our hands. The common man has lost faith in the government because the government's failed them. The public craves order; without it, chaos.

"Observe the lessons of history: after the bloodshed of the French Revolution the people welcomed the Emperor Napoleon. For decades our Congress and the courts attempted to forestall secession. And in the end, Lincoln fought a war to force order. And out of the Civil War grew the industrial might we used to challenge and ultimately eclipse the established regimes of Old Europe. Now we dither while the Empire of the East builds its economic and military might. The Chinese know discipline.

"Michael Neumann was right. Don't look so surprised. His Samsa blogs exposed the failures of democracy as none before. But he came to the wrong conclusion. Let us not perpetuate his mistake.

"The Arab fanatics will detonate the plutonium device at Camp David. They will be caught and exposed. Senator Gregory will ascend to the Presidency and declare martial law. We will attack the Middle East in force and control the oil which has crippled our economy and drive the anarchists back into the sand. The public will hail us as conquering heroes. They will be too prosperous to worry about petty freedoms.

"Our propaganda machine will turn other democracies to our side or we will roll over them. That is why, Jeremiah, you must position the Senator as our only hope. Have you been following this Dialogos banter from those Neumann brats? They're making our case for us. They are abominations but they will serve us well. Once we have them under our control we will use them to continue their debate. They will be a tool to spread our message of peace and prosperity ushering a new golden age for the West, at least for any who understands our wisdom. Those who do not will reap the whirlwind.

"What if those kids don't agree to cooperate?" asked Scott.

"We'll have their parents. It's amazing what a little pain can accomplish when applied intelligently, right my friend?"

Gates looked up at The Man standing behind him. Those watching did not mistake the smirk cross his face.

"Which, General, brings us to the abduction. How are your preparations coming?"

"We're set to go. Two Achilles recruits survived this latest induction. They will lead the small assault team on the Neumann home. The Neumann's have stepped up security but it'll be no match for us. We'll take them like we did in Italy."

"I wish for my friend here to accompany you," said Gates. "That won't be a problem will it?"

"We strike tomorrow during the testimony," replied Scott.

"I have a jet waiting to transport him as we speak."

"The facilities at the Peacemaker compound in Virginia have been readied", said Scott. "The children will be kept under sedation until their parents are in our custody. A message will be sent after the hearings. It will instruct them to go to a hidden location where we will render them unconscious, just to be safe, and bring them to the compound."

"Very good," said Gates. "It appears we have planned for every contingency."

Gates stroked his hand as though it were a favored pet.

"We will not communicate again until we have the situation well in hand. A good day to all of you."

Gates pushed a button terminating transmission.

"They have not anticipated every contingency," he said to The Man without turning to look at him. "I want you there every step of the way. You are my eyes, my ears, and yes, my hand. I want you to remain at the Compound until the Neumanns are under our control."

"Michael Neumann will not stand in your way," said The Man. "I will not underestimate him again."

"You may have your fun with him and his wife but I need them intact, for now. Once I have finished with them you may have them to do with as you please. The doctor is attractive, no?"

The Man smiled. "I better go catch my flight. Don't want to keep the General waiting."

Gates smiled to himself. Generations of preparation were finally bearing fruit.

§

His course was set in his fourteenth year. His grandfather had sent him into the woods with only a knife. His task: to kill and bring back to camp the largest animal he could find. He knew the rules by heart; his grandfather reciting them from the time he was only five.

You will go into the forest with only a knife and your wits. You will sleep on the cold ground; you will take no modern conveniences. If you must build a fire you will kindle it with only those materials you find around you. Use your strength and cunning. Your character, your fate will be determined by killing and bringing back to camp the largest animal you can; the greater the beast, the greater your destiny.

His ancestors all had been great men. He learned their stories passed down through tales told and retold. Ricard Gates, born in 1833, was the first child born to Helmut Gatessprung who immigrated to Baltimore from Central Europe that same year. At sixteen Ricard was kicked out of his father's house and told to earn a living against the protestations of his mother. He took a job on the new Baltimore and Ohio Railroad. His superiors took advantage of this bright, industrious worker who rose quickly through the ranks excelling at whatever job they threw at him. As the railroad swept westward, Ricard, now Richard, went with it. The Pacific Railroad Act of 1862, perhaps one of the most corrupt pieces of legislation ever to come out of the US Congress, "loaned" over a quarter of a million square miles to the railroads, an area larger than the state of Texas, opening the West to economic development.

Young Gates saw opportunity in westward expansion and oversaw the sale of parcels to settlers, farmers, and ranchers in the new state of Kansas and the Colorado Territory, robbing land from the Indians in treaty and awarding to those who would make him rich. He took advantage of his position selling parcels at lower than market prices if the purchasers would cede partial ownership to him. Before long he left the railroad and became a successful land speculator. Ultimately settling down in the Colorado Territory his first son was born in the same year Colorado joined the Union and the centennial anniversary of the Declaration of Independence: 1876.

Richard continued to grow what was becoming an empire expanding his interests into mining. Living out in the middle of nowhere, unlike the other robber barons of his age, Richard maintained a low profile. His son, Richard Jr., followed in his father's footsteps, dramatically increasing the family fortune. He expanded their mining interests into oil and gas cementing the future for Gates family.

Richard Jr.'s son and Stanford's grandfather, Ivan, born shortly after the turn of the century exhibited the same industry and acquisitiveness of his forbearers. Schooled at the knee of his father and grandfather, Ivan learned every detail of his family's successes and failures. They spared no specific from their lofty goals to their Machiavellian manipulations. From infancy they instilled austerity and discipline in their young charge.

As Ivan grew to manhood during the Great Depression he came to despise the weakness of the suffering masses and consequently a government which made excuses using his money, or worse, money that didn't exist to fund social welfare programs protecting the weakest of the herd. His father and grandfather chaffed under the draconian regulations aimed at tying the hands of business enterprise during the Theodore Roosevelt administration but this latest Roosevelt took government interference to a whole new level.

Ivan was the first of the clan to graduate from college. There he learned of social Darwinism: to structure a society so that only the strongest survive while the weak weed themselves out of the pack. Thus was born his philosophy of business and government: a vision wherein the human species

243

would excel through unfettered competition with the potential for wealth limited only by the lack of imagination and will; the only purpose of government, to provide the means to make that possible.

Disenchanted with the American attachment to social welfare he looked to models overseas and found them wanting as well. He looked first to Germany. He thought the National Socialists captured much of his selfsame beliefs, and while he appreciated how Hitler's scapegoating of the Jews, Communists, and others served to align the masses, Hitler's obsession with those he deemed inferior for purely racial reasons repelled Ivan who saw their extermination as a wasteful use of resources, at best, and a profound error in judgment at worst, given that some of the best minds in Europe, Rothschild, Einstein, and Spinoza had come from that stock. He examined only briefly the reign of the Communists and Stalin finding their collectivism inherently counter to the economic freedom vital to foster growth and innovation.

Thus he realized that he must create something wholly new. He saw little use for nations or boundaries except as they provided a means to power. America could provide the raw materials but was heading for disaster. He knew the next stage for the family would be to cultivate a position with Washington whereby the government would serve his ends, not the other way around. By the time his son was born in the early 1940's with keen foresight Ivan knew he would be the one to sow the seeds of revolution but that it would be for one who was to come after to see it through.

That one was born in 1976, two centuries after the founding of the nation and one century after the birth of Ivan's father. Ivan viewed Stanford's birth as an auspicious omen seeing in him the potential for greatness he never saw in his own son, a weak pretender to the family. Ivan bullied his way into the boy's life causing the boy's mother to depart in hurt and anger and his father to descend into family obscurity. Stanford worshipped his hard-driving grandfather rising to every challenge placed before him.

Ivan instructed his grandson as he prepared for his test, the ultimate test, of his manhood. This was not a test he would pass or fail but a trial which would determine whether he was the one to lead the family to greatness.

Stanford spent a largely sleepless night under the pine boughs. He found flint in the rocky soil and so built a fire to keep warm. He cut a swath from his coat fashioning it into a sling. If he were to fell a large animal he would need a way to stun his prey so he could approach the animal and use his knife to deliver the killing blow.

Throughout the night he sat with his back against an old Ponderosa pine periodically feeding the fire. Every time he started to doze off some noise in the forest would startle him. Eventually, as the sun rose and the forest floor began to brighten he extinguished the smoldering embers and prepared to find his quarry.

He trudged through the woods searching for rocks suitable for the sling. He came over a rise and saw an adult black bear in the distance. Stanford quietly crouched down to study his quarry unobserved.

The bear bent over a stream, drinking; oblivious to the adolescent hiding just 100 feet away. Still stooped, Stanford noticed he was next to a pile of rocks. He saw one, near the bottom of the pile which would serve him well. It looked to be just the right size and shape. As he attempted to dig it out with his right hand, the other stones came loose causing a minor avalanche sending Stanford rolling backward while the bear looked up wondering what the noise was all about and then calmly wandered back into the woods.

When Stanford and the rocks came to rest he found his left hand pinned by a boulder. What little he could see made him realize that his hand lay crushed under a stone too large to move. He would die if he spent even one night out there damaged, in the cold.

His wrist lay exposed. Stanford pulled the knife from his belt. Through the swelling pain, he reasoned that if he cut through his wrist and around the bones he would be able to extricate himself from the now worthless appendage. He hoped that the wrist bones had been sufficiently shattered to complete the amputation before he passed out from pain. He found skin and ligament offered little resistance to the knife; its edge sharpened to a fine edge in preparation for the outing. As he reached the shattered bones of his wrist he found he could work around them but the tough tendons proved more difficult than expected.

With the force of sheer will he retained consciousness as he finally pulled his arm free of the boulder. Using the sling he bound the wound to control the bleeding and shakily got to his feet.

Ivan stirred the smoldering dross in the burn pile on the back of his property. In his late 80's, he still retained much of the vigor of his youth even if he moved more slowly. Throughout his life Ivan delighted in the rugged terrain of the Colorado wilderness. Though he employed a staff to work the estate, he could still be seen doing chores which would tax a younger man. It would be three more years before a stroke would fell him.

Staring into the blaze, smelling the burning wood and leaves, Ivan found he could admit fear for the boy. All that which could befall him raced through his mind, but he had faith, faith in his young charge despite his age. Ivan had schooled him well. The boy possessed a mental toughness none could match. This was not some soft child, but a proto-man, one who knew no sentimental attachments, one who reveled in a manifest destiny. Yes, the boy had learned his lessons well.

Something made him look up and coming across the field he saw a small form staggering toward him. Stanford was almost upon Ivan before he recognized the boy and caught him just before he fell.

Ivan saw the wound, the blood oozing from the makeshift bandage. He knew he had to stop the bleeding or the boy would die. Ivan looked around and found an iron rod, the remnant of an old farm implement, lying with one end in the fire.

Ivan removed the cloth from the end of the boy's arm. With a gloved hand he reached down, grabbed the iron bar and pressed the red hot end of the firebrand against Stanford's ragged stump.

Both men screamed: Stanford with the pain of searing flesh and Ivan with the heat traveling through his glove scorching his hand. The smell of burnt skin and cloth filled their nostrils as both lost consciousness.

Others came running in response to the cries.

Ivan was sitting at Stanford's side in the hospital when he regained consciousness.

"How do you feel, boy?" he asked.

"Okay, I guess."

"Tell me what happened."

As he staggered back from the forest to his house Stanford's fevered mind conceived the story.

"I found a bear, a black bear. I was above him on a hill. I stunned him with my sling. I ran down the hill but before I could finish him he attacked me, took my hand but not before I killed him. Sorry I couldn't bring him back to you."

"Do you think you could remember where that was? I could send someone back out and find him."

"I don't know, Grandfather. I might. It's all pretty hazy."

Ivan knew his grandson was lying. But he saw promise in the story. A great leader needed a great legend to establish his manhood. Anyone who looked at Stanford, his left hand missing, would see the truth of the story. The outcome was better than Ivan could have hoped.

While Stanford recuperated in the hospital Ivan sent three men to find the black bear, any black bear, kill it, and bring it back to be stuffed and mounted.

§

Stanford was never the same after the accident. He kept to his story never divulging what really happened. In time he came to believe the lie along with every other lie he told himself. His grandfather passed away one month before Stanford left for college, Stanford having nursed the vegetable who had once been the center of his universe. He knew he had a task, no, a great calling. He would fulfill his grandfather's dream.

Chapter 29

"I said stop it; that's enough."

Gabby's overnight bag stopped bouncing as Alex and Kerry dropped to a sitting position on the bed and stared at their mother.

"I'm sorry to be so short with you but I've got a lot on my mind."

"We do too," said Kerry.

Gabby placed a folded sweater in the bag.

"Why would Dad do this?" asked Alex.

"I'm sure your father has a perfectly good reason."

"He's not mad at us," said Kerry.

"No. That's not it."

"Then what is it?" they asked in unison.

Gabby dropped a pair of pumps in the bag and sat on the bed. While any other parent might have tried to candy coat their concerns, Gabby knew she was dealing with children wise beyond their years. There was no benefit to shading the truth.

"It's a few things. He's worried about the hearings. He believes that the outcome is a foregone conclusion and that the government will attempt to curtail our civil rights. He's worried he can't protect us and so is trying to figure out what to do."

"But the Constitution guarantees our freedom," said Alex.

"It does," replied Gabby. "But at times our country, our leaders and our fellow citizens, haven't always lived up to that promise. I know you've been studying history. You know about the internment camps during World War Two, the Communist scares following the War, and you're aware of any number of minorities denied their rights because the majority was uncomfortable with them. Your father, no, all of us, are concerned that this may be one of those times. I believe your father may be able to use the hearings to our advantage but he isn't so sure."

The children nodded. "Even if he doesn't show up, we have faith in you, Mom," said Alex.

"Thank you. I think I can hold my own."

The children laughed.

"You said there was something else," said Kerry.

"You know about your father's dreams. He takes them very seriously. He had a dream and he believes if he testifies that some harm will come to the two of you. He couldn't bear to put you in harm's way."

"But that could happen even if he doesn't testify," said Kerry.

"It might. That's why we now have extra security."

"We do?" said the kids.

"I didn't see anyone," said Alex.

"They're out at the road. They're keeping an eye on anyone coming or going."

Gabby kept her great fear to herself. Michael was becoming increasingly agitated; taking risks he shouldn't, running from others he should face. In light of her medical training she couldn't help but wonder whether his mental state was deteriorating, his behavior bordering on paranoia. He confided his fears to her on more than one occasion worried he might be experiencing negative side effect of the Treatment, side effects which might eventually plague all the Voyagers.

And yet, for some reason she had faith, faith in him, faith in the two of them, faith in where this journey was taking them. There were too many positives arising out of it for all this to be an illusion.

"Or am I just fooling myself?" she wondered.

Alex disrupted her reverie.

"You're not tewwing us everything."

Sometimes Gabby wished she had normal children, ones she might hide her true feelings from, protecting them from the harsh, uncertain truth.

"I'm telling you what I need to. Everything else is speculation."

"But if we know more about what's worrying you, we might come to a different concwusion," said Kerry.

Gabby zipped her bag.

"C'mon, let's go find Bobby and Dawn," she said, sidestepping her children's concerns.

Standing in the foyer Gabby said, "I have to go. Where's Bobby?"

"He's in his room and won't come out," said Dawn. "He's in another one of his dark moods. I don't know what to do when he's like this. I'm worthless with him."

"Stop it," said Gabby. "He's gone through a terrible trauma, losing his mother like that. There's only so much you or anyone can do. His healing will take time. He knows we all love him. Kids, give me a hug."

Gabby felt the same vibration she had felt before but said nothing.

As she stood she said, "I'll be back soon. I will call you with regular updates from Washington. I'm not going to use the BRIDG Communicator since I want you to stay off the computer. Now, why don't you go find Bobby? I want to talk with Dawn for a minute."

The twins ran off in the direction of the bedrooms.

"Dawn, I know you don't think so but you can handle Bobby."

Dawn shook her head violently.

"There are times when he's so sweet", said Dawn, "but then others when he gets like this. I know he likes me but when he's in this mood there's no controlling him. I'm helpless. He's like a demon possessed."

"And you want to take away his pain."

Dawn nodded; a small tear creased the corner of her eye.

"You can't, no one can."

"But he's normally such a good kid. I wish I could take him in my arms and tell him everything's going to be all right."

"Every parent feels that way," said Gabby. "But you can't protect him. He's suffered more tragedy than any one person should. You can't change the past. You can only show him he has a future."

"What future? How can I tell him he's going to be okay when I won't be around to see it?"

"I spoke with your oncologist," said Gabby. "I know the prognosis is grim. You can't lose hope."

"I lost hope a long time ago and I'm not going to pretend everything's all right."

Dawn took a step back without thinking. Despite her small stature the person Dawn saw before her now seemed to tower over her, Gabby's presence filling the room.

Gabby took one step forward.

"Don't . . you . . dare talk to *me* about false hope. I know more about false hope than you could ever imagine. I spent years hoping my mother would get better. Michael accused me of holding out false hope when I told him I could cure him. You think words are all I have at my disposal? Do . . . not . . . underestimate me. I'm not dispensing platitudes to make myself feel good."

Dawn found it difficult to catch her breath.

"We're not playing games here. You think you should leave us? Do you think Michael brought you here by accident? We have so much more to do and," Gabby's voice lost its force, "we need you here. Understood?"

"Michael said pretty much the same thing," responded Dawn recovering her composure.

"He's very wise," said Gabby. "Not as wise as me but he's working on it."

Dawn smiled in spite of herself.

Gabby reached into her purse and pulled out a device about the size of a cell phone, its only feature: a button.

"What's this?" asked Dawn. "Another one of your communicators?"

"Think of it as a panic button. If anything happens that scares you; push that button and hold it."

"What does it do? Call the cavalry?"

"Close enough. I'll call you each morning and evening to give you an update and check on the kids. Hang in there. We'll get this figured out."

Gabby picked up her bag, turned, and headed for the garage.

Dawn couldn't help but hope against hope that Gabby was right.

Chapter 30

"Leave me alone."

Bobby's bedroom looked as though a marauding gang of Huns had come through, taken all his things and thrown them about with no thought for order. A child's tablet computer sat on the floor, smashed. The blankets and sheets from his twin bed sat in a heap in the middle of the room. Bobby sat in the corner scowling, knees pulled up to his chest. Alex and Kerry stood just inside the door taking in the childlike carnage. They took another a step into the room and Kerry closed the door behind her.

Kerry looked at Alex. "Maybe it's time."

Alex shrugged.

"Just stop it," said Bobby. "I hate when you do that."

"Do what?" asked Kerry.

"You know," said Bobby sullenly.

The twins didn't move.

"I said, get out."

Alex easily dodged the book Bobby hurled at his head.

"It's time," agreed Alex. "Dad weft, Mom's gone. We can handow Dawn."

"What're you talking about?" asked Bobby who couldn't help wondering what plan the twins might be hatching. Despite his anger and the age difference, he enjoyed their company. But at times he felt a resentment he couldn't control. Though he didn't yet possess the ability to articulate his frustration; Bobby never felt he fit in at the Neumann household; and didn't dare give voice to the fear that someday he would have to leave their sanctuary.

§

Bobby and his Mom had been with the Neumann's for over a year. Gabby and Michael hired Grace as their nanny and Bobby felt like he came in the bargain. Now he had to share his Mom with two more kids, but that was okay. He found he liked the twins even though he often didn't understand them.

Before they came to the Neumann's his Mom had a good job but got laid off and had difficulty finding work. The Neumann's, looking for a nanny, hired his Mom and took an easy liking to Bobby, too. Everyone was nice enough. They tried hard to make him feel included. But they were so different from anyone else he knew.

For so long it had been only the two of them. When he was old enough to wonder, he asked his mother about his father and she had said 'you're all the love I will ever need in the whole, wide world'. That made Bobby feel warm inside and he hugged her.

One day they were out running errands. His Mom was driving and Bobby was sitting on a booster in the back seat on the other side of the car. He complained to her when she strapped him in the seat.

"Why can't I sit on the seat like you?"

"Because I want you to be safe."

Grace had taken Bobby grocery shopping. The twins were at home with their mother. Bobby liked it when just the two of them went out together. It made him feel special.

Grace had just pulled away from a stop when the driver of a speeding car ignored their stop sign and t-boned Bobby's car on his mother's side careening them through the intersection and lodging them against a tree.

"Are you okay, Bobby?"

"I think so." Bobby felt better hearing his mother's strong voice. He looked around him and saw shards of metal and glass everywhere. He saw his mother look down in her lap.

Bobby heard the quaver in his mother's voice.

"Bobby, you be a good boy, now, you hear? The Neumanns're good people."

Bobby heard sirens in the distance.

"I love you, baby."

Those were the last words Bobby ever heard his mother say.

Gabby and the twins met him and his Mom at the hospital. She had taken charge as soon as they arrived. He saw the twins hang back but could see their concern despite their young ages.

Eventually a doctor came out and spoke to Gabby. He saw her nod.

Gabby walked over to Bobby and knelt in front of him.

"Bobby, the doctors tried everything they could but your Mom was hurt too badly. I'm so sorry, dear, but she's gone."

Bobby didn't know what to say, an unbearable sadness filled him. Then he asked her, "Where will I go?"

"Oh, honey," Gabby pulled him close, "you're not going anywhere. You will stay with us. You will be a part of our family forever and ever."

That made Bobby feel safe, but he didn't feel happy.

§

"You're upset 'cause you don't feeow wike you fit in," said Kerry.

"So?" said Bobby still sitting in the corner, staring at nothing.

"So, we think it's time you had the Uwysses Treatment," said Alex.

Bobby looked up at the twins. "Really?"

They nodded in unison.

Bobby jumped up and then stopped.

"What will Dawn say?"

"She doesn't have to know," said Kerry.

"Mom biwt an induction room in the basement not too far from our pwayroom." said Alex.

"I wondered what that room was," said Bobby.

"Wet's go down there and get started," said Alex.

"Now?"

"Sure. Mom and Dad are away. It's the best time. Unwess, you don't want to," said Kerry. "It's up to you."

"No, I want to. Let's go."

They kids ran out of Bobby's room and headed for the stairs.

Dawn, hearing the stampede coming from the second floor, called out, "where're you going?"

All three yelled, "we're gonna play in the basement."

She watched as they ran around the corner past her and headed for the basement stairs.

257

An hour later Dawn walked down to the basement to check on them. She saw Kerry and Bobby playing together at an air hockey table. Bobby stood while Kerry kneeled on a chair.

"Where's Alex?" asked Dawn.

"He went back upstairs," said Kerry. "He's probabwy pwaying in his room."

"Okay. I'm going outside for a smoke. Be back in a few."

Dawn walked back up the stairs, grabbed her coat, cigarettes, and lighter and walked out the back door and into the yard. She sat down on a patio chair, lit her cigarette, and stared off into the distance absently flicking her ashes in an ash tray she kept there for just this purpose. As Dawn gazed in the direction of the stream she thought she saw movement among the trees on the other side.

Probably just some animal, she thought.

Alex emerged from the induction room and walked over to where the two were playing.

"I'm ready."

Kerry turned off the power to the hockey table while Bobby followed Alex into the makeshift hospital room.

"Now wie on the bed," said Alex.

"Have you done this before?" asked Bobby.

"No, but we watched Mom do it a bunch 'a times."

Bobby saw a fluid-filled clear plastic bag hanging on a pole with a tube coming out of it.

Alex stepped up on a stool next to Bobby on the right side of the bed. Kerry, on the other side, pushed over a box and stood on it so she could see, too.

Alex tore open a packet with an alcohol wipe and swabbed the back of Bobby's right hand. Bobby could practically feel Alex's intense focus.

Then Alex reached down, pulled up the tubing, and exposed a small needle.

Bobby tensed.

"Wait a minute. You didn't tell me you were gonna use a needle."

Kerry, standing on the other side patted Bobby's other hand and said, soothingly, "It's okay. It'ow just sting for a second.

Bobby looked back at Alex. "Didja ever do this before?"

"No, but I watched Mom do it. It doesn't wook too hard."

"I don' know."

"Bobby, wook at me," commanded Kerry. "Awex and I have practiced with our toys and with an orange. Awex wiw do just fine."

As she spoke Bobby felt a sharp prick and the needle was in his hand.

"That wasn't too bad." While Alex taped the needle in place Bobby asked, "What's in the bag?"

"You wiw be asweep for about twenty-four hours," said Kerry. "This is to make sure you get pwenty of fwuids and nutrients."

"Now Bobby, look at me," said Alex.

Bobby turned his head and saw Alex holding a syringe.

"Oh, no. You're not gonna give me a shot."

"I won't", said Alex. "I wiw just inject this into the tube at this opening here." Alex pointed to a yellow seal on a Y connector on Bobby's IV. "This wiw put you to sweep. Once you're unconscious we'oh give you the virus."

"A virus? I don't wanna get sick!"

259

"It's not that kinda virus," said Kerry.

"OK." Bobby swallowed hard.

Alex looked at Kerry raising his eyebrows. She nodded.

"Now, you're getting a wohwer dose of the medicine to make you sweep. Since you have a smawwer body than an aduwt it takes wess. I've cawcuwated the right dosage for you."

Alex inserted the needle into the tubing and slowly pushed the plunger.

The twins watched as Bobby's eyes fluttered and he drifted into unconsciousness.

After waiting a few minutes Alex picked up another syringe containing a yellowish liquid.

"Can I do it?" asked Kerry.

"No, I wanna," replied Alex.

"You got to do everything else," said Kerry.

"Yeah, but this is the most important part," said Alex.

Kerry folded her arms across her chest and stared at Alex who smiled in return.

She stepped down off her box and Alex stepped down from the stool. She got up on the stool and he stood next to her, barely able to see over the bed. Kerry picked up the syringe, pausing for a moment to gaze at the pale, yellow fluid.

"Amazing isn't it?" she said. "That something so smaww, so simpow, can be so profound."

"Isn't that the way it awways is?" replied Alex. "Awexander the Great conquered the wowd but was fewwed by a tiny mosquito carrying the even tinier mawaria parasite. Did you know over 2,500 years ago a Sanskrit medicow text described mawaria as being carried by mosquitos?"

"Oh, Awex."

Kerry turned and with grim concentration inserted the needle in the tube and injected the fluid. She watched Bobby and, seeing no signs of change, got down from the stool.

"Now we wait," said Alex.

"Dawn should be back inside soon," said Kerry. "You think she'ew push that panic button Mom gave her?"

"Probabwy," said Alex. "But it's too wate to do anything, now." He smiled and settled in to wait for Dawn's arrival.

Looks like it's gonna rain, thought Dawn. She picked up her cigarette pack and lighter. *I was going to bring them outside but I think I'll just let 'em play in the basement while I read.*

Dawn turned and walked back into the house oblivious to the men in the bushes patiently waiting for the signal to descend.

Chapter 31

Dawn woke with a start. She'd been sitting on the couch in the den reading and drifted off to sleep. She rubbed her face and wondered, *how long have I been out?* She looked over at the clock. *It's almost three. The kids are awfully quiet. I'd better check on them.*

Rising from the couch she walked to the stairs to see if they were playing in their bedrooms. It wasn't unusual for Alex and Kerry to take naps at this time of day. She checked all the bedrooms and finding no one upstairs headed for the basement.

The signal came mid-afternoon. There were five of them: the squad leader, two Achilles warriors, a technician to control the warriors, and the Man. He had been a sniper in a past life and yearned to exercise his skills. The order had been given for there to be no witnesses and no disturbances to arouse suspicion. The house sat well apart from others in the area making it an easy target.

The squad leader nodded to the Man who silently moved to the left circling towards the front of the property and took his position behind a tree with a clear line of sight to take out the surveillance team.

Anchoring his silenced rifle against the tree the Man sighted his targets, released the safety, and placed his finger on the trigger. The first shot would be easy. The second shot would have to be quick.

No different than shooting fish in a barrel.

The Man slowed his breathing. A shallow intake of breath followed by two rapid squeezes of the trigger and he rendered the surveillance team impotent.

Maybe I'll take out Neumann the same way. Won't escape next time. Never see it coming.

"Where's Bobby?" asked Dawn. She found Kerry and Alex in the basement quietly reading while they sat on the floor. Dawn noticed the book titles: Kerry engrossed in a text on astrophysics, Alex studying the macroeconomics of developing countries. They never ceased to amaze her.

"Isn't he with you?" said Alex.

"No."

"He's probabwy in his room," said Kerry.

Dawn shook her head. "I've been upstairs and he isn't up there either." Something didn't seem right.

"What are you two up to?"

"Nothing," said the twins in unison.

"Bobby?" she called.

No reply.

Dawn noticed one of the basement doors was ajar, the one leading into Gabby's treatment room. Dawn learned of the room during her first tour of the house but had yet to witness an induction.

Is Bobby playing in there? Gabby will have a fit.

Kerry and Alex watched as Dawn opened the door looking questioningly at each other.

"What have you done?!" screamed Dawn.

The twins ran to the doorway. They saw Dawn standing next to the bed, shaking.

"He's okay," said Kerry.

"The hell he is," replied Dawn. "What have you done to him?"

"We induced him," replied Alex. "He wanted to."

"That doesn't make it right," said Dawn barely able to contain her panic. Instinctively she felt Bobby's face; his skin cool to her touch. She noticed he was breathing regularly.

"Your mother's gonna kill me," she said under her breath. "I'll be fired for sure. And I should be."

"He'ww be okay," said Alex. "He'ww be happier."

"You don't get it," said Dawn shaking her head. "What if he's hurt? What if he dies? I could never forgive myself; that sweet boy."

Turning to the twins, "He never hurt you."

Kerry walked over to where Dawn stood. "We're sorry to upset you. But he's going to be fine."

"I'm calling your mother. She'll know what to do."

Dawn remembered the panic button Gabby had given her. She reached into her pocket.

The Man shouldered his rifle and moved to a window on the back side of the house. He didn't detect any movement inside. Just as he had done in Italy, he took out a tool and cut a small hole, almost too small to be seen, in the lower right hand corner of a window pane.

After donning his gas mask he inserted a thin tube, half the diameter of a pencil, through the hole and into the room. He then connected the tube to a small pressurized tank and turned the valve releasing the gas.

Within minutes the odorless, colorless fumes would fill the house rendering everyone inside unconscious. The Man gave the signal for the others to join him.

Kerry noticed it first; a barely perceptible change in her awareness. Instinctively she mentally reached for Alex who noticed the same feeling. Each perceived the attackers preparing to enter the house. Simultaneously they felt the sleep agent coursing through their veins. Their minds worked as fast as anyone alive but not fast enough. Before they could alter their blood chemistry to neutralize the poison they collapsed where they stood.

In Washington, Gabby noticed an odd sensation which disappeared as quickly as it came. She dismissed the feeling, picked up her briefcase and left the hotel room for the briefing with the BDT attorneys.

They stood in the kitchen on the back side of the house.
Through his mask the Man said, "Search the entire house. Remember, no witnesses."
One Achilles warrior, Frank, leaped up the stairway four risers at a time to search the second floor. The other warrior, Tom Talbot, found the basement stairs and headed down. Despite the emotional control elicited by the chip embedded in his shoulder, he continued to seethe.
Why am I invading a civilian house? What kind of threat are these people? Those idiots I work for; what insanity have they roped me into? And what choice do I have? They control me, for now.
He came across a finished space which looked like a playroom and seeing no one explored further. He entered

what appeared to be a hospital room and saw two small children passed out on the floor along with a young woman. *Probably the nanny, but who's the kid in the bed?*

Tom returned to the kitchen.

"Everyone's downstairs," he reported. "The targets are alone with their nanny and an older child asleep in a hospital bed."

"We were told to take only the twins," said the squad leader. "Frank you and Tom get the kids. I'll figure out what to do with the other two.

The Achilles warriors returned carrying Kerry and Alex. A black panel truck had pulled into the garage to load the hostages out of sight. When Frank and Tom returned they found the Man and the squad leader arguing.

"We take the other kid, too," said the Man. "No telling what kind of leverage he'll bring us."

"Those were not our orders," replied the squad leader.

The Man took one step toward him.

"Screw orders, this is a field decision. Do you really want to argue about this?"

The Man took out his silenced pistol.

"Talbot, go get the other kid," he said. "Take care of the nanny. Remember, no witnesses. I'll make sure things are set up for the other kid in the van."

He handed Tom the gun.

Tom nodded and headed back downstairs.

Tom stood over the hospital bed looking down at Bobby. He disconnected the leads from the EKG. He removed the IV bag from its pole and gently placed it on Bobby's stomach.

Why do I feel like I've done this before?

266

He walked over to where Dawn slept. Tom raised his pistol to shoot; aiming at Dawn's head.

Doesn't seem right. She looks so vulnerable.

Tom felt a memory on the edge of his awareness. No, more like a feeling, a perspective.

I'm supposed to help those who are in trouble.

Tom felt a momentary thrill tenuously breaking through the haze.

My Purpose, this has something to do with my Purpose.

Tom's pulse quickened.

I'm on the right track.

For one brief moment he felt exhilaration unlike any experience in his foggy memory.

She's no witness; didn't see a thing. She'll wake up tomorrow with a hell of a headache and that's about it.

Tom raised his pistol and fired twice into a chair standing next to the door. He walked over to the bed, gently lifted Bobby, and headed for the stairs confident he did the right thing, hoping he was on the right path, the path to his Purpose.

Chapter 32

The priest watched as the bus pulled away. He stood on the deserted street clutching his cloth duffel in one hand and the briefcase holding his laptop and papers in the other. The trip had not been particularly easy. It began with a flight from Rome to Istanbul, then a smaller airplane to Adana in the south of Turkey. From there he took a series of conveyances which finally dropped him off in a small community along the shores of Lake Van in eastern Turkey. He gazed at the mountain peaks in the distance as he pulled his coat tightly around him. Spring did not come quickly at this elevation.

A less educated man might have thought himself in the middle of nowhere but the priest knew better. He appreciated the ground beneath his feet knowing full well he stood at the crossroads of civilization. To the east, Mount Ararat, the fabled final resting place of Noah's ark; to the west, the headwaters of the Tigris and Euphrates rivers. Across millennia a succession of uncounted armies had passed through this region in search of riches and glory whether the Assyrians, the Ottomans, the Persians, the Romans, or the Byzantines. Now ruins of those forgotten dynasties dotted the landscape.

The priest pulled a piece of paper from his pocket. He attempted to follow the crude map as best he could finding himself turned around twice in the process. Finally, on a quiet, out of the way, street he came to the dark wooden door set in an ancient stone structure. Next to the door on a small plaque stood the name of the monastery in a language unknown (probably Armenian) but which conformed to the lettering on the map. He raised and released the door knocker waiting in the shadows for someone to grant him entrance. Father Juan couldn't help but wonder if the old Cardinal had sent him on a wild goose chase.

§

Father Juan sat at one end of long oak table studying an historical discourse on the Book of Daniel while taking notes on his laptop. Using the BRIDG would have proven faster than to manually type the words but lacking access to a computer with the circuit and, in fact, feeling more comfortable with the older method he continued to record his thoughts. An older priest worked at the other end of the table as few frequented the Vatican Archives at this late hour.

Juan was so engrossed in his work he didn't see the other prelate enter until the massive form of Cardinal Mbanugo blocked the light overhead.

"Eminence?" said Father Juan.

The Cardinal said nothing but stared at the other researcher in the room who finally got the hint, packed up his materials, and left the Library.

"May I take a seat?"

"Please."

The priest pulled out a chair and sat next to Juan. Even at this level the Cardinal's frame could be intimidating. Despite his gray hair, he still looked hale and hearty, all six and a half feet of him.

"What are you working on?" asked Mbanugo who, in fact, chaired the Commission investigating the NextAge Movement and served as Father Juan's mentor.

Juan turned to face Mbanugo.

"The Ulysses Treatment . . . "

"Please keep your voice down. Others need not hear our discussion."

"I'm sorry Eminence. As I was saying, the Ulysses Treatment imbues its charges with enhanced intuition; but not intuition in the typical sense. We're capable of evaluating multiple factors at once, understand the implications of the forces at play and thereby prepare for the likely future. That makes it possible for one who has undergone the Transformation to make better strategic decisions which have the greatest likelihood of success."

"I understand."

"Good. Now, throughout history there have been prophets who, in essence, saw into the future and were able to anticipate the results of actions thus warning or preparing the people for what was to come. So much of that prophecy, however, is couched in the culture and language of the time, thus making it difficult to interpret what the prophets' messages might mean for our more modern time and place. I want to better understand the nature of that prophecy whether from biblical times or among the more recent mystics to see what insight I can gain by pooling their visions."

"But if their 'intuition', as you call it, is biased by culture and language, how will you come to understand the true nature of their visions? And if their visions are based on

270

knowledge of their day, how could they see so far into the future?"

"To answer your second question, we in the West have this notion of linear time. Some other cultures believe that time is cyclical. And some physicist believe that time is an artificial construct all together. What if the Voyagers could exist outside of time?"

"And you have experienced this?"

"Not yet."

The Cardinal nodded.

"As to your first question, I am reading numerous accounts. I am hoping to piece together a truth from among the perspectives."

"You have an academic background, my son. Didn't you learn that it is better to form conclusions from primary rather than secondary sources?"

"Of course, but where am I to find a primary source? Are you suggesting the Bible? I'm sorry Eminence, but I have read and reread the Bible so many times I'm afraid I will bring my own bias to my readings."

"While inspired by God, the Scriptures have been written by man. They are hardly a primary source. I know you have studied the history of the Gospels and know the difficulties in determining true authority and authorship."

"So, what do you suggest I do? Travel back in time?"

"Didn't you say time was an illusion, according to the physicists?"

"You mock me. At least for the time being, I'm stuck in the here and now."

Cardinal Mbanugo reached into his jacket pocket, pulled out a piece of paper, and slid it across the table to Father Juan.

"There is a monastery in Eastern Turkey along Lake Van. It has been kept since time immemorial by our brethren of the Armenian Apostolic Church. There you may find what you seek. They will be expecting you."

The Cardinal rose, again blocking the light fixture. As Father Juan looked up at him he couldn't help but see the old priest's head framed in the light. He couldn't help but think he saw a halo.

"Go with God, my son."

§

The monastery door opened to reveal a monk dressed all in black who looked at Father Juan with questions in his eyes. Not knowing a word of Armenian, the priest began in English, "My name is Father Juan DeLeon. I am here to see the Abbot."

The monk nodded and escorted Father Juan along ancient stone corridors lit nevertheless by electric light. Before long they arrived at another door. The monk knocked twice and left the priest standing alone.

Juan gazed down the intersecting corridors looking for some sign of life but found the halls deserted; no sound to disturb the peace. Were it not for his Transformation, Father Juan would have been startled when, suddenly, the door in front of him opened and there stood a man, about the same height as the priest with graying hair at his temples.

The man nodded in greeting, opened the door wider and motioned for the priest to enter. As Juan crossed the threshold the Abbot moved behind a massive wooden desk and indicated for Juan to take a seat in one of the chairs facing his desk. Behind his host Juan could look out the window and see a rocky shoreline descending into the lake, mountains in the distance. The room was filled with dark wooden bookcases lined with books of multiple genres and in multiple languages. Along one wall hung maps, most appearing to be as old as the room in which he sat.

The only item out of place in this 19th century bastion of academic order was a very modern computer monitor sitting on the priest's desk. Juan placed his bags next to the chair and sat.

The priest leaned forward with his hands clasped and asked, "parlez vous Francais?"

"No. Habla Español?

"English, then?"

"Yes," said Juan with relief.

"Very well. My name is Albert and I serve as the Abbot of this monastery. How may I help you?"

"To be perfectly frank, I'm not sure."

"Cardinal Mbanugo didn't tell you what we do here, did he, Roman?"

"I'm afraid not."

The man sat lost in thought for what seemed forever. He appeared to be wrestling with what to say next. Father Juan didn't know how much to reveal to this stranger in such an isolated setting; whether about his research and certainly his newfound perspective. Juan didn't sense hostility, only profound caution. As a result he reasoned that he should be the one to break the ice. Maybe he could reveal something without giving up his deepest secrets.

"Perhaps if I shared my research interests with you that may help."

The other man nodded.

"I am exploring the nature of prophecy. I wish to better understand how to interpret the visions of the prophets and mystics, to determine if I can find common threads in their visions to better interpret their words. So often their language is wrapped up in symbol and metaphor making it difficult to understand the true meaning of their revelations."

"We live in a literal time," replied the Abbot. "We expect to be spoon-fed meaning rather than glory in the difficult journey to find the truth."

"The labor in search of true faith and understanding is never easy," said Juan. "If it were, the world would be a different place than it is now. My search lies along a different path. I believe, in my struggle to understand prophecy, I am unable to understand the words and visions as they were spoken because they have been filtered through many minds and cultures. The writers and editors, while well-meaning and perhaps inspired by the Holy Spirit, nevertheless may lose the impact and meaning of the original words spoken by the prophets."

Juan sensed he had roused the Abbot's curiosity though his features remained impassive.

"I hope I haven't offended you by speaking so plainly."

"I am well aware of the limitations of your scriptures. I possess a doctorate from the Sorbonne in theology and history."

Father Juan couldn't help but show his surprise but then asked, "What do you mean, 'your scriptures'? There are differences to be sure between the Roman and Eastern rite's canon but they aren't substantial; at least not for our purposes here."

"You are missing the point, but that is to be expected. What is your facility in ancient languages?" said the Abbot as he leaned back in his chair.

"I am fluent in ancient Greek, Aramaic, and Hebrew."

The Abbot nodded again, considering what to say next.

"Now I must test your sincerity," said the Abbot. "Can I count on your discretion, that you will reveal none of what you see or hear in this monastery to anyone outside of these four walls for any reason upon pain of death?"

"Excuse me?"

"Can I count on your discretion . . ?"

"I heard you the first time. I don't know what all this need for secrecy is about; but "pain of death"? Doesn't my word as a priest count for something?"

"It does, but you must understand the gravity of your oath. It cannot be entered into lightly."

Father Juan sensed sincerity, and, yes, fear, in the Abbot. This wasn't some power play on the part of the man behind the desk. He truly worried that some dark secret might be revealed.

"May I speak to Cardinal Mbanugo of what I learn?"

"You may speak to no one outside of these four walls. The Cardinal said nothing to *you*, did he?"

Father Juan nodded. "I agree, upon pain of death, not to reveal anything that I should learn here today." He sensed the man behind the desk relax.

"Father Juan, we are a research institution but one unlike any you have known before. Other research institutions exist to advance knowledge and share findings from their investigations. But we serve a different function. While others seek to grow knowledge, we seek to preserve it. But the knowledge we possess could pose a grave threat to humanity."

Juan sensed the priest's sincerity but nevertheless challenged, "Whatever secrets you may possess, I don't understand how they could pose such a threat."

The Abbot rose. "You may leave your bags here. They will be taken to your room."

"I'll need my laptop," replied Father Juan but the Abbot shook his head.

Rather than argue, the Father followed the Abbot out of his office and down the hall.

"Do you have a cell phone?" asked the Abbot.

Father Juan reached into his pocket and handed the device to the priest.

"It will be returned when you depart."

They came to a flight of ancient stone stairs and walked down what Father Juan estimated was about twenty feet. They came to another wooden door but this one had a keypad next to it. The Abbot punched in a code and opened the door. Father Juan found himself in a room with a metal door on the far side. Along the right-hand wall stood shelves with cardboard boxes containing surgical garb and latex gloves. Following the abbot's lead he donned a suit which covered him from head to toe except for his feet, hands, and face. He placed paper shoe covers on his feet, a surgical mask over his mouth and nose. Finally he donned the latex gloves.

Without a word, the Abbot pushed a button releasing the metal door at the far side of the room with a hiss. Father Juan found himself in another, smaller room with an identical metal door on the far side. They walked to the other door and once the door behind them closed with that same hiss, the

Abbot punched in another code on the keypad opening the door to the room beyond.

Father Juan stepped through and caught his breath. Carved into the rock and for almost a hundred feet on either side and ahead of him were stacks of metal shelving. The nearest shelves held books, some of which he had heard of but never seen. He saw what appeared to be a Guttenberg Bible and a copy of Isaac Newton's Principia. The Abbot led him to the center of the room and raised his arms to take in the whole of what the room contained.

"We are the Keepers of the Story. You will find all the sacred tales here; many in the original documents. We believe the oldest to be the original stone tablets with the Code of Hammurabi," he said pointing to the back of the room.

"I don't know what to say," began Father Juan in wonder. "I could spend a lifetime down here and not begin to grasp what I see before me." He walked further and paused next to a plaque which he read in Greek.

"These are the proceedings of the First Council of Nicaea!" he exclaimed.

"Written in the original hand. This monastery was founded early in the fourth century as a library. The bishops wished to retain the original documents from the Council which chronicled the debate but the Roman Emperor decreed that these should be destroyed lest anyone wish to revive the controversies. A bishop of the Armenian Church secreted them here and they formed the basis of our collection. Given the Emperor's decree they rightly reasoned that no one should know of the library and we have kept it secret ever since.

"The first Abbot of this monastery saw wisdom in the Bishop's decision but he saw further and recognized the need to preserve original documents from all corners of the earth. He broadened our mission to catalogue and maintain the collection you see around you. It is arranged chronologically by culture. You will find the original writings of the ancient Hebrews over here including an original Jerusalem and Babylonian Talmud. We have documents from all Christian denominations. You could lose yourself in the versions of Gospels alone. And over here: writings of the followers of Mohammed."

"Why have you not revealed its existence?"

"People want to believe there is one truth, one certainty that they can rely upon. The human race struggles to maintain the truth of conflicting ideas and thoughts. How would mankind fare if the unity of religious truth within their denomination where to be called into question? Can you imagine the chaos?"

"I can appreciate your caution."

"And do you now understand now what I meant by 'your scriptures'?"

Father Juan nodded. "There is greater depth and complexity to the true story than mankind is aware."

"So you see why we must count on your discretion. Did you notice the vacant halls above? Our monks travel the globe in search of hidden treasures. It is their job to authenticate and acquire. Most of what they find is not worth the trip but from time to time, their discoveries provide profound insights."

"How do you fund all of this? The travel, this high-tech, hermitically sealed room?"

"We are provided for. The details are unimportant but, as you can imagine, any institution that has been around as long as we have would have access to sufficient resources to maintain our mission. Until recently, access to the collection has been limited but new technology, such as what you are wearing and the climate control of this room has made protecting our treasures easier. There is less need for restoration as in the past."

"While I understand your reasons for keeping this phenomenal cache secret, it seems such a shame to keep so much wealth hidden," replied Juan. "Do you ever see a time when it will be revealed?"

"We call it the Time for Telling. It is said there will be a sign. What it will be, no one knows. Now, is there any place or time in particular you wish to begin?"

"I have been studying the prophecies of Daniel."

"Ah, you are in luck. Daniel lived in Babylon during the rise of the Sopherim. Are you familiar?"

"Yes. The Sopherim were the Hebrew scribes."

The Abbot led the priest to a stack near the back of the room. Juan noticed animal skins in scrolls wrapped around thick cylinders of wood.

Pointing to the scrolls the Abbot said, "Many of Daniel's later prophecies were transcribed by one Yaakov ben David."

"What about that one, there?" asked Juan pointing at a scroll sticking out from among the others.

The Abbot smiled. "You have a good eye. You will notice that most of the scrolls are clean and well kept. The Sopherim utilized a prescribed discipline for transcribing their works. It appears this one was never formally written down and doesn't appear in any scriptures. We call it the Lost Prophecy of Daniel."

"May I?" said Juan as he reached for the scroll.

Juan walked to the shelves and reverently removed a document looking more worn than the others. He took the scroll to a table and began to unroll it; mindful of its age and history.

"How do you authenticate the collection?" asked Juan absently.

"We look for consistency of style, proper use of language for the time, and carbon-dating where possible."

Father Juan bent over the scroll and began to read. He felt the constraint of the latex gloves, longed to touch the pages. He found the text challenging. It seemed to have been transcribed in a hurry in ancient Aramaic.

Yes, this certainly reads like prophecy from the period.

Father Juan caught his breath. He read and reread the passage. He felt his skin tingle with excitement. A broad smile broke out on his face.

It could be just a coincidence. But there's more to it. There must be.

Juan stood up straight, first considering and now certain in the revelation.

And they don't even know. But what would Michael think even if he knew? He'd find some way to discount the truth. Or perhaps he does know. But what does it mean? I'm out of my depth here.

Do I contact them? I should say something, but I gave my word.

He looked at the Abbot, longing with every fiber of his being to say something to someone, anyone but couldn't speak without revealing his true nature, the purpose of his visit.

"You seem to have found something you were looking for," said the Abbot. "I can see it in your eyes."

Startled out of his reverie, Father Juan responded through his mask, "I wasn't looking for *this*."

Mistaking his intent and sharing the priest's contagious excitement the Abbot asked, "Perhaps you would want to join us?"

"Join you?" Father Juan laughed. "Soon you will want to join me."

"I don't understand."

"It seems your 'Time for Telling' is at hand."

The abbot's eyes went wide above his mask.

"But how would you know?"

"I have given my word not only to you but to others. More I cannot say."

Chapter 33

The stretch limousine came to a stop just beyond the steps in front of the Capitol. Gabby waited for the security detail to emerge from the lead car. During the briefing with their attorneys the previous afternoon a man from the security firm Arthur employed interrupted their preparation to go over the procedures. As a result, the meeting had gone longer than expected and Gabby didn't get a chance to call home to check on the kids.

The lead security officer opened the limo door. As arranged, Arthur exited first followed by Peter and then Jules. Bright sunlight momentarily blinded Gabby as she stepped out of the car. Shielding her eyes she gazed across the limo's roof at the milling, noisesome crowd; the bobbing placards drawing her attention. She read signs saying 'Stop the Infection' and 'The Godless Shall Perish" before turning to look at the Capitol.

When she was ten years old Gabby's mother and her Aunt Gertie brought her to Washington. They had taken in all the usual tourist sites: the Washington Monument, the Lincoln Memorial, the White House, the Smithsonian; but she'd been most impressed by the US Capitol Building. The structure spoke to her. She perceived a potency in the marble structure which reached beyond the edifice itself. To that young mind, the Capitol represented everything that was right about

America, the highest aspirations of the human race: equality, justice, mercy, and the rule of law over the whims of man.

As she gazed at the dome she couldn't help but wonder, *what's become of us? We've fallen so far. Personal whims have become the law, not the other way around. Michael's right. Four years ago he was right. His blogs showed us how far we've fallen, how our animal nature thwarts our high aspirations. Our only hope is to rise above our innate limitations. That's why today is so important. We have to show the world a way out. We have to make it clear that the power brokers' divide and conquer strategy diminishes us all.*

"Gabby, come on," shouted Peter.

"Gabby, are you okay?" asked Jules as they ascended the marble steps. "I sense your uncertainty. You're certainly capable of handling this without Michael."

"That's not it," she replied. "I'm not worried about the Committee. I feel like I'm missing something important. I sense big changes coming."

"So do I," confessed Jules.

"I wish Michael were here. I miss him. He should *be* with us. Maybe it's just after all we've been through, to not feel the connection, I don't know. I wish I knew what he was up to."

The BDT lawyers explained that most hearings were held in the various Congressional Office buildings but Gregory had chosen the Capitol building to highlight the importance of today's session.

Once inside as they passed through the metal detectors the security guard stared at Gabby unblinking. From his outward appearance she might have thought him hostile but Gabby sensed he had undergone the Treatment. *We have friends everywhere. I wonder how many are here today.*

As Gabby walked down the corridor flanked by staffers and reporters, the bright lights on the video cameras and the flashes from the photographers' cameras made it difficult to make out any details among the amassed throng. She noticed Jeremiah Barnum standing immediately outside the hearing room. He spoke into a microphone while his cameraman stood behind him and scanned the approaching Voyagers. Gabby noticed a teleprompter standing out of the way.

"How did he get such a plum position?" she asked in an aside to Jules.

"He's Gregory's mouthpiece."

"Still, the favoritism is pretty blatant. What's Gregory got up his sleeve?" she asked to no one in particular.

Jeremiah Barnum stood ready for them. This would be his shining hour.

"Ladies and Gentlemen, Here they come, their faces familiar to all of you: Arthur Paulson, Peter Keyes, Jules Allen, and, of course, Dr. Gabriella Neumann. But where is her husband?"

As the four of them turned to enter the hearing room Barnum stepped in front of Gabby, shoved the microphone in her face and asked, "Where's your husband. Where's Michael Neumann?"

Gabby continued walking, ignored the camera, and responded, "Isn't he already here?" leaving a confused Barnum in her wake.

Gabby and Arthur walked deliberately to the table placed in front of the dais. Gabby took the center seat with Arthur to her left while their attorneys sat on either side. Gabby turned to look at the one vacant seat on the far left side of the table. *Where is he?* She reached for him but still felt nothing.

Jules and Peter took their seats in the gallery directly behind Gabby and waited for the senators to arrive. Two already had taken their seats and appeared to be studying their materials. Behind them against the wall milled multiple staffers. Peter tried to catch Cheryl's eye to no avail.

"Are you ready, Gabby?" asked Arthur. "I've done this before, you haven't."

"I'm getting a sense for Gregory now. I have a plan."

Cheryl noticed Peter's entrance but chose not to acknowledge him. There was too much to do. This was the day for which she had planned so meticulously. The briefing books sat in front of each seat. Each staffer knew their role.

She stepped over to her media coordinator.

"Any last minute issues?" she asked.

"We're set to go," replied Marylyn. "We've wired the microphones into the sound and recording system and into the network feeds as well. People will even be able to watch or listen on our internet channel.

Cheryl nodded and went back to surveying the crowd.

She avoided Peter's eye, despite an almost overwhelming need to connect with him, unsure she could hold it together much longer. The past few days had been almost unbearable, the headache constant.

Marylyn leaned toward Cheryl, "the Senators are about ready to enter. I'll cue Barnum."

"Ladies and gentlemen, today is the day you've been waiting for." Barnum stood in front of the open doors to the hearing room, his cameraman and teleprompter stationed directly across the hallway.

"The scene outside the Capitol building tells it all. Thousands have come to demonstrate their displeasure with the Samsamites. They're angry. And they should be. They've had enough. And haven't we all.

"Dr. Neumann and Arthur Paulson have been called to testify before this court of inquiry. I have questions, you have questions, we all have questions. But will they answer them? Will they finally come clean? Will they produce the names of everyone who has gone through the so-called 'Treatment'?

"And where is Michael Neumann? Is he too cowardly to show? As I told you during yesterday's broadcast: he's missing in action. Make no mistake, he's smart. He knows what's coming. But rather than face the music, he turns tail and runs away. Ladies and gentlemen, today is the beginning of the end for their NextAge Movement.

"If you've been following these hearings you know these people have broken many laws. We are a nation of laws. But you also know we don't yet have laws on the books to deal with threats like the Ulysses Treatment or their BRIDG. Our legal system struggles to keep up with the evolution in technology. The Congress will use the testimony given in these hearings to craft new laws to protect all of us.

"But every one of us must step up, must make sure our elected officials hear from us, know where we stand, know that we will not tolerate the Samsamite in our midst."

"But where are our elected leaders in this important hour? The President sits in comfort at Camp David with the Vice President and the Speaker of the House. Why aren't they here? Why? I'll tell you why. Because few have the courage to stand up for what is right, what is just.

"There aren't many like him. Like Abraham Lincoln, Senator Paul Gregory came from humble beginnings. Like Thomas Jefferson he has excels at everything he attempts. Like George Washington he is a man of fierce principles. And like Ronald Reagan he will not tolerate the enemy in our midst. He clearly sees we stand on a precipice poised between our foes foreign and domestic. Paul Gregory is principled, courageous, and decisive. It was wise for the President to trust the Senator to chair this Committee; to root out all the enemies of this great Republic and bring them to account.

"Ladies and Gentlemen, my fellow Americans, we are a nation of laws. Let's take our cameras inside the hearing room for the swearing in."

"I want to thank you for agreeing to testify here today," intoned Gregory in his most solicitous manner. "But, Mrs. Neumann, I have to ask you, where is your husband?"

"It's Dr. Neumann."

"Yes, well, we'll see about that. Where is he?"

"He isn't here."

"I can see that."

"Then why did you ask me?"

"Dr. Neumann," said Gregory emphasizing her title, "if you continue in this vein, I will hold you in contempt.

"Senator, I don't know where my husband is. Perhaps he was attacked by that crazed mob I saw outside.

"Do you and your husband think the laws of this nation don't apply to you?"

"No sir, I'm not a Senator."

"That's quite enough," Gregory practically shouted.

Cheryl noticed he was coming close to losing control.

Calmly Gabby continued, "What I'm trying to say Senator is that I'm a doctor. I call it like I see it."

Cheryl, acutely aware of Gregory's moods didn't like where this was going. *He's going off the rails. If he doesn't get control we could be headed for disaster.*

Unobtrusively she leaned toward the Senator and whispered in his ear.

"Dr. Neumann, we'll deal with your husband's absence later", continued a more contained Gregory. "This Committee is charged with protecting the Republic from enemies both foreign and domestic. You and your cohorts as citizens of these United States, enjoy all the liberties granted under the Constitution. However, we have heard testimony over the past several weeks which causes us to believe that you would use these same liberties to undermine not only this great nation but our entire way of life. You take the freedoms we hold so dear and use them against us. You may be well-meaning but, can you see our dilemma?"

"Senator, as a physician and a scientist I was trained to be a skeptic; to question what I assume to be true; a process whereby I learned that through rigorous discipline and objective analysis I could come to learn the truth.

"This Committee has seen a parade of hand-picked pundits who have done nothing but confirm and reinforce your preconceived notions. There has been no objective inquiry."

"Dr. Neumann, this Committee was not charged with determining the proper role, if any, for you and your NextAge Movement, in our society. Our role is instead to determine if a credible threat exists and if so, how best to deal with it. And I must confess, your combative manner hasn't increased my comfort."

Cheryl smiled. *Now we're on track.*

"Your so-called dilemma is of your own making," replied Gabby. "You and others like you have sown fear and hatred. You use emotion to cloud the real issues."

"No, Dr. Neumann," he replied. "You have broken the laws of this nation. You use the freedoms guaranteed by the Bill of Rights for your own corrupt ends. You pervert the intentions of our Founding Fathers.

"Two hundred and fifty years ago a group of men got together and threw off the yoke of tyranny. Now you would replace their greatness with a tyranny of the elite, or so you think yourselves."

"Senator, those men were an imperfect lot doing the best they could in a world still steeped in monarchy. But they were never of one mind. Their only unifying vision was one of liberty and the right of man for self-governance. There were some among them who thought the elites should continue to rule. They didn't trust the common man. They created a Senate appointed by the state legislatures. Others were more egalitarian preferring direct representation and thus was borne the House of Representatives.

"Over time these institutions have evolved, the Constitution has evolved to recognize the changes in our society and our own understanding of what it means to be free. I believe the Constitution was written by men to govern our imperfect nature; a garment, if you will, which clothes our beliefs and principles. But there is a spirit or soul behind those principles which has been lost in all this rhetoric."

"Fine words," said Gregory. "We could debate the finer points of democracy all day, but it wouldn't change the fact that you pose an imminent threat to our well-being."

"An imminent threat?" responded Gabby incredulous. "If anyone faces an imminent threat, it's us. Our people are attacked around the world. You need look no further than that mob out front. You, Senator, and others like you, have stirred up those people."

Gregory looked down, shaking his head. When he looked up he said, "Dr. Neumann, they're afraid; and for good reason. You and your people, you've modified yourselves in an attempt to lord it over the rest of us. You may think you're trying to do good and you may believe that we're acting out of some paranoid fantasy. But make no mistake, the very uncertainty of this Ulysses Treatment and its long term effects leave us no choice."

"You have a choice, you all have a choice," Gabby said looking at each of the Committee members in turn, some wincing under her gaze. "You can embrace the future or crawl into your holes and demonize us in a vain attempt to prevent society from evolving. And if you make that choice, you're no different from the Dominican Inquisitors or the witch trial judges.

"Enough!" Gregory slammed his fist on the table.

Cheryl started. Gregory was not used to being challenged so overtly.

"This is not a debate," said Gregory. "You give me no choice but to . . .

Cheryl heard a commotion in the back of the hearing room. She craned her neck to see what had interrupted Gregory.

"What in the hell is going on?" Gregory shouted.

I'll have to put a stop to this. He's coming unglued, thought Cheryl.

Gabby turned her head to catch a glimpse of what was causing the disruption. From her position she could see little but that didn't stop her. A wry smile creased her face.

Perfect timing.

Chapter 34

Michael Neumann broke from the crowd and walked to the front of the room, stopping just short. Peter rose and stepped around others in his row. Gabby watched as Michael whispered in Peter's ear. *What's he planning?*

Arthur moved over one seat to make a place for Michael next to Gabby.

"Nice entrance," said Gabby shaking her head. "We have a few things to settle, but I'm glad you're here."

Michael turned to face her. As their eyes met Gabby caught her breath. Gazing into those eyes she saw something intolerably attractive. They seemed to sparkle. Then the vision vanished.

"What happened to you?" she asked.

"I love you."

"I know that. What happened to you?"

"We'll talk later; first things first."

Cheryl noticed an uneasiness winding through her gut. She sensed images floating in the back of her mind, just out of reach. She felt the pain increasing, laser-like in her forehead, her thoughts, starting to become disjointed.

Instinctively, she looked at Peter but he seemed unaware of what was going on around him. *Gabby said we didn't want Michael Neumann to testify. What's he up to?*

The pain intensified as her disorientation grew. Then she heard Senator Gregory's voice, centering her.

"Mr. Neumann, thank you so much for agreeing to join us today," said Gregory, his voice dripping with sarcasm.

"Mr. Chairman, members of the Committee, I want to apologize to you for my late arrival. I have been unavoidably detained due to circumstances outside of my control. I certainly meant no disrespect. I wanted to get here sooner but had no doubt my dear wife would acquit herself well. I will do my level best to respond to any and all of your questions."

Now's his chance, thought Cheryl. *He's ready. All my preparation will come to fruition.*

At the same time, try as she might, Cheryl couldn't ignore another feeling, pushing against her enthusiasm: *something is very wrong.*

Gregory stared at Michael Neumann. *I'm ready. I'll get him to take the bait and then I'll spring the trap. I'll put him on the defensive, isolate him. I'll bring him down and set the stage for Operation Liberty. By midnight tonight I'll be President.*

"Mr. Neumann, you've been summoned before this Committee to testify in your role as the leader of the NextAge Movement. You are its leader, are you not?"

"I suppose I am, Senator," responded Michael, "I'm certainly seen that way by many though it's a mantle I never sought. I suspect people see me as the leader because I was the first or maybe it's because of my commitment."

Perfect, thought Gregory, *he's made himself the focal point. I'll discredit him as an irresponsible dreamer with delusions of grandeur.*

Gregory felt the question come. Somewhere in the back of his mind he knew he shouldn't voice it but some misplaced curiosity caused him to wonder, "and what is it you are so committed to?"

"I'm glad you asked, Senator. On my way here I listened to my wife's testimony over the internet. I think she made some fine points, but I thought you did, too. People are afraid and they're afraid with good reason."

Where's he going with this? wondered Gregory. *This is too easy.*

"Let's look at the 20th century," continued Michael. "We like to think ourselves civilized but the past 100 years have been mankind's most brutal losing over 150 million people in various wars and genocides. That's a million and a half people a year. Every day, we're discovering more efficient ways to maim and kill our fellow man. And science is making that possible. Let me give you one example."

"Mr. Neumann, that's quite enough. We don't need another history lesson," said Gregory though no one could hear him. He looked questioningly at Cheryl. She walked over to where he sat.

"My microphone isn't working," he whispered.

Cheryl frowned and walked unobtrusively to the techies at the audiovisual control station.

"Fritz Haber won the Noble Prize for chemistry in 1918," continued Michael. "Several years earlier he developed the means for extracting nitrogen from the atmosphere and by combining it with hydrogen made possible the cheap production of synthetic fertilizer thus inaugurated high production farming on a scale unimaginable before, feeding millions.

"He is the same man who developed the means to deliver chlorine gas during the First World War. It's said his wife committed suicide in their garden using her husband's gun distraught over what he had done. He on the other hand, saw nothing wrong with gas as a weapon as death is death no matter how inflicted. He saw his role as a patriot defending his country."

Cheryl leaned over the techies' console. Fretting over the controls the head-phoned lead techie looked up at Cheryl and shook his head. Instinctively she looked at the crowd and noticed Peter seemingly lost in thought. *Could he . . . ?*

"Following the war," Michael continued, "his Institute developed a means for delivering cyanide gas as an insecticide to be sprayed in grain stores. He called it Zyklon A.

"Haber left Germany in 1933. Though he converted to Lutheranism in his 20's Haber was born a Jew. He knew his service during the war and scientific genius wouldn't protect him from Hitler's plan. He never returned to Germany. The Nazi's reformulated Zyklon A to the more effective Zyklon B which was then used to murder Haber's relatives along with millions of other undesirables.

"Senator you are right to fear the advancement of science. Human ingenuity has proven remarkably resilient in turning even the most benign inventions into engines of destruction. But how are you going to stop it? By putting us in concentration, I'm sorry, I mean, quarantine camps? You can no more stop the tide of scientific advancement than you can turn the flow of the mighty Mississippi.

"Governments have been unable to stop man's destructive tendencies. Even this great nation will start a war to satisfy the bloodlust of its leaders. Can we look to religion? Man's inhumanity to man is no more evident than in those who, professing to follow Jesus, Mohammed, or so many others bringing hate and destruction in their name. There is no moral high ground.

"Or let's talk economics. Our economic freedom has brought great wealth and with each year we're seeing that wealth concentrated in fewer and fewer people.

"And now we are killing off the ability of this planet to sustain life. It's only a matter of time, a long time to be sure, but unavoidable if we remain on our current path. Mankind has proven itself too self-absorbed, too self-interested to tackle these problems head-on. If your committee is truly interested in the safety of this Republic and its citizens, that's the kind of issue you should be considering.

Cheryl looked over at Gregory. She could practically feel the anger emanating from him.

"Can you cut the internet feed?" she asked the techie.

"Senator, you asked what I was committed to. I'm committed to a better way, a new approach. One that recognizes our limitations and does whatever is necessary to rise above them. Our fundamental problem lies in our DNA and unless we adapt we will go the way of the dinosaur.

"I don't know about you but when you look up into the night sky and behold the vastness of space; I still retain a sense of wonder when I see the incomprehensibly infinite cosmos. You and I are too young to know, but I remember talking with my father about the race to the moon. The science, the technology captured the imagination of the entire country, even the world. He told me that every time a new mission launched, even if it was just to orbit the earth, televisions were brought into every classroom so that students could witness the new voyage of discovery. Why do you think we're programmed to hope, to aspire, to behold with awe the magnificence of this creation?

"We've buried our sense of wonder in our quest for control; each person shouting louder and louder only to be drowned out by the next person wanting only to be heard, only to get what's rightfully theirs.

"Senator, we are not the enemy, we are your only hope. I'm not saying we're better or worse, but those of us who have gone through the Transformation see a higher purpose, a higher goal with a clarity which prevents the self-dealing which has frozen mankind, yes, even this Senate for years. The Treatment is not an end in itself but a means. I'm trying to build a bridge from where we stand today to where we could be. If it's a choice between transformation or self-destruction, I choose life."

"Cut the internet feed," said Cheryl to the techie.
He removed his headphones. "What did you say?"
"Cut the internet feed."
The man shrugged went to his keyboard and began uncoupling the transmission from the internet.

Gregory could no longer contain himself. Cheryl had made a mess of things making him look like a dupe; and this on the verge of his greatest triumph. He would be heard, microphone or not.

"Enough!" he shouted as he slammed his hand on the table. At that same moment his microphone reactivated causing his voice to echo loudly against the chamber walls startling all who could hear.

Michael sat before Committee patiently waiting. Gabby marveled at his calm, his control.

"Who are you to lecture me?" roared Gregory, the other Committee members cowed beneath his anger. "You've had your say, now I will have mine. I will ask you now and I will not ask you again. Mr. Neumann, will you provide this Committee with the names of those who have undergone the Ulysses Treatment?"

"Senator, I respectfully decline," replied Michael.

"Dr. Neumann, will you provide this Committee with the names of those who have undergone the Ulysses Treatment?"

"Senator, I respectfully decline," responded Gabby.

"And Mr. Paulson, will you provide this Committee with the names of those who have undergone the Ulysses Treatment?"

"Sorry Senator, I respectfully decline."

"Then you leave me no choice . . ."

Cheryl heard another commotion near the entrance to the hearing room. The doors opened and two people entered flanked by Capitol security. She thought she recognized one but she couldn't place the woman.

Senator Gregory raised his arms in violent supplication. "What now?" he asked, exasperated.

"Senator, I am deputy director Harrison Gage of the FBI. The woman accompanying me is Dawn Frame."

"Let me through", Dawn pleaded attempting to part the crowd at the rear of the hearing room. When Dawn finally saw her she couldn't help but blurt out "Gabby, someone took the kids!"

Chapter 35

Instinctively Gabby and Michael reached for the twins but felt them only faintly.

"My dream," said Michael unable to articulate more as he took Gabby's hand.

Dawn practically ran to the witness table as the hearing room erupted with the news of the kidnapping, the cacophony drowning out any attempt at order.

A quick thinking BDT attorney grabbed Michael's microphone, "Mr. Chairman, it appears the Neumann children have been kidnapped. We ask for a postponement at this time."

Gregory hesitated for a moment and then banged his gavel without a word.

Cheryl watched as her boss and lover abruptly stood and exited the hearing room, but not before he shot her a sidelong glance telegraphing his displeasure. It was clear he didn't want to be anywhere near her. She immediately began wondering how she would get back in his good graces. But try as she might, Cheryl could barely think, the pain behind her eyes unbearable.

Cheryl stood behind the sound table, frozen, chaos all around her. *What am I going to do?*

The small knot of people standing at the witness table attracted her attention. She saw the woman (Dawn was it?) talking excitedly with Gabby and Michael. Peter and Jules joined them, their distress apparent.

She couldn't take her eyes off them.

Should I go over there?

She knew she wouldn't be welcome. She'd certainly given those people no reason to accept her. She was the enemy. And now Paul had just rejected her. Cheryl looked down at her feet, unwilling to make eye contact with anyone.

They're all looking at me. They know I screwed up. Am I on my own? Will Paul take me back or will he shut me out? He loves me, I know he does. But that may not be enough. I've made such a mess of things. He'll freeze me out. I've seen him do it before. Was he just using me?

Cheryl felt her emotions spinning out of control. Fear, pain, anxiety, panic all seemed to merge at once blotting out everything around her. Her breaths were now coming in short gasps. The floor seemed to shift beneath her feet.

I'm losing it. It's finally happening. I knew it would. Peter was right. I can't keep it together. I have to get out of here, go somewhere, anywhere. Can't be around anyone. They'll see me, know I'm going.

"Cheryl, come with me. We don't have much time".

Cheryl looked up to see Peter standing in front of her. She couldn't meet his gaze, couldn't let him see her shame.

"Peter, go away. I have to get away. I can't stay here."

Calmly Peter instructed her, "Cheryl, there's nowhere to run. You're safe with me."

She wanted to be safe, she wanted the pain to go away, that's all that mattered. Cheryl looked up into Peter's eyes,

301

her supplication written across her face. He seemed so real, so solid.

Peter took her hand. "Come with me."

Like a small child she followed him to where the others were standing. The tight knit group parted including her in their circle. She couldn't look at any of them.

She heard his voice. It sounded like the soothing rain of a spring shower.

"Can you help us?" asked Michael.

And then she felt them. With the chaos all around her, reporters trying to squeeze their way past the security guards, others, like the FBI director talking on his phone; she felt them. It was as though she had stepped into the eye of a hurricane. She looked up into their faces. The pain began to recede, her breath calming.

Gabby now stood in front of her, that woman she had treated so badly just a few weeks before. As Cheryl looked into her face she saw only kindness, compassion.

Who are these people? I don't deserve this.

"Cheryl, do you have any idea where my children are?" Gabby asked gently.

"H-H-how could I know?"

They terrified her, these people. But why?

Is it them or is it me? What did Peter say? 'I've stopped lying to myself. Now it's time for you to stop, too. You can't deny who you are any longer.' He's right. I've been so caught up in Paul's world I've lost sight. No, it wasn't Paul. That's an excuse. It's what I wanted. I've been running away from who I really am for years caught up in what I thought I wanted to be. No more.

But who am I? What am I? Was I really so wrong? When did I go off the rails? That thing with Margie? Was that it? Was that the start? Have I been avoiding myself all this time?

"Cheryl", it was Peter talking to her again. "Take deep breaths. We need you here with us now."

"We believe Senator Gregory may be behind this," said Gabby. "Could you have possibly heard anything which might give us a clue?"

How could they think I know anything?

She looked from Peter to Michael, to Gabby, everyone crowded around her. She took her first calming breath, trying to find her center.

"I don't know how I could . . . I . . . I would never. . ."

But I would, I could, I did.

The revelation of her involvement rather than push her over the edge had a calming effect on Cheryl. For the first time in years uncounted she began to return to her core.

Is there a way out?

As her mind calmed, clarity began to return, and something else. A quiet resolve began to build, borne of desperate need, rising within her, like a rocket rising from its launch pad, instilled with incomprehensible power, building speed, filling her, freeing her from her fear. She remembered hearing something, what was it?

Now anger.

What has he done to me? What did he make me a part of?

With the sure knowledge of where the Neumann children had been taken and with the full humiliation of her complicity Cheryl blurted out, "I heard them talking once. They said something about Dialogos and 'removing them to the Compound'."

Gabby glanced at Michael.

"I'm so sorry; I didn't know who they were talking about. I never ..."

"There'll be time for that later," said Michael. "Do you know where the Compound is?"

Cheryl nodded. "I was there once, a few weeks ago. It's the Peacekeeper installation in the Virginia countryside; the notch where Maryland, Virginia, and West Virginia come together, not too far from Camp David.

Cheryl noticed Harrison Gage had been listening and now moved off to communicate with his staff.

Within moments he came back. "They're on their way. Let's take this outside."

Cheryl turned to walk away. Peter grabbed her arm.

"Where do you think you're going?" he asked.

Cheryl looked into his face. She shrugged. "Honestly, I don't have a clue; just somewhere away from here."

"You're coming with us," countered Peter.

"What?"

"You've been there, right? You know the place, know where they might be?"

Cheryl nodded.

"Then we need you to come with us. I wouldn't ask this of you if it weren't absolutely necessary."

Michael walking toward the exit at a brisk pace called over his shoulder, "come on, you two."

They crowded together standing on the deck on the west side of the Capitol Building overlooking the Mall, the spire of the Washington Monument silhouetted in front of the setting sun cast its shadow toward the milling crowd.

Onlookers and reporters stood near the Voyagers awaiting some word on the fate of the children. Michael and Arthur stood off to the side speaking excitedly with Harrison.

"How can you take me with you after what I've done?" asked Cheryl.

"You've done quite a bit, haven't you?" said Gabby. "We can't turn back the clock or erase what's happened, but you can use this opportunity to redeem yourself."

"But how can you trust me?"

"My dear, you still don't get it, do you?" said Gabby. "This whole connection thing is very real. I have no doubt we can trust you now and, frankly, you have something else to do here. I don't know what it is but I sense you have a greater role to play. Something the rest of us can't do."

"I don't understand. What could I possible do what you can't?" said Cheryl.

"I don't get it either," Gabby responded. "But I've learned to trust my instincts. In time, you will, too."

Michael walked over to where they were standing. "They should be here shortly. We have to figure out who's going. Of course Gabby and I along with Peter and Cheryl."

Michael looked at Cheryl questioningly and she responded with a tentative nod.

"Good," he said. "Arthur, I think you and Jules should stay here and control the situation from this end. Something's brewing."

"I'm coming with you," said Dawn.

"No you're not," he responded.

"Yes, I am."

"Dawn, it's too dangerous," said Gabby.

Dawn crossed her arms.

"Look here," she said. "They were taken while I was watching them. I don't care what you think. I owe it to them to see this through."

"Who are you?" asked Michael.

"What?" responded Dawn frowning.

"You're not the same person I accosted a few weeks ago."

"Hey, when this is all over, I'm still leaving. But I have to come with you, make sure they're okay. And, uh, I have something to confess. This is as good a time as any."

Michael and Gabby looked at Dawn, questions in their eyes.

"It's about Bobby. Right before they were taken. The twins; they gave him the Ulysses treatment."

"They what?" exploded Gabby.

"I was upstairs. I thought they were playing. I never imagined they might do something like that. I screwed up."

"Yes, you did," said Gabby. "But it isn't the first time they've put something over on an adult. Even Michael and I struggle to keep up with them sometimes. Don't blame yourself too much."

Gabby stepped over to Dawn and embraced her.

"I just reached for Bobby to see how he's doing," said Michael. "I feel him faintly like the kids but he seems ok. Hmmmm, interesting."

"What is it?" asked Gabby.

"I'm not sure," replied Michael.

Cheryl and Peter stood off to the side both staring across the National Mall.

Finally she looked up at Peter. "It feels right, being here with all of you. I feel safer than I have in a long time."

"You are. There's no more need for fear."

He took her hand.

"I don't know what they think they can do," said Cheryl absently.

"Who?"

"Michael and Gabby. They're stepping right into the lion's den."

Peter looked down at Cheryl, "I've been through quite a lot with them. I wouldn't worry too much. Heaven help anyone who gets in their way."

Peter lifted his head, and gazed into the distance.

She saw them before she heard them. Two Black Hawk helicopters banked over the Smithsonian on the south side of the Mall and headed directly for them.

As they landed, Cheryl watched as Gabby, Michael, and Harrison possessed of incredible speed sprinted for the first helicopter and leaped in as it rose off the ground having barely touched down.

Cheryl walked swiftly down the steps of the Capitol with Peter and Dawn and boarded the second helicopter. As she climbed in Cheryl noticed the sigil of the FBI's vaunted Hostage Rescue Team emblazed on the side of the craft. She took some comfort knowing from her work on the Committee that the Team had been developed primarily for hostage rescue and counterterrorism. These operators, as they're called, are specially trained in low light and rural environments; skills they would need where they were going. And something else occurred to her. She remembered some of them had been Navy Seals before joining the FBI.

Why did I think about the Seals?

The operator sitting across from her handed her a bullet-proof vest and helmet. After she donned them he handed her a headset to muffle the noise of the helicopter and so she could listen to the assault plan.

"Do you know how to shoot?" he asked.

"My dad taught me."

He handed her a gun.

"What am I supposed to do with this?" she practically shouted into her headset.

"We don't know what we're going to find when we get there," said the operator. "Better to have some protection than none."

Chapter 36

Cheryl gazed out the window of the Blackhawk as it descended. She saw three helicopters on the large concrete pad she noticed when she had first come to the Achilles facility. She watched as the main rotor of one of the helicopters cycled down and though the sun had set and darkness enveloped the Compound she could still make out Michael Neumann as the first to emerge.

Despite having visited the compound a few weeks before, as Cheryl stepped from the helicopter her impressions shifted radically. Bodies littered the ground, some moaning but most still and silent. The smell of fresh spilled blood and the lingering scent of expended gunpowder assaulted her sense of order. She saw Michael, Gabby, and Harrison talking near the entrance to the facility with one of the assault team. She guessed two of the helicopters had arrived earlier and paved their way. She walked quickly over to where they stood trying to ignore the battle scene around her.

"Two of my men are down; taken out by a sniper on the roof," said the man who appeared to be the commander of the assault team. "Good shot. We laid down fire but he escaped before we could take him out. Appeared to be a trained operative. He may still be in the vicinity. Keep an eye out.

"Come here. I want to show you something." The commander turned and walked toward a corpse at the entrance to the bunker, his body stuck in the doorway preventing the entrance from closing.

As they looked down the commander continued, "He wore no body armor. I couldn't tell you how many bullets we pumped into him before he finally collapsed and it still took a while for him to die. Damndest thing I ever saw. We're going to have to be very careful when we go in there. Don't know how many like him there are."

Michael turned to Cheryl. "Have you been in here?"

"Yes. Inside there's a waiting room with a door on the left and one on the right. The one on the left leads to the laboratories, the one on the right to the training facility. I remember there's an infirmary on that side, that's probably where the kids are. But there's a security station between the two you'll have to get around somehow if you're going to get through."

The commander motioned for two of his team to remove the Achilles warrior from the entrance. "I'm going in first with three of my men. We'll let you know when you can follow."

After hearing the all clear the group proceeded. But before she could enter, Gabby turned to Dawn and said, "Dawn, you'd better stay out here and wait for us; no telling what we'll find."

Dawn stepped back as Gabby turned to enter the reception area.

As the team cautiously walked into the vestibule, they noticed the room was vacant save for one individual standing behind the glass of the security station. As they approached the cubicle to assess the situation they pulled up short.

"What is that?" Harrison asked. The man behind the glass looked ready to pounce, clenching and unclenching his fists; a look of pure fury emanating from his gaze.

"It's the result of the Achilles Treatment. What have I done?" said Gabby shaking her head. "What have I done?"

"But something isn't right," she continued. "His skin, it's mottled and lumpy. I can't imagine that's from the Achilles virus."

"I think I know what it is," said Cheryl. "During my tour they explained they were using spider's milk to make them bullet proof."

"That would explain the defender in the doorway," said Peter.

"What else can you tell us?" said Michael.

"The guy who did this, his name is Dr. Simon Meyerhoff, said something about implanting a chip for control" said Cheryl. "Apparently the Treatment makes them very aggressive. The chip controls them but I don't know how except that it's wired into their brains."

Gabby nodded. "I had the same problem with my lab rats."

They stood motionless staring at the defender, shocked at the sight before them and unsure how to proceed. Finally Harrison spoke.

"What are our options, commander?"

"I don't see how we can get through the security station. We can blow the door but that might bring others and we're in a vulnerable position in this waiting room."

While they debated what to do Cheryl took a step closer to the glass.

"Tom?"

The warrior appeared to hold his breath. Cheryl turned to the team, "I know him. I think he recognizes me."

Cheryl took a step forward.

Peter caught her arm. "Cheryl, wait. You don't know what he'll do."

"I can't tell you why but I don't think he'll hurt me." Her voice softened, "Peter, I have to do this." She hesitated for only a moment. "It's my turn now."

Cheryl walked alone to the doorway on the right. The others attempted to follow but stopped short when they saw the Achilles warrior brandishing his weapon.

"No!" he said in a voice strained with control.

They watched as Cheryl entered the control center. They watched as she cautiously approached the warrior. They watched as she reached up and tentatively placed her right palm over Tom Talbot's heart.

§

A group of teens clustered in the high school parking lot; the water vapor in their breath visibly carrying their laughter in the cold, night air.

They cheered as the football team sauntered out of the locker room and headed in their direction. The Jaguars had just squeaked out a win against their cross town rivals 31-30 taking the conference championship. The gathered crowd's attention couldn't help but be drawn to two of the players: the quarterback and his best friend and tight end, Tommy Talbot. They made an imposing pair; both well over six feet and clearly well-muscled beneath their letter jackets.

They walked over to where the group was standing. "Nice job, Kevin," said one of the kids to the quarterback.

"Thanks but we couldn't have done it without Tommy here", said the quarterback. "He won the game."

"That catch was amazing!" gushed Gloria as she hurried over and took Tommy's arm. "You tossed that tackle on his ass, ran into the end-zone and made that amazing catch. I've never seen you jump like that."

"Thanks, Glo. No big deal."

"Yes, it was."

Tommy grinned, "Yeah, you're right. It felt pretty cool. C'mon, let's get over to Sam's and celebrate before we get any colder standing around here."

They walked arm in arm to Tommy's car. He opened the passenger door for Gloria, closed it after she got in, and went around to his side.

As they pulled away Gloria asked, "What did the coach say?"

"The usual. But he's right. We won because of hard work and discipline."

"But now the season's over. We get to spend time together."

Tommy didn't say anything but stared straight ahead as he drove out of the parking lot.

"Tommy, you promised. You said when the season was over that was it for athletics. You said you weren't going to swim again. It's our senior year. We should be having fun."

"I am having fun. And I didn't promise. I said I'd think about it."

Tommy didn't tell her the swim coach and his teammates had descended on him, cajoling him into one more year.

"I came so close last year. I could win State. Plus, you used to tell me how much you liked to watch me parade around in my tank suit."

Tommy poked her in the ribs with his finger in an attempt to make her laugh.

Gloria didn't take the bait but stared straight ahead, silent until they pulled up at the party. She climbed out of the car before Tommy could open her door and quickly walked the two blocks past a herd of cars, Tommy walking swiftly to catch up. Bright light, raucous music, and the smell of cigarettes, pot, and beer escaped as the door opened and they entered the revelry. Gloria immediately latched on to her girlfriends while Tommy broke off and stood around talking with his buddies all the while looking at Gloria out of the corner of his eye.

While he talked football and swimming one teen ran by them and out the front door desperately trying to avoid the embarrassment of disgorging his stomach contents in front of everyone. In another corner of the dining room another group stood around laughing as they passed a pipe.

Feeling increasingly uncomfortable, Tommy broke off from the conversation looking for his girlfriend and a way out of the chaos. He found her flirting with one of the basketball players. She held a beer in her hand and it was obvious from her breath and her behavior that it wasn't her first. He took Gloria's arm and said "c'mon, let' go."

"No, I'm having a good time."

She pulled away.

"You've had enough to drink. I'm taking you home."

"Let go of me!"

"Look, Tommy, she's okay. I'll bring her home." said the boy she was flirting with as Tommy suffered under her hostile glare.

"Fine," spat Tommy as he turned heel and walked out into the night.

Keyed up from the game and annoyed with Gloria's behavior Tommy walked deliberately to his car not ready to call it a night having nowhere else to go, wondering what to do, feeling rudderless.

Halfway to his car he heard a commotion off to his left. Without hesitation he walked quickly in the direction of the noise.

"Let me go." Tommy heard a female voice, pleading. As he came upon the scene he saw two troublemakers he knew from school pushing a smaller girl around.

"C'mon, let's have some fun. You'll like it."

Tommy stopped just five feet away. "Let her go."

The boys, obviously intoxicated, looked up from their intended victim.

"Ooooh, the big, bad football player," said the larger of the two. "You want a piece of this? You'll have to wait your turn." He laughed looking over at his accomplice.

Tommy held his ground.

"Look guys. Let her go. I don't want any trouble."

The smaller one came at Tommy, who took a half step to his left, turned and caught his assailant easily with a powerful upper cut to the solar plexus. The boy collapsed in a heap but not before the larger one threw a right hook and split Tommy's left cheek throwing him off balance. Momentarily dazed, Tommy quickly recovered and leveled the second scum with a roundhouse to the side of his head dropping him to his knees.

"Let's get out of here."

Tommy took the girl by the arm leading her away. They walked quickly to his car, where he helped her get in, closed the door, went around to his side, got in and turned the ignition. He drove about half a mile before pulling over.

"Are you okay?" asked Tommy.

"Yeah, I'm fine. Thanks."

Tommy heard the uncertainty in her voice.

"You're hurt," said the girl. "Look at me."

Tommy turned to look at her, sensing he knew her. She took a piece of tissue from her purse and dabbed at his cut. He wanted to wince but didn't.

"You're going to have quite a shiner."

He angled the rear-view mirror to look at the damage. "It's not too bad." Turning back to her, he added, "You look familiar."

She sighed. "You really don't remember me? I was your lab partner in biology two years ago. Cheryl, Cheryl Cooper?"

"I'm so sorry. Of course." Tommy looked truly contrite.

"Don't worry about it. I was just a freshman."

"Just a freshman. You were the smartest one in the class."

"Whatever."

"What were you doing out here all alone?"

"The party was boring and the people I came with didn't want to leave so I figured I'd walk home."

"I'll take you."

She told him where she lived but added, "Would you mind driving around for a little while? I'm still a little shaken up and don't think I can face my parents right now.

Driving through quiet neighborhoods, they bantered about nothing in particular until Cheryl asked, "I couldn't help but notice your girlfriend isn't with you. What happened? You two break up?"

"I think so."

"I'm so sorry. I didn't mean anything by it. I was just joking. There I go again; talking before I engaged my mind. I'm sorry."

"Don't worry about it. We'd run our course. I think I knew this was coming."

Neither said anything for a while and then Cheryl asked, "What are you going to do next year? Do you have a college picked out?"

"I'm not going to go."

"What do you mean?" Cheryl asked incredulous.

"College isn't for me. I might be able to get a scholarship. But if I went to college it would be for an education not football or swimming. I don't know what I want to do. My dad was in the Navy. He went in during the Vietnam War. I could use the time to get my head on straight."

"Get your head on straight? You have so much going for you."

"You sound like my parents."

"People look at you and see the whole package. You're bright, a great athlete, and, I might say, almost too good-looking."

"Almost?"

"I don't want you to get a swelled head."

"My head is already swollen from tonight's outing."

Cheryl giggled. "I'm sorry. I feel so stupid."

"You have no idea what's going on in my head. I don't know who I am, what I want. Sports are just fun and games. I need to do something where I can make a difference. I just don't know what it is."

They pulled to a stop beside the curb in front of Cheryl's house.

"You may not know who you are but I do. I know all about you. When you were twelve you tried to save your brother from drowning."

Tommy turned his head and stared out the window.

"And I see the pain that still lingers. You poured yourself into sports. When you were fourteen you became an Eagle Scout. You've dated the same girl for three years. What you do speaks volumes about who you are."

Still looking out the window Tommy challenged, "Who are you, my stalker? If you're trying to make me feel better, you're doing a damn poor job of it."

"Look at me," Cheryl commanded.

Unable to control himself, Tommy turned his head, looked into Cheryl's eyes and saw a depth he had never recognized until now.

"You know more about what you want than you know. You've already suffered more tragedy than anyone should."

She reached out with her right hand and gently placed her palm over his heart.

"I see who you are and I know that you will spend all your energy searching for meaning, but the purpose you're looking for will elude you. You'll find yourself running in circles. But a time will come when you will have the chance to make everything right. And I will be there."

Cheryl blinked and the look was gone.

Tommy stared at her unable to respond, shaken to his core.

"I'd better go," said Cheryl. "My parents are probably watching out the window wondering what I'm up to. I feel one of my world-class headaches coming on. Thanks for taking care of those animals back there."

Cheryl grabbed the handle and opened the car door.

As she stepped out Tommy leaned across the passenger seat and said, "Wait. What *was* that?"

Cheryl shrugged. "Don't know. It happens sometimes. Forget about it."

§

As the thing that had been Tommy Talbot looked down at Cheryl a lone tear tracked slowly down his cheek. It may as well have been a torrent.

Cheryl turned toward Peter, anguish written across her features, "Do something! Help him!"

Not a command but a plea for compassion and release, a plea to the one person she knew would understand her need.

"Peter, there may be a way to control the chip," said Michael.

But Peter already knew what to do. He bowed his head and closed his eyes. His consciousness reached out entering the vast BRIDG network like a surfer riding the ultimate wave carried along and reveling in the sheer exhilaration arising from freedom carried by the flow. He located his virtual self and, thinking in tandem, downloaded the problem. His virtual mind, grasping the task at hand, independently leapt through the Web Gateway, moving at the speed of light, seeking the chip controller.

Located in a matter of milliseconds, Peter's new mind quickly grasped the design and took control.

"He seems to be relaxing," said Gabby.

"I found the controller. It's a primitive design but I'm getting the hang of it," marveled Peter. "Fortunately this is all connected through the internet so I could easily access it. Once we get through this we might be able to develop a more sophisticated form of control."

"Cheryl?"

"He recognizes you," said Michael.

319

Cheryl looked up into Tommy's eyes. "Yes, Tommy it's me. I'm so sorry."

"My Purpose. Tell me. Have to know."

"Oh, Tommy, I can't. I wish I could. I don't know your Purpose."

Peter walked up to the glass. He turned to Cheryl and said, "I think you do."

"No, I don't. How could I?"

"You just connected with him, broke through the haze, helped him see who he really is. You're here for a reason. You know what he has to do."

Cheryl stared at Peter, struggling, searching for insight.

How am I supposed to know his purpose?

Then Cheryl remembered how she calmed herself in the hearing room. She began taking slow deep breaths while looking at Peter.

I can do this. I have to. Just relax. Let my intuition take over.

With no headache to distract her the images came; first one, then another, then more, faster and faster, flowing through her mind. They seemed to drift randomly in her consciousness now. Cheryl picked one and concentrated on it. The other images coalesced around it, her mind bringing order to the chaos.

Cheryl stepped back overwhelmed in wonder.

She looked at Peter. "I know. I know."

The smile disappeared from her face as she turned to Tommy.

"Tommy, I can't tell you your purpose. You have to find that for yourself. But I can show you the path. I know what you have to do. There is a way for you to find refuge. These people here; they're our hope. They have a way out of all this

320

insanity. We have to rescue their kids. You must lead us to them and find a way for us to get out of here. Along that path lies your redemption."

Chapter 37

Hesitating for only a moment, Talbot reached for the switch and released the door allowing the others to enter. The assault team entered first, checking for a trap. After giving the all-clear, Gabby, Michael, and Peter followed.

"Basement," said Tommy his voice clipped, struggling for control. "The infirmary."

Cheryl looked up at him. "Oh, Tommy, what have they done to you?"

"The last one. The rest, dead. When they got here," Tommy nodded at the FBI operators, "they placed a last guard on the infirmary. I'll take you."

They walked quickly down a dimly lit corridor and came to an elevator.

"Elevator's shut down. Take the stairs." Tommy swiped his badge and the door opened. They descended to the basement but Talbot stopped short of opening the door.

"One guard outside the infirmary. I'll lead. Stay out of sight. Cover me. In case."

Tommy stole down the corridor with the three members of the assault team right behind. Cheryl could see where the corridor bent to the left. He stopped at the bend and signaled for the operators to wait.

Talbot calmly turned left to walk down the hallway; the others waiting for the signal to move. Cheryl heard a brief scuffle and Tommy returned.

"Coast is clear."

They followed quietly behind Talbot and came to the door marked 'INFIRMARY'. A soldier lay unconscious at their feet.

"Will there be a guard inside?" Michael whispered.

Tommy shrugged. "I'll enter first."

He took a deep breath and pushed the door open. The others followed.

On the far wall stood occupied three beds; their occupants unconscious, or worse. On the one closest to the door lay Bobby, next to him Alex. As they moved into the room they saw Kerry in the third bed, sleeping like the rest, their sepulchral forms simultaneously horrifying and sobering.

Gabby took a step forward to check on them but Michael stopped her.

She saw him, a man in a white lab coat standing next to Kerry's bed. He held a scalpel against her neck and directly over Kerry's gently pulsing carotid artery. One slip and she would be dead in moments.

"Welcome. It's good to see you again Ms. Keyes."

"Dr. Meyerhoff."

"You remember me. I'm honored. Now, I certainly recognize you Mr. Neumann, and you Dr. Neumann. I must say I love your work. I may be your biggest fan. I've spent years studying your notes. We really must sit down some time and chat. We have much in common.

"And you, Ms. Keyes. It looks like you've gone over to the other side. The senator will be so disappointed. But from the way you're standing it looks to me like you've reconciled with your ex."

Cheryl hadn't realized it but she was standing very close to Peter. She looked up at him and smiled. *I guess I have.*

"I do so love family reunions," continued Meyerhoff, "which brings me to our dilemma here. Amazing specimens, aren't they? Don't worry they're fine. Just a drug induced sleep. By the way, who is that third child? I can only deduce from his condition that he was induced with the Ulysses virus before they were whisked away. Who did that? Certainly not the nanny. Hmmmm. Mysteries within mysteries.

"Where was I? Oh, yes. While I'm sure you want to be reunited with these sweet darlings I'm going to need some guarantee for my safety. Now, I know you won't do anything which might bring harm to your children. Biology is a wonderful thing, isn't it Dr. Neumann? That protection instinct, it's programmed into you, into all of us. It's our biological imperative. We pride ourselves as a species on our rationality but when it gets down to brass tacks, we're all about survival. While some might disagree I believe the strongest instinct in any animal, including the human variety is the preservation of the species. Dr. Neumann, I suspect you would do anything to save your children, wouldn't you?"

Gabby stared at him.

"Wouldn't you!" he demanded.

"Yes," her voice dripping with menace.

"I thought so. Now we can all be reasonable here. But first I suspect you want to play doctor. Go ahead. Examine them."

Meyerhoff swept his right arm indicating the other two beds.

She went first to Bobby's bed. She saw a penlight next to the bed, grabbed it, lifted Bobby's eyelids and found his pupils reactive. She checked his pulse, strong and regular.

She turned around and before she could examine Alex she felt the tears well in her eyes. He looked so small, so helpless. She stroked his cheek lovingly.

She recognized the feeling. She felt it in the delivery room when they were born; seeing them in the incubators. She wanted nothing more than to nurture and protect them. Meyerhoff was right. There *is* an instinct more powerful than any rational thought. She felt an anger such as she had never experienced growing inside of her, threatening to consume her, but with the power of the Ulysses Treatment she resolved to channel that anger, that instinct. She would find the time, the right time, and in that moment he would know the extremity of his error.

She examined Alex and found him to be unconscious but in good condition, like Bobby.

"Would you like to examine the girl?"

"Yes."

"Well then, come over here, my dear."

Gabby crossed over to the other bed but Meyerhoff corrected her.

"No, no, no. Come over here on my side."

He stepped back just a bit to allow her to get close to Kerry all the while holding the scalpel against Kerry's neck. She looked down but before she could touch her daughter, Meyerhoff grabbed Gabby in a vise-like grip with his right arm. He was much stronger than he looked.

Michael took a step forward but stopped.

"Uh, uh uh, not yet," said the doctor.

Meyerhoff pulled Gabby firmly against him. "Much better. Very nice."

Gabby felt his hot breath on her neck his right arm pushing against her breasts, his whole body pressing against her. Rather than look at Kerry she stared helpless at Michael. She could sense his anger, his frustration.

"Here's what we're going to do," said Meyerhoff. "You are going to lift your daughter out of this bed while I continue to hold the scalpel against her neck. You're going to be very careful because one false move and, well, I don't have to tell you.

"Everyone else will remain down here. You and I are going to get into one of those helicopters up there. You will sit next to the pilot while I take care of this little girl."

"And then what?" Gabby asked through clenched teeth.

"Oh, I'll save the surprise for later. I do so love surprises, don't you? Now, do we have an agreement?"

Gabby looked at Michael imploring him with every fiber of her being, knowing full well he could do nothing. From him she felt radiating confidence. She knew he trusted her fully. He had always been so strong and now he felt even stronger than before. What had changed?

Meyerhoff's voice brought her thoughts back into focus.

"Do we have an agreement Dr. Neumann?"

"We have agreement," she intoned. She needed one moment, just one moment, one slip.

"Okay. Now, all of you move away from the doorway," said Meyerhoff. "That's good."

Meyerhoff felt Gabby's body relax slightly in surrender. His body relaxed in sympathy and to move aside for her to take Kerry. But in that split second, sensing victory, he unconsciously let down his guard, minutely to be sure, but just enough. Faster than his limited cortex could process Gabby shoved the doctor's left hand away from Kerry's neck. Pivoting on her left heel she thrust her right elbow back,

326

shattering the doctor's larynx. He fell to his knees, unable to breathe and looked up at her with questions in his eyes.

"You're wondering how I could go back on our agreement. But you see, doctor, we do agree. There is no biological imperative greater than a mother's love for her child. But with your twisted mind you could never see the depth of that connection. You crossed the line to a point from which there is no return."

She watched his eyes glaze over and pushed him to the floor with her foot. Michael rushed to her side taking her in his arms.

As the adrenalin rush which propelled her attack subsided she began to sob uncontrollably.

Michael whispered in her ear, "I love your bony elbows."

Gabby pulled back. "Stop it. I just killed a man."

"You had no choice," said Michael.

"Still, it hurts. I felt the life go out of him, felt the Break."

Gabby wiped her eyes, calmed herself. "Let's wake them up and see how they're doing. Michael, Peter, can you help me?"

It remained quiet outside the bunker. A medical chopper had just taken off airlifting the two wounded FBI agents to safety. Dawn paced back and forth waiting for news.

Why is it taking so long?

She watched the remaining assault team patrol the perimeter. The agent supervising the cleanup sent two agents as scouts to determine if they could expect any action from other Peacekeeper soldiers elsewhere in the compound. This installation was well known to the FBI and they estimated a force of as many as five hundred soldiers on site at any one time. The scouts had just returned.

"It's odd," one reported. "There's no one else here."

"I just downloaded an NSA satellite feed," replied the lead agent. "It confirmed a large troop movement leaving the compound earlier today. But we lost contact around noon."

"They could be anywhere by now," replied the agent.

"I have a bad feeling about this." replied his supervisor.

Out of the corner of her eye, Dawn thought she saw movement on the roof of the bunker but when she turned her head she saw nothing. *Must be my imagination; the shadows playing tricks with my eyes. What's going on? When are they coming out?*

"Can I get you something?"

"Excuse me?" she replied.

"Can I get you something?" asked the lead agent.

Dawn thought to mention that she may have seen something on the roof but the thought passed quickly out of her mind.

"No, I'm just waiting to see that they're all right."

"I wouldn't worry, ma'am. They're fine"

"How would you know . . . oh, you're one of them."

"'Fraid so."

"The kids?"

"Don't know for sure yet."

Dawn nodded.

"You live with them," said the agent.

"Yeah, I do."

"What are they like?"

"Like anyone else, I guess, only, they're so direct, so driven. I'm not used to that."

"And the kids?"

"They're something else but I've grown to really care about them."

"I heard there's another child, an older one."

"Yes. Bobby. I hope he's okay. He's been through so much."

"You really like him."

"I don't know what it is but he touches something inside of me."

The agent noticed Dawn ringing her hands.

"They should be out soon," he said.

The Man positioned himself out of sight on the roof of the bunker, waiting patiently for his quarry to emerge.

Chapter 38

The first to emerge were Peter and Cheryl with the twins. Dawn couldn't help but smile as they ran to her.

"I've been so worried about the both of you. But where's Bobby?" she asked with more than a shade of worry.

"He's fine," said Alex.

"He's the youngest person ever to be induced," said Kerry.

"If you don't count those of us born with it," continued Alex.

Dawn watched the door anxious for the sight of him but then she began to wonder. *He's had the Treatment. What will he be like? Will he be different? Will he still . . .* Dawn's thoughts trailed off.

"He's coming out of it," observed Gabby.

Bobby's eyes fluttered open, taking in the space around him. He sat up with a start.

"Where am I?"

"You're in a hospital bed," responded Gabby. "Do you remember what happened?"

Bobby thought hard. "I was in the basement with Kerry and Alex." He paused. "They gave me the Treatment. Did it work?"

"You tell me," replied Gabby.

"I don't understand," he replied. "I thought, I don't know, I thought things would be different; that I'd feel different."

330

"Bobby, look at me."

Bobby turned his head to look at Michael.

"What do you want?" said Michael.

"What do you mean?"

"More than anything in the world, what do you want?"

Bobby thought for a moment.

"I don't want to feel alone anymore. I don't want to be angry."

"Did you know that's what you wanted before the Treatment?"

Bobby thought, he thought hard. He realized he had never been able to put his feelings so easily into words before. His pulse began to race with excitement. He looked at Gabby. She smiled at him and he knew.

"It's working! I can feel you. And I can tell how you feel. I'm not alone. I feel like we're connected. I can't tell how, but I feel it. Wow!"

Bobby looked around the room.

"How did I get here?"

"You and the twins were kidnapped but you're safe now," replied Gabby.

"Where are they?"

"They're outside," said Michael.

"Don't be mad at them," pleaded Bobby.

"We'll see," said Gabby. "We're just glad you pulled through it okay."

"I want to go see them."

"I bet you do," Michael replied. "Let's go."

Bobby practically jumped out of the bed.

As they reached the top of the stairs Michael said, "Peter's here too, and Dawn."

"Dawn's here?" Bobby stopped in his tracks, his heartbeat accelerating. His eyes went wide as he looked up at Gabby. He broke into a run.

Dawn stared at the doorway waiting for Bobby to emerge. Alex and Kerry stood on either side of her.

Dawn barely noticed as the twins chanted, "we know something you don't know," as Bobby emerged.

A broad smile exploded on her face.

Bobby stopped at the door staring at her and then stepped tentatively through.

"Oh, Bobby, you're okay," she said.

Bobby took one step.

"Mom?"

"What?" said Dawn.

Bobby took another step.

"Mom." No longer a question.

"What's he talking about?" she said to no one in particular.

"You're his mother," said Kerry.

"I can't be. His mother died in a car accident." Dawn became alarmed thinking Bobby's brain had been damaged somehow.

Bobby now stood directly in front of Dawn, Michael, and Gabby standing behind him.

"Grace adopted Bobby as an infant," said Gabby. "We all sensed something special the first time we saw the two of you together but we had no idea. It took Bobby's Transformation to reveal the truth."

"You're my son, my baby?"

"Uh, huh," Bobby said with a smile of pure liberation. He took one last step and hugged Dawn with all the feeling an eight year old can muster.

Dawn returned the embrace with all the emotion of a mother who thought her child lost to her forever, tears streaming down her face.

She held him tight, afraid to let go, wanting the moment to last forever. And then she remembered.

Dawn looked up at the sky and screamed, "No, not now!"

Shaking with anger, Dawn collapsed in a heap.

"What is it?" Bobby asked. "You're so torn up, but we're together again. It'll be okay."

"No, it won't." Dawn looked at the ground refusing to tell him.

Gabby looked at Michael. She knelt down and Bobby turned to her.

"Bobby, there's no good way to tell you this. Your mother has cancer."

"How bad is it?"

Gabby looked up at Michael and then back at Bobby. She looked to Dawn but Dawn wouldn't meet her gaze.

"She's dying, Bobby."

"No, not again. I can't do this again. I can't. It's so unfair." Bobby looked imploringly at Gabby hoping for some solution. She could only stare back at him in mute silence.

"What good is all this?" screamed Bobby. "I went through this for nothing."

"Not for nothing," said Alex. "Bobby, take my hand."

Alex placed his left hand on Dawn's right shoulder. Bobby held Alex's other hand.

"Not for nothing," said Kerry; her right hand on Dawn's other shoulder. Bobby took Kerry's left hand.

All the Voyagers present felt it: Peter, Harrison, Michael, Gabby, even Cheryl. It began as a hum, a rumble too low to be heard, but deep, nonetheless; like the feeling one might get standing next to a powerful subwoofer. The vibration swelled, took on other shades, tonalities pulsing around and through all of them.

Dawn began to sweat; her body temperature rose. No one moved for what seemed like an eternity. Finally Alex and Kerry simultaneously broke the circuit. Dawn swooned, exhausted. Bobby caught her and she rested comfortably against him.

"What just happened?" she asked.

"I'm not sure," said Gabby, "but I have a hunch. How do you feel?"

"I feel lighter, better. I can't feel the pain."

"Our bodies are amazing machines. We have the capacity to heal ourselves. We do it every day, a small cut, a cold. It's our immune system. Many of our diseases are either the result of our immune system run amok, like diabetes and lupus, or it's inadequacies like with AIDS or cancer. We're just now discovering how the mind can drive our own immunity. We've identified nerves connected to the spleen and bone marrow, vital components in our arsenal to fight disease.

"In fact, when Michael was shot four years ago he accelerated his blood clotting factors to prevent himself from bleeding to death. Somehow Bobby and the twins were able to activate a hyper-immune state in you."

"Am I cured?" said Dawn.

"I'll want to run some tests," said Gabby. "But I suspect the fix is temporary."

"Of course," said Dawn, her dejection readily apparent.

Gabby squatted in front of Dawn.

"You have a choice, Dawn. If you decide to undergo the Transformation you will, in all likelihood, be able to control

334

the disease such that you either cure it or at least it will never become a problem. But, if you don't, well . . . you know what will happen."

Dawn turned to look at Bobby, saw his expectant expression.

Without taking her eyes off him Dawn said to Gabby, "You're wrong. I have no choice. For the first time in my life I'm absolutely certain what I have to do."

Michael turned to address the twins. "That was quite something. How did you discover it?"

"We weren't sure what would happen," said Kerry.

"It seemed like the right thing to do," continued Alex.

"I think we needed Bobby 'cause of his connection with her," observed Kerry.

"This bears more examination but we'll have to wait until we get home," said Gabby.

Just then the last of the FBI operators exited the building with Tommy in tow.

"There's no one else in there," said the FBI commander. "Someone must have sent out the alarm when you were notified of the kidnapping or maybe they planned this all along. The labs are empty, too. Talbot here says he was the last one. Only two of them made it through the last induction and the other, Frank, died over there in the doorway."

Michael walked over to where Talbot stood.

"So, what do we do with you?" he asked to no one in particular.

"He's suffering, can't you see?" said Cheryl. "Help him. I know you can."

"Peter, what do you think?" asked Michael.

"I'm able to control the chip for now but that's a short term solution. At least until I can jump the gap."

"Jump the gap?" asked Michael.

"I sensed a new solution when I reached out to take control the chip. This virtual mind I have, it's only part of the answer. The solution is too incremental but it's all I have for now."

Peter looked at Tommy and then at Cheryl.

"You know, Gabby could induce him," said Peter. "With the full benefit of the Ulysses treatment, might be interesting."

"Is that your answer for everything?" asked Cheryl.

"Do you have a better idea?" said Peter.

"No."

"Well, then maybe you ought to be thinking about this for yourself."

"Me?"

"Yeah, it might make you a little less belligerent", said Peter. "Mellow you out a bit."

"As if you guys are easygoing?" said Cheryl as she playfully swatted Peter with the back of her hand.

"Point taken."

Cheryl looked at Tommy. "Tommy, I'll do it if you will."

Talbot nodded. "Worth a try. Anything's better'n this."

"Then it's settled," said Cheryl with a smile. "Peter, I have to confess, I never thought this would happen."

"What, the Treatment or you and me?"

"I guess both but I was talking about you and me. I don't want to rush this but, do you think there's a chance for us?"

"Cheryl, you can't see it yet, but we share a strong connection, and it's only grown in the past few hours. We're different people than we were six years ago. We both have a clearer idea of who we are and what we want. And with Gregory out of the picture . . ."

At the mention of Gregory's name Cheryl took a step back.

"Peter, there's something I have to tell you. Gather the others. They'll need to hear this, too."

In a few moments Gabby, Harrison, and the group commander joined them.

"What is it?" asked Gage.

"I remember a conversation I overheard a week or so ago. I was in a meeting with Paul and General Scott. They kicked me out but I listened in anyway. They were talking about something called Operation Liberty. Kidnapping the kids was the first part but they also talked about Stage 2."

"Any idea what they were referring to?" asked Gage.

"Something about multiple intermediaries and the President, Vice President, and the Speaker at Camp David. I got the sense that Paul scheduled your hearing so that he wouldn't have to attend."

"We have a problem," said Gage.

"What is it?" asked Michael.

"The NSA, with the help of Peter's de-encryption algorithms has surfaced a potential domestic terrorist threat. They may be connected. But I don't see how a full-on assault on the compound would work. That place is impregnable."

"Earlier today I would have told you there's no way Paul would do anything like that but after the kidnapping, there's probably more I missed," responded Cheryl. "Now so many of the things he told me start to make sense."

"If there were a successful attack, he would be next in line for the Presidency," said Michael. "Harrison, can you raise anyone at Camp David?"

Gage was already on his phone.

Michael lifted his chin and stared off in the distance. "It's too late," he said a moment before the night sky to the east lit up like daytime.

"We're forty miles away. For us to have seen it, that had to be a nuclear device," said Gage. "We should feel the pressure wave in about three minutes. But we're in no immediate danger."

"The operative word being 'immediate'," said Michael. "This changes everything. With Gregory taking control of the government we'll have to go underground."

"Do you think he'll blame you?" asked Cheryl.

"We won't be the only ones," said Michael. "He'll use the assassination to galvanize the nation against anyone who he believes will stand in his way or anyone he can use to political advantage."

"What have I done?" said Cheryl. "I can't believe I played a part in all this. I was so blinded by my own ambition I couldn't see Paul's ambition for what it was."

Michael chuckled. "Cheryl, sorry to disappoint you but when the history books are written you won't even rate an asterix."

"Maybe not but I'll know I helped to bring this about."

"You're not the only one," said Gabby. "I could blame myself. I created the Achilles virus. No doubt Gregory will use his newfound authority to create legions of Achilles warriors. If it hadn't been for Michael getting injured in that accident I wouldn't have even started down this path."

"We're all here as a result of our justifiable intentions," said Michael. "And we didn't arrive at this point as a result of the actions of a few megalomaniacs like Gregory or Scott. All of us bear some responsibility for what we've come to. We want easy solutions to complex problems. Scientific and political advances of the past few hundred years have caused us to believe that with the right law, the right technology, we can cure disease, feed the hungry, and eliminate oppression. The real problem lies buried deeply within us.

"As a people we've focused more on indulging our individual need for survival and success at the expense of what's good for the whole. By avoiding today's pain, we've sacrificed our future. We've been building to this point for quite a while. We've reached the tipping point I predicted four long years ago."

"So what do we do now?" asked Cheryl.

"We knew this day might come," said Peter. "You know that server farm you saw at BDT? We've built several in hardened secure spots around the world. We have secret manufacturing sites for building the BRIDG circuit."

"We have caches of the virus in hidden laboratories on every continent," added Gabby. "Induction facilities can be activated at a moment's notice."

"So you see, we're prepared," said Michael. "Some of us will go underground. Others will be rounded up and 'quarantined' as your former boss put it." Michael shook his head. "He just doesn't get it. We can't be confined by the limitations of time and space.

"We have our work cut out for us. Extremism breeds extremism. The NextAge Movement has been a reaction to a world increasingly untenable. Gregory and those like him came together, in part, as a response to what we've been doing. Now we'll up the ante.

"Despite what I've been saying, I have faith in humankind. People will chafe under Gregory's new world order. And they will find us. Our numbers will grow even faster. In the end we will prevail. But for now, we'll all have to sacrifice, live on the run. We can't go back to what we had before."

"Maybe I can," said Cheryl. "You'll need someone on the inside."

"How can you go back?" asked Peter. "Too many people saw you leave with us."

"I can go back to Gregory. Tell him I left with you to see what you were up to."

"You're playing a dangerous game," said Peter. "You aren't trained in counterespionage. And I don't want to lose you now that I've found you again."

"Peter, you won't lose me. Once I have the Treatment we'll always have that connection. I have to do something to make up for what I did here."

"I can prepare you," said Harrison. "We'll find a way for you to move back and forth between both camps."

"Gabby, can you induce me tonight?" asked Cheryl.
Gabby nodded.
"Then it's settled."

Michael and Gabby stood apart from the others.

"It's good to see Peter and Cheryl standing there together, don't you think?" said Gabby. "I wonder if they'll rekindle what they had."

"Peter looks content, at least for the moment, and Cheryl seems to be on the road to conquering her demons," replied Michael. "She's a strong woman. I should know. I married one."

"Yes you did."

Gabby looked at the children playing with Dawn.

"Bobby looks happier than I've ever seen him," she observed. "All of them, even Dawn, look so carefree. What kind of world have we created for them, Michael?"

"One where they have a real future; one where superficial happiness will give way to true purpose and fulfillment, not only for them but for their children and the generations to come.

"Michael what happened to you?" asked Gabby. "Did you have another Encounter?"

"I suppose so."

"What did you learn?"

"What I am. What we are."

"And what is that?"

"Ah, now that will take a while. For good or ill each of us must discover that on our own, just like Tommy and his Purpose."

"Okay Mr. Cryptic, I'll accept that answer for now. We've made it this far together. I can exercise a little patience."

"My dear," said Michael looking at Gabby with deep affection, "you have me for all eternity. But the stakes are far greater than you and I; far greater than Gregory realizes."

Michael took Gabby in his arms and kissed her. As she surrendered she felt Michael reaching for her through their connection. Like rivers of energy his strength wound through her. Reveling in the totality of the experience she mentally reached for him, their souls bound inextricably together.

Michael released her, took her hands in his, a smile of pure peace written across his face.

He took a step back still holding her hands.

Gabby smiled in return but she could not still her mind as the torrent of his connection receded. All Voyagers were imbued with the gift of foresight. Though at times that same foresight might be wrapped in clouds of mystery as in a dream, at other times the future, especially the immediate future, could reveal itself with terrifying clarity. Gabby watched as those same clouds of mystery were swept aside; as fate pulled back the veil, if for just a moment.

A cry of unspeakable anguish escaped from her throat. "No!"

The twins' heads flipped around in alarm staring at their father.

Michael took another step back, releasing Gabby's hands, his face now serious; his eyes betraying a profound focus.

"Find me."

The muted crack of a sniper's rifle split the air less than a breath before a small, dark spot formed on Michael's forehead.

Epilogue

Late morning rainwater dripped in a steady rhythm from the eaves. Two days prior the priests proclaimed the end of the winter rains heralding the coming of spring.

Yaakov ben David strode purposefully along the quiet street, his mind on his destination.

"Come, come, Yitzhak, we must hurry. The great one has summoned me."

"Thank you father for bringing me along," said the boy. "But where are we going?"

Yaakov stopped.

He turned and quietly instructed his son, "You must learn to hold your tongue. You will find you learn more by listening than speaking. And what we do is for no other ears than ours. Now, stay close to me. We must make haste and these streets are not safe."

The eight year old had to walk swiftly to keep up with his father. They had left the district occupied by his people and were entering a new neighborhood with larger homes. Yitzhak struggled to hold his tongue.

"These homes are so much larger than ours, father. Why can't we live here?"

"Because we must live with our people. We have suffered in this land for two generations but we won't be here forever, God willing."

After several minutes Yaakov turned to his right and entered a large home. Another young boy perhaps a few years older than Yitzhak asked them to wait. Yitzhak marveled at the fine furnishings in the foyer.

"This is such a wondrous place," said the boy.

"Yes it is, but do not think you shall ever attain such wealth," replied his father. "I have brought you here today so that you might begin to learn my trade. You are doing well with your letters. It is my hope that one day, God willing, you will be a scribe like me."

"Oh father, to be one of the Sopherim; there is no higher calling. I will feel truly blessed. Thank you for bringing me along, but where are we?"

"You are in the home of rav Daniel."

The boy gasped. "Rav Daniel? Will I get to see him?"

"Yes, my son. But do not speak unless spoken to."

"Oh, I won't father. I'll keep quiet. I promise."

"We shall see," said Yaakov absently.

After a moment the young boy said, "My friend Eli told me that God speaks to Daniel in dreams."

Yaakov smiled. *Keep quiet, indeed.*

"He does. I am here to inscribe his dream. We will listen to his revelation and I will write what he tells me word for word. When we return to our home I will transfer his words in the prescribed fashion."

"How do you do that?"

"You are just full of questions today, aren't you? Well, I suppose it is time for you to learn. I will find a clean animal skin on which to write his words, not in Aramaic but in Hebrew. Each column shall have no less than forty-eight nor any more than sixty lines. I will use a black ink prepared according to a special recipe."

344

"I remember. I helped you do that once."

"Yes, you did." The man patted the boy on his head. "I will say each word aloud as I write. And finally, and this is most important, every time before I write the most holy name of God I must wipe the pen clean and wash my entire body."

"Wow. I bet you hope rav Daniel doesn't say the Lord's name very often."

Yitzhak smiled as his father tousled his hair.

The young boy returned and ushered them into Daniel's chamber. Yitzhak saw an old man reclining on cushions. Daniel motioned for them to take a seat. Yaakov sat in front of a writing table and arranged his materials.

"Thank you for coming so quickly, Yaakov," said the older man. "I want to make sure you capture my entire dream. But before I recount my vision, who is this you have brought with you?"

"This is my son, Yitzhak, rav Daniel," said Yaakov.

"Are you going to be a scribe like your father?"

"I hope so, sir."

"It is a noble profession," said the prophet. "Future generations must know what happened here today. They must know what is to become of our people."

A young woman entered with a tray of drinks offering them first to Daniel and then to Yaakov and his son in turn. Once they took their cups she quietly exited.

"My friend Eli says that rav Ezekiel called you a 'pattern of righteousness'. What does that mean?"

"Hush," scolded the boy's father.

Daniel laughed. "That's all right, Yaakov. Do you know the difference between a truth and a lie, my boy?"

"Oh yes, sir."

"Good. Then you also know the difference between a story, a fiction, and what truly happens in this world?"

The boy nodded.

"Much will be said of me. The truth of my life will grow with the telling. Legends borne of truth will evolve into myth and superstition. It is my hope that my words will survive but in generations to come much will be made of deeds which never occurred. Do you understand?"

"I think so."

"That is why it is so important for your father to record my words exactly, though I fear others will come along and pervert them for their own ends despite what I say. Such is the way of man.

"However, it will be said of me that I utilized the past to unlock the future. You must remember that.

"Now, where was I? I apologize, I am getting old. Ah yes, my dream."

"Is it true that God speaks to you in your dreams?" asked Yitzhak.

"Son! I am sorry rav Daniel," said Yaakov. "I should not have brought him."

"Curiosity feeds the mind and the soul," replied Daniel. "Yes, boy, he does."

"What does God look like?"

Daniel's countenance darkened. "One may not look upon the face of the Almighty and live."

"Then how do you know what he's saying?"

"The Lord communicates in ways we mortals can comprehend. Years ago, when we were first brought to Babylon I began to have dreams, dreams which revealed the Lord's will and His plans for our people. He sends dreams to man so that we may know His word and do His bidding."

346

"It is time to stop with your questioning," said Yaakov to his son. "Can't you see Daniel is tired? You do look tired, my friend."

"I am old Yaakov. My time is upon me."

"Oh, that you would return with us to Jerusalem."

"I would not survive the journey. It is my hope that you and your family will return in your lifetime. I have had another dream, one last vision."

Yitzhak watched Daniel's demeanor change, his eyes gazing into the distance, focused on nothing. Yitzhak felt himself falling under Daniel's spell. He saw a similar change in his father as he prepared to scribe.

"Last night as I slept I was filled with the wonder of the Lord. I stood in the Great River, the one the Babylonians call the Ufratu which shall someday be named Euphrates by some other conqueror. I felt the water flowing against my ankles. The Lord called to me. As I stepped further into the deep I felt the flow pulling at me. Though I was filled with fear, I walked into the river and let the current take me knowing that was the will of the Lord."

Yitzhak began to be afraid. Rav Daniel was no longer the kindly old man who instructed him so gently before. Now the boy saw all that one might imagine a prophet to be, one possessed of the fire of the Lord. Yitzhak watched as his father furiously transcribed all that he heard.

"I traveled with the current until the river spit me out on dry land. Dark clouds bore down on me with lightning and thunder. And the Lord spoke to me out of the whirlwind and He said, 'I will deliver you to Jerusalem. And you shall rebuild My temple. But you shall reside in the Promised Land for few generations, My people scattered across the deep. And despite all that man does, despair will reign across all My dominion. I will send many to guide and teach them; to prepare the way. In his wisdom man will devise great wonders and magics but it will avail him not. Decadence and decay shall reign for that is lot of mankind. I put them in that state so that they should seek for Me.

"But all is not lost for you are my people. At the appointed hour I will send the Archangel Michael and the Archangel Gabriel to Earth. And they shall walk among the people as mortals. And they shall gather about them others who shall become like them and ascend to heaven.

"And the forces of darkness will gather, too. They will profess to do the Lord's bidding while committing great evil in My Name. And they will bring terrible fire on mankind.

"And the Dark ones will beset the land with their evil and all will bend to the lash. All save the Voyagers. Their kind will multiply and oppose darkness, and they will ascend to heaven as they do my bidding on Earth. They shall build a glorious bridge and the children will throw wide the luminous gates. They shall lead my people to Me."

Daniel leaned back on his pillow, exhausted.

Yaakov spoke as he rolled his scroll and placed it in a fold of his tunic.

"These are grim tidings, my friend. Do you know when they shall come to pass?"

"Not in our lifetime."

The young girl entered the room

"My grandfather tires."

"You had better leave," said Daniel. "My head pains me as it often does after my dreams."

348

Yaakov and his son walked swiftly back to their district winding through alleyways, past homes and shops now teeming with people,

"Father I don't understand. What does it all mean?"

Yaakov saw the stricken look on his son's face.

"These are the words of the Lord and so are sacred. You are young yet and must continue your studies if you are to understand his visions."

"You are old, father. Can you explain them to me?"

Yaakov smiled.

"Not old enough. I confess that I do not understand them myself."

As the two rounded a corner they found themselves confronted by a gang of thieves.

"Please, let us pass" said Yaakov.

"Where are you going in such a hurry?" asked the lead man. Yaakov noticed he was short and walked with a limp.

"We only want to return to our home."

"You are not in your appointed area, Judean. You do not belong here."

Yaakov, having just spent time with great prophet found himself filled with potency.

"We did not come here by choice. We were stolen out of our land and some day we shall return."

"Then you must pay a toll to pass," said one of the other brutes who pushed Yaakov back with the larger end of his cudgel.

"I have no money," said Yaakov.

"What's this then?" said another thief as he pulled the scroll from Yaakov's robes.

"It's nothing," said their leader and the thief discarded the scroll in the dirt.

Yitzhak's eyes went wide. *That's the sacred word of God.* The boy dove for the scroll. Mistaking Yitzhak's lunge for an attack the leader struck the boy in the temple with his club dropping him in the dust.

Yacov fell to his knees cradling the head of his boy's now lifeless body.

"My son, my son," he wept.

The leader raised his club again and struck Yaakov in the head crushing his skull. Under his breath he uttered, "Filthy Judeans. . ." as he and his gang lumbered off in search of easier pickings.

Before long, an old woman came across the site of the attack. She saw a man hunched in death holding his son. She might have felt a modicum of pity, but for the fact that death was an all too common occurrence. Then, out of the corner of her eye, she saw it.

She bent down, picked up the scroll and secreted it within her robes. Perhaps it would be worth something to someone someday.

Acknowledgements

Confrontation proposes how the circumstances and the characters first imagined in *Connections* might evolve in the context of our culture and society. You might envision something different and if so I would like to hear from you.

While a work of fiction, I conducted a considerable amount of research to lend it an air of believability. Some of the research was performed on-line, some in hard copy, and some through interviews. Chief among the valuable sources was J.E. Garvey whose experience with the Navy informed my take on Navy Seals.

The usual cast of characters (and I do mean characters) read early manuscripts and offered invaluable insight making this a much better work that it would have been otherwise. These include C. Werner, M. Lucius, F.T. Pandora, M. Goldmann, K. Goldmann, and M. Venditti. If I missed you, I apologize and please let me know.

As to the writing itself, I want to thank George Gopen, recently retired professor at Duke University. He was my professor for expository writing my freshman year in college. A few weeks into the course he said to me, "It's not your fault but you don't know how to write", or something to that effect. He proceeded to work with me on-on-one for an entire academic year using poetry as a means to instruct me in the glory and nuance of the written word. There should be more like him.

If you like the cover art, the credit goes to Dana Feiwus.

To my family, especially my wife Pam, who put up with my sequestering myself in the study for hours at a time and who has been with me through the highs and lows of the process and who never let me know how crazy she thought I was.

Finally, dear reader, rather than keep you awake nights worrying "what will happen next?", or more precisely, "does this guy have

351

any clue where he's going with this story?" rest assured I have already imagined the ending in considerable detail. Whether it will take one or two more books to get there (I'm hoping for one more) remains to be seen.

Jim Goldmann
June 17, 2013